Chasing Mayan Dreams

Chasing Mayan Dreams

◆

Adventures in the Mexican Rain Forest

A Novel

Michael Cantwell

iUniverse, Inc.

New York Bloomington Shanghai

Chasing Mayan Dreams
Adventures in the Mexican Rain Forest

iUniverse books may be ordered through booksellers or by contacting:

iUniverse
1663 Liberty Drive
Bloomington, IN 47403
www.iuniverse.com
1-800-Authors (1-800-288-4677)

Because of the dynamic nature of the Internet, any Web addresses or links contained in this book may have changed since publication and may no longer be valid.

This is a work of fiction. All of the characters, names, incidents, organizations, and dialogue in this novel are either the products of the author's imagination or are used fictitiously.

ISBN: 978-0-595-47065-5 (pbk)
ISBN: 978-0-595-70928-1 (cloth)
ISBN: 978-0-595-91347-3 (ebk)

Printed in the United States of America

The idea for *Chasing Mayan Dreams* grew out of the author's friendship with Gertrude (Trudi) Duby Blom, the Swiss-born journalist and photographer who devoted much of her life to the preservation of the Mexican rain forest and the Lacandons who live there today. Trudi agreed with the author that a literary work of the imagination was an excellent way to tell her story and the meaning it holds for all of us.

Gertrude Duby Blom died in 1994 at the age of ninety-two. In honor of her vision and courage, this novel is dedicated to her.

Acknowledgments

I would like to thank all the people who have given me encouragement, suggestions or other kinds of help as I wrote this novel—Anne-Marie Cantwell, Barry and Joan Norris, the staff of Na-Bolom, Robert Bruce, Ken Nelson, Richard Walton, John R. Humphreys, Barbara Kouts, Harold Schmidt, Didier Boramanse, Chankin Viejo, Kayum Yuk Maax, Susan Di Raimo, Olga Consuelo Lopez Santos, Mary Hughes, Elsa Guzman, Robert Markens, Michael Karp, Arnel Cruz, Gail Rogers, Sharon and John Carson, Claudia Dias, Ross von Burg, Dennis Switzer, Betty Spence, Kathleen Daniel, Edward Margolies, Sidney Furst, Herbert Engelhardt and Larry Stroher, Gloria Stevenson, Ali Sutjianto, and the editorial staff of iUniverse.

Several sources were invaluable to me in my research for the novel. Prime among them were *La Selva Lacandona* by Gertrude Duby Blom, *Lacandon Dream Symbolism* by Robert Bruce, *Hach Winik, The Lacandon Maya* by Didier Boramanse, *Frans Blom* by Robert Brunhouse, *Tribes and Temples* by Frans Blom, *Forest of Kings* by Linda Schele and David Friedel.

Michael Cantwell

PROLOGUE

Prologue

Now I know that Las Casas is a city of underground gods. By day they hide inside the statues of the saints in the churches. Some of them dwell in the surrounding mountains where they herd the spirits of animals in subterranean corrals. The oldest of them inhabit ruined temples in the far off jungles.

The marketing Indians abandon Las Casas to return to their hamlets in the hills before the setting of the sun. The Ladino shopkeepers retreat behind closed doors shortly afterward. Save for a few determined lovers, the squares are deserted before midnight. It is then, when the night mists fill the valley, that delegations of gods from the jungle and the mountains converge upon the town. The gods from the statues in the churches, some of them still wearing their saint apparel, gather with them. They patrol the cobblestone streets to see if anything that belongs to them was stolen or defiled during the preceding day. Then they climb the long stairway to the church of San Cristobal and hold councils in the dead of night. Their edicts are circulated through the dreams of sleeping men as signs for them to follow when the morning star brings the sun and the first vultures stare blankly from the red-tiled rooftops.

I have come to believe that whether or not we will be saved depends on how well we remember our dreams.

But when I first saw Casa Balam standing in a meadow on the edge of Las Casas like a great, walled monastery, I knew nothing about dreams or gods. I wanted nothing more than a mountain hideaway—no dazzling revelations, or orgies of consciousness, just peace and time to write a book version of my ten year-old-Master's thesis, "English Authors Who Hated Their School Days." Gasping for the thin, mountain air and weary from a long journey, I knocked on the great, carved wooden door over which a painted image of a jaguar pranced. A handsome young man who reminded me of the Prince Valiant of my youth admitted me into a large, flower-filled patio.

"My name is Philip Nason," I began.

"Yes, Mr. Nason. From New York. We were expecting you earlier. You're too late for *comida*."

The voice was dry and flat. I detected a trace of contempt in the gaze that met mine. I lifted my heavy pack to my shoulders, hoping the young man would pick up my portable typewriter but he did not. Despite the urging of friends, I preferred to work on a typewriter rather than a computer. Perhaps, for me, the clicking sound was music to accompany my writing.

We walked through iron gates from one patio to another. "Be sure to close each gate after you've passed through," he said, slamming a latch in place. My guide was wearing a long white Indian shirt with a kind of cross design woven in red and yellow on both sides. Clanging another gate behind us, he led me up some metal stairs that ran alongside the house. I was out of breath when we got to the top. I noticed three doors off the balcony on which we stood. Prince Valiant opened the first door and ushered me inside.

"This is your room. It is called Jatate. It has a lot of light for a writer."

Then he was gone and I achieved what I had come for, and what the 1990 guidebook to Mexico had promised. I was alone—suddenly, miserably, alone. On the white stucco walls above the raised fireplace in my room, men in white smocks poled dugout canoes and women sat before stone tables grinding corn. The photographs were all signed, Erika Christian Boeshure. The eyes in the photographs followed me as I unpacked. I was delighted to discover that the fireplace was stacked with wood and all I had to do to get a roaring blaze was strike a match.

I parted half-drawn curtains to close the windows, and beheld a garden of breathtaking beauty. Tall native pines rose from beds of tiger lilies, Canterbury bells, and orchids. Then, as the sun hid behind a cloud, an inexplicable sadness came over me.

To shake off my mood, I took a stroll through the garden and roamed the arch-lined patios of the house. I entered a handsome wood-paneled library which appeared to be a treasure trove of the lore of the region. *Yes, I thought, here is where I can spend hours working on my book.*

But the greatest marvel in the house was the adjoining museum containing archaeological findings. I admired animal figures carved in rock. On a pedestal sat a classic Mayan head. High on the wall was a splendid photograph of a man in the prime of life. He was squatting in a grave gazing at a human skull he held in his hand. This photograph too was signed Erika Boeshure.

A young woman was dusting artifacts and I called to her.

"This extraordinary photograph—Who is that man?"

"That's Claus Boehm," she said with a vaguely German accent.

"Who is he?"

"You don't know? He's Erika's husband, the Mayan explorer."

"Is he in the house now?"

"Oh no, he's dead."

"When did he die?"

"Years ago. I don't know. Erika won't talk about it. There are books by him in the library."

I stood fascinated with the spectacle of the man, so handsome and full of life, holding a dead man's skull in his hands.

Back in my room, I heard the sound of far-off thunder. As it got dark, I turned on the lamp on the night stand and picked up the little booklet that lay there. There was a note of welcome and a list of rules to be observed while staying in Casa Balam. Lights were to be turned off when not in use. Gates were to be kept shut at all times so that dogs would not stray. No alcohol was permitted in the dining room. If I'd wanted a monastery, I had found one.

My eyes were drawn once again to the faces on the wall that looked back with a disturbing gaze. Then the closet door creaked open and two green eyes peered out of the dark. A black cat strode into the room. I realized then why the eyes in the photographs were disturbing. They looked at you with gaze of a cat, empty, serene, and contemptuous.

I opened the door to usher the cat out onto the balcony. The animal screeched as it leapt over something that lay in front of the door. My heart beat quickly. Through the darkness, I made out a human form wrapped in something like a sheet. Just as I was convinced that it was a dead body, the shape moved. I stood frozen with fear. A red glowing ash traced a circle in the dark. Then a soft unearthly giggle rose. The lump at my doorstep was an Indian with long straggly black hair, who was wearing nothing more than a sackcloth. He was leaning on one elbow and smoking a cigar held in his other hand. His eyes, reflecting the light from my room, were the same as the eyes on the wall. He held the cigar up to me. I was surprised by this small offer of friendship from a man whose world was as remote from mine as Mars. I took a deep puff. It was strong tobacco all right and it sent me into a fit of coughing.

I squeaked out a "*muchas gracias*," and hastened back inside my room. I couldn't look at the Indian faces on my walls and I couldn't deal with the Indian outside my door.

I was greatly relieved when I heard the dinner gong. When I glanced outside, the Indian was gone. The rain was coming down very hard now so I steered a course under the balconies and eaves to keep dry. As I passed under the archway that opened upon the main patio, I heard the gong again, louder this time. I was surprised to see that the big hammer was being wielded by an old woman in a long purple gown.

She placed the hammer on its hook and, looking at me, said, "Buenas noches," in a deep Germanic voice. I realized I was standing before Erika Boeshure herself.

She looked like a mother queen and for a moment I thought she was wearing a crown on her head. Her neat, coiffured hair seemed to possess the luster of the pearls that hung around her neck. Her face, though webbed with age, shone with an intense vitality. Perhaps it was the eyes that gave the overall impression of sparkle. To be sure, they were set off by dark mascara, but they were as bright as a child's and held me in their gaze.

"Where is everybody? Don't they hear the bell?" She spoke to me as if, by my very punctuality, I had joined her battle against tardiness.

I followed her into a vast, empty dining room. She sat at the head of a long row of tables that appeared to be set for a royal banquet. Two tall lighted candelabra stood on either side of her. There were other candles on the tables. I stood, paralyzed in my shyness, not knowing where to sit.

"Well, why do you hesitate? Sit next to me!"

I felt as I did in dreams when I was called to the teacher's desk only to find myself naked from the waist down.

"Have you made yourself at home?" she asked cordially, tucking her napkin in her lap.

"Yes," I began nervously, following her example with the napkin.

"I don't think Kayum will be joining us." She gazed at the empty room. "He isn't well. But where are the others? Didn't they hear the bell? You are in the back of the house and you heard it."

"It was very quiet in my room," I said.

"I should hope so. Where do you live?"

"New York City."

Her cropped eyebrows arched and she looked at me with wonder.

"How can you possibly survive in that place? I think the only possible solution for New York City is a forced march of the population into the countryside."

I didn't know quite how to respond. "We don't have any countryside to go to."

"You mean you've destroyed it already?"

Just then, a half dozen young people trooped in on guilty feet. I took them to be her volunteer staff. They were followed by the more casual entrance of three mature looking couples whom I took to be my fellow guests.

"Don't you people hear the bell? Peter, where is Didier?"

"He's eating in town," Prince Valiant called Peter said.

"Eating in town is he? He should tell us when he eats in town. How many others are eating in town? Micheline, you can start serving."

The girl I'd seen in the museum began serving bowls of soup and circulating plates of sweet, freshly baked bread. The couple who sat on Erika's other side turned out to be a Harvard professor and his wife. Farther down the table, a man and a woman were conversing in French to two serious looking men who appeared to be German. The soup was followed by crisp turkey enchiladas in mole sauce. Erika was soon surrounded by pots of tea, which she poured into cups.

"Peter, do you have the seedlings ready for tomorrow morning?" She looked up at my medieval prince who was standing before the serving window. "It is important that we plant that side of the mountain behind Guadalupe. The erosion there is terrible."

"Do you own land up there?" I asked innocently.

Erika shot me a look of rebuke for my ignorance and then explained patiently. "No. The land belongs to Mexico. I am giving a lecture on this subject in the museum Wednesday night. You may find it interesting."

She spoke French to the couple down the table and, just as easily, addressed the two men in German. I was enjoying my dessert of fresh apple pie drowned in cream when Erika's voice cut back into English.

"Listen, everybody, there is a movie, *The Great Dictator*, with Charles Chaplin showing in the civic center in town on Sunday night. There are free tickets available in the office."

I'd been in Las Casas less than a day, but the very suggestion of something out of my north of the border past was like the announcement of a visit by an old friend.

"I saw it years ago, but I'd love to see it again," I said.

"It's a marvelous picture," Erika said to me. "Do you remember the scene where the dictator dances with the big, balloon map of the earth?" To my amazement, Erika Boeshure rose from her high-back chair and danced, in Chaplinesque pantomime, lifting her heel high into the air behind her back to kick an imaginary balloon.

Everyone looked on wide-eyed. I sensed a general concern that she might cause some injury to herself as she executed her comic dance.

"Of course, Chaplin didn't know about the concentration camps at the time or he would not have poked fun as he did," she said resuming her seat. "Not even the Swiss embassy knew about them until they discovered that I was in one of them." She said the last as matter-of-factly as the rest.

She went on to discuss, with a trace of nostalgia, the flourish of artistic achievement in Germany.

"The Nazis took over much of the art and the artists of the time for their own purposes."

I knew I was treading dangerous ground but the imp of the perverse prompted me to say, "Yes, of course, the anthem that was played every time Hitler made an appearance was from a quartet Haydn called his greatest work."

"I am glad you can see the beauty through the propaganda." She strummed her fingers on the table and then began to hum the theme. "Do I have it right?" she asked me.

I felt my face turn red as I answered, "Yes."

All conversation around the table stopped. Erika looked up at the ceiling, her voice lifting as she boomed out, "Deutschland, Deutschland uber alles," tapping the side of her teacup with her spoon all the while. The two Germans stormed out of the room. Everyone else looked on aghast. I trembled with embarrassment for having provoked the scene.

"Erika, that is simply in bad taste," Peter said when the performance was over.

"Nonsense," Erika held her head up high. "It is beautiful music despite the fact that it was taken over by the Nazis. There was much beautiful music."

When I returned to my room, the questions in my mind fell over one another. Who was this incredible woman? Was she a saint, an actress, a hideous joke? How had she come to live in this house? Why was it like a monastery? What of the Dane holding the skull? And who is the crazy Indian I now hear coughing on the other side of my wall?

But as my mind raced, my body was overcome with tiredness. I undressed, letting my clothes lie where they fell and crawled into bed.

My mind did not rest. Indian eyes drifted in circles across the screen of my closed eyelids. They were replaced by images of Prince Valiant walking around in his white Indian shirt with the big fiery crosses. The sound of slamming gates rang in my ears as did the exasperated voice of Erika Boeshure. Then I was riding on a mule, like those I'd seen on the bus ride up the mountain. I was riding through a pine forest, climbing higher and higher until the pines were replaced by thorny bushes and big rocks. The trail wound precariously around mist-filled ravines. Vultures sat atop bare branches. To my alarm, a band of armed men, looking like the revolutionaries in Diego Rivera murals, appeared, blocking my way. Cartridge belts were slung across their chests and they carried rifles over their shoulders. They looked at me menacingly, their moustachios drooping. Suddenly, the three men broke into howling laughter. I began to believe they were not going to do me any harm and started to laugh with them.

"Buenos dias," the man in the middle, whose big belly shook with his laughter, said, "We see that you are in good company."

All along I'd had the feeling that I was traveling with a silent companion, that at my back there was a clopping of another mule, although, whenever I'd turned around to look, I'd seen no one.

"But, I'm alone," I said.

"You are not alone, señor. You will never be alone again until the instant of your death." All the men laughed. The man in the middle leaned toward me in a gesture of confidence. "Your companion, señor, is a good friend of ours. But what have you done to him?" The two men on either side of the fat one lifted their rifles from their shoulders and cocked them. My curiosity overcame me even in the face of what appeared to be my imminent extinction. I looked back. There, only five yards behind my own mule stood another with a man seated on its back. My heart began to pound violently as I realized that my secret companion of the trail had no head on his shoulders but, instead, carried one in a net bag dangling from the side of the mule. Long gnarled black hair stained with blood streamed across the disembodied face. I turned to my executioners who were aiming their rifles at my chest. "We must pay you for what you have done to our friend, Mateo."

"But I don't know anybody named Mateo. I have never met this man," I protested, my voice shaking. "Please don't shoot me!"

I woke up to the pounding of my heart. I did not dare go back to sleep and spent the rest of the night waiting for the dawn. With the first glimmer of light, I heard Erika rising to talk to her cats in German. Afterward, I heard the cooks coming into the kitchen and the clatter of pots and dishes.

Erika came into the dining room while I sat alone with my breakfast. She was wearing riding clothes and holding a trowel in one hand. I told her about my dream.

"Have you read about Mateo in the papers?" she asked.

"I can't read Spanish. Who is Mateo? What would he have to do with my dream?"

She lifted the coffee warmer from the pot. "Mateo is a revolutionary leader from this region who was killed in Guatemala by federal soldiers there. It happened just last week. They say he was captured alive and then beheaded." Then she paused, holding the pot, and gave me a surprised look. She appeared older, stripped of the makeup from the night before, but the eyes shone with the same incandescence. "There was another Mateo—many years ago. Of course, Kayum is next door to you, isn't he? The Lacandon Indians believe in a dream soul that wanders outside the body during sleep and sometimes visits the dream spirit of another. Kayum may have left you a calling card last night."

"I believe in a rational explanation for everything, even dreams, don't you?" I said, an edge of desperation creeping into my voice.

"Of course, but what is rational and what is known science, don't always coincide, do they?"

I returned to my room and began to pack. Casa Balam was not the haven I had been looking for. There would be no quiet days of writing here. I pulled my shirts off the hangers in the wall closet. I was almost completely packed when Micheline walked into my room carrying a bouquet of flowers.

"What are these for?" I asked incredulously.

"It is the flower renewal ceremony," she smiled. "Every room gets fresh flowers in the morning. It is a rule of the house."

When she left, I drew back the curtains from all of the windows. The sun was shining in the garden which beckoned me with its lush imprint of creation. No, it wasn't the place to write "English Authors Who Hated Their School Days." But it might be the place to do something else. I sat down on the bed listening to the Indian who was coughing on the other side of the wall.

Then I went to the library and asked the bosomy peach-skinned girl in the Chamula sweater to recommend some books about the region. Before I could finish my request, she placed a stack of books and papers in my arms.

"Erika told me to give you these," the girl said, speaking with Alpine resonances. "When you're finished, I will give you others. Are you writing her story?"

"I was writing a book of literary criticism. Her story, you say?"

I began to spend my days going from the library to the patio to the garden, following the course of the sun. I found my thoughts ticking back and forth through time as I chased down the events in Erika's life, the odyssey of Claus Boehm, and the extraordinary history of the Lacandon Indians. The girl in the library was right. I decided in the end that the story of Erika and Claus and Kayum should be placed in a kind of literary capsule and sent across the galaxies as a last appeal on behalf of humanity.

Let me start at the beginning. But how can I speak of beginnings any longer? I have learned to think in Mayan time where the future flows relentlessly into the past and the present is a point on the rim of eternity.

I am a child at a Mexican carnival. Instead of the wheel of fortune, a Mayan calendar spins. I put my pesos on the board. Where the wheel stops, I begin the story.

PART I

OCOSINGO

Chapter One

Perhaps the plane would come today. If it did not come today, then surely it would come tomorrow. Or the next day. Perhaps. It was the way things happened in Mexico. Erika had discovered that her mother's Swiss watch had few uses in this country. And when the plane came, there was no guarantee that the famous Pancho Balam would be on it. She'd been waiting a week.

The muddy square of Ocosingo was bordered by orange trees. Erika had been pleased to discover that in the morning, she could order coffee and tortillas from the gaseoso stalls and then simply raise her hand above her head to pluck an orange.

Now it was afternoon. She sat at an unsteady water-soaked table, drinking coffee and looking out over the square. A train of mules passed by, headed for the distant *chicle* camps. Erika knew it was early in the season for the chewing gum gatherers. She regarded the stuffed, life-size figure of Judas hanging from a tree in front of the church. It was Good Friday and Erika had been told that the Indians would burn the straw Judas on Easter morning. The town of almost identical whitewashed plaster covered houses with faded red tile roofs, was asleep. The square was strewn, even at mid-day, with the recumbent bodies of Indians and *chicleros* who had carried the night in the numerous saloons. Erika had read that on his first visit to Ocosingo in 1925, Pancho Balam had failed in his intention to measure the average height of the Indians of Ocosingo as he could never get one to stand up long enough to be measured.

Erika wondered if this town had changed at all since then. Eighteen years. Her own world had changed completely in that time. It was now 1943 and she was an exile from a country at war, waiting in this jungle outpost for a man she'd only read about. Erika was angry at herself for having brought the wrong clothes. The square was hot and humid. She felt uncomfortable and ridiculous in her heavy straw hat and dark, tight-fitting linen dress with the padded shoulders. She removed her hat but the shade from the trees moved until the sun was strong on her head and she had to put the hat back on. Erika had brought only one change of clothes and it was just as wrong. But she hadn't expected to be sitting in this cafe for so many days. Her money was running out, and if Pancho Balam didn't come, what then? She was counting on an interview with him to give her article about the jungle the slant that *Collier's* magazine wanted. The editor she'd met in Mexico City had shown an interest when Erika had suggested putting in the explorer. The article needed a hero. And she needed the money from the magazine to start her life over again. But she couldn't think about that now. She just wished she had brought different clothes.

Erika watched small boys leap over the bodies of sleeping drunks as they carried out a game of baseball. The doors of the church were open and the Indians inside were chanting in a blue haze. Erika loved the singing, the thumping of drums, and the smell of incense.

Two men sat at a nearby table. One had strong Mexican features while the other had the rugged looks Erika associated with the American north. They were speaking in English and their accents confirmed their nationalities.

A boy placed a bottle half-filled with rum and a shot glass before the Mexican and a setting of coffee before the American. Both men were dark from the sun and wore the same loose fitting Indian shirts. The American's face seemed composed of hard, wind-sculpted granite. The dark eyes brooding under the beetle brow and the hawk beak reminded Erika of illustrations for stories of Edgar Allan Poe. The man with the rum had the suffering eyes of Mexico, but the mouth and jowls were full with the consolations of sensuality. Erika turned her glance back on the square, picking up her dropped thoughts.

"I don't think old Pancho Balam will show up in this shit-ass town," she overheard the American say.

"But Señor Barnes, this is his last chance," the Mexican said. "He needs this expedition."

"He left his last chance in New Orleans and he knows it. It's going to be all ours, Pepe."

Erika found the conversation disturbing. But curious as she was, she didn't want to talk to the men. They reminded her of the vultures that squatted in the courtyard of her hotel. Then the men were talking about her.

"I tell you, it is the one," the Mexican was saying.

It dawned on Erika that the Mexican was Pepe Quarles, a well-known commercial photographer whom she had never met but had seen strutting with gay señoritas in the zona rosa of Mexico City.

"Naw, not the type," the American said. "That boudoir flower can't be the lady reporter you've been gabbing about. But she's a refugee all right."

"It's her, I tell you," the other insisted. "My friends told me she was coming here to get a story. She's a story in herself. They say she rides a horse better than a man. She outwitted the Nazis for years until they finally caught her. Even then, the Swiss government was able to strike a deal for her release from the concentration camp."

Out of the corner of her eye, Erika saw the men staring at her, but she refused to look their way. Didn't it occur to the fools that she might understand English?"

"She's a looker all right," the American said with a hissing laugh. "How's your French, sprechen sie Deutsche? You say she's a Jew?"

"She's Swiss as I've told you," the Mexican said, lowering his voice. "Her mother was Jewish. I don't think the Nazis knew that when they arrested her. She was charged with unpatriorice acts … writing articles unfriendly to der Fuhrer, that sort of thing."

"Not only a Jew but a dumb one." The American lowered his own voice although Erika could still hear what the men were saying. "But she sure is well-stacked," the American went on. "Shall we introduce ourselves? I know some German."

Erika was prepared to turn down an imminent invitation in whatever language when she saw Manuel Castellanos coming toward the cafe. His immaculate white suit and polished boots seemed almost as out of place as Erika's wardrobe.

The two men rose to greet the mayor of Ocosingo, but he only nodded to them and went directly to Erika's table.

Manuel Castellanos lifted his panama hat from his head and Erika asked him to sit down. Despite his punctilious manners, Erika saw a carnal longing in the mayor's eyes whenever he gazed at her. She had encountered the same look in almost every plump, middle-aged official she'd met in Mexico. Her curiosity had never been strong enough to encourage the peeping lust but she liked Manuel Castellanos and was flattered by his attentions.

"Tell me, is there any news?" Erika asked when the mayor sat down.

"Yes, there is good news. It came over the telegraph."

Erika felt as if a refreshing breeze had fluttered across the afternoon. "Is Pancho Balam coming?" she asked excitedly.

"The news is not about Pancho Balam."

The breeze fell as suddenly as it had risen and Erika felt trapped in the hot, motionless air. But the mayor was brimming over with his tidings. "Governor Alvarez has approved the funds for the expedition I have proposed. Not as much as is needed, but it gives the project an official stamp, so to speak."

It was a zephyr of hope. "Marvelous!" she forced herself to be cheerful. "The governor's backing may be all you need to persuade Pancho Balam to lead the expedition. I'm sure he can prevail upon his rich friends to contribute."

"I don't think he has rich friends anymore." Manuel Castellanos shook his head sadly and turned the brim of his hat slowly in his hands.

"Why do you say that?" Erika was surprised. The mayor placed his hat on the table and shrugged.

"He went to the northern plains of Chiapas to look for abandoned oil wells for the Toltec Oil and Gas Company. Those are his only expeditions nowadays."

Erika felt uneasy. Castellanos knew something that could change the whole line of her story.

"I thought you wanted him to head the expedition," she said.

"Oh, there is no question that Claus Boehm, or Pancho Balam, as the Indians call him, is the best man for the job. But frankly, he's not a youngster any longer. Things have happened to him in New Orleans. I don't know. He's my choice, but well, I'm referring the names of all candidates to the governor. Alvarez could veto my choice in any case...."

Castellanos pulled himself up in his chair and attempted to regain his composure. He went on to speak about how important the expedition was to the State of Chiapas and, for that matter, to all of Mexico. Governor Alvarez liked the idea and had told Manuel personally that it was high time somebody charted the unknown parts of the Lacandon Rain Forest. The discovery of any Mayan treasures would be a bonus. Castellanos had reason to believe the plan had backers in Mexico, although the governor never referred to them and insisted that funds were limited. But the mayor went on to say that interests in Mexico and elsewhere wanted to know how much of the rain forest could be leveled for commercial use. He didn't like the deforestation aspect of it himself. The jungle had always been part of his life. But he had become mayor of Ocosingo by being a realist. If converting the jungle into farm land was good for Mexico, then he would do his part. Besides, the jungle would grow back. It always had. Didn't it swallow up the Mayans?

"What I'm hoping to get out of it is a road that will someday be built linking Ocosingo with the Yucatan," he said finally. "Ocosingo has been a poor cow town for all its existence."

Erika was aware that the two men at the next table were watching and listening intently.

"Why do you have reservations about Claus Boehm?" she asked.

The mayor was looking out over the square as if he were imagining his new Ocosingo. He shrugged and sighed deeply.

Erika's heart sank. Her article was in serious trouble. The editor wanted a story about a conquering hero. She pressed Castellanos for details.

"I only know there are stories of fancy cars his beautiful young wife drove through the streets of New Orleans. It is said she had expensive tastes and he couldn't keep up with them. But if you want to know my personal theory, I think it has to do with the fact that they took him away from the jungle. The last time Claus Boehm had come to the jungle was in 1932. He did not see it again until a visit in 1941. When a man has lived in the jungle as Claus Boehm has, he cannot be away from it for very long without risking his sanity. I have seen the effects of the jungle on men. When a man is in the jungle, his senses become completely alive. He must constantly think and act according to the reality around him. But when he is away from that reality, his mind is like a machine that keeps running after its purposes have been served. The man finds that he does not know how to turn off the machinery in his head."

"If Claus Boehm loved the jungle so much, why didn't he return to it long ago?" Erika asked.

Manuel Castellanos asked if he could light up a cigar. Erika had no objection. The aroma sweetened the smell of incense coming from the church.

"Claus Boehm made his famous expeditions in the twenties," Castellanos explained. "The University of New Orleans rewarded him by making him Director of Meso-American Studies. What man in his prime of life wouldn't have taken the job? But as years passed, there were fewer expeditions." Castellanos knew from his own experience that the tedium of administrative work could take a heavy toll on the soul. He had learned to live with it. But surely in the case of Claus, it was a waste of an enormous talent. Maybe Claus hadn't understood his need for the jungle.

They fell silent for a while, looking over the square and listening to the flies buzz around them. A baseball hit by a small boy struck the hanging figure of Judas causing it to swing back and forth. The church bells tolled. It was two o'clock. The plane would come soon or not at all. The winds came up in the late afternoon, making it difficult for pilots to land a plane in the small cow pasture that was the landing field of Ocosingo.

The Yankee at the next table took advantage of the silence. "Señor Castellanos, I don't think the plane from Villahermosa is coming today," he called.

The mayor gave a short nod of his head, but did not answer.

Erika was about to ask Castellanos who the man was when he stood up and came toward them. Erika was surprised that he was tall. He appeared to be in his mid-forties. His small bird-like eyes peered at her inquisitively over the large hawk nose that protruded out of a bony face. With his large brow and chinless jaw, he looked like the harsh schoolmaster of children's stories. But his thin mouth was set in a lewd, egoistic smile.

"Señor Castellanos, forgive my intrusion, but I'm waiting for your opinion of my proposal. Have you read it?"

Castellanos looked impatiently at the man, and replied with an edge of irritation in his voice.

"I have. It's very professional, of course. But Señor Barnes, as I told you, I am referring the names of all candidates and relevant papers to the governor."

The man persisted. "But what is your opinion? Surely, your recommendation will mean a lot."

Castellanos scowled and tugged at the collar of his shirt.

"I've just told you—"

The man laughed derisively. "I hope your loyalty to fallen friends has not outweighed your concern for the future of your town?"

He pulled his chair over to their table and sat with them. Erika was annoyed at his presumption. He looked at her with unabashed prurience and winked.

"Since our honorable mayor is not polite enough to introduce us, allow me. I am David Barnes, Associate Professor of Middle American Studies at New Orleans. My good friend Manuel tells me you have been waiting for Pancho Balam for some time."

She felt his foul breath on her face when he laughed. He leaned toward her confidentially. She was sickened by the closeness of the impudent eyes. "Let me assure you that it is better for you if he doesn't come here. I knew Claus in New Orleans," he continued. "Of course, they had to let him go. Why, I've seen him stagger drunkenly to the lectern in embarrassing attempts to make fund raising speeches he couldn't finish. How many times since then have I seen him in the streets wearing the same shirt day after day, reeking with the stench of gin? But I can't pity him."

Barnes leaned almost out of his chair, toward Erika, his hot, acrid breath mixing with the scent of spoiled fruit in the tropical air. "But, say, won't you and the mayor join us in a drink? I'll call the waiter for more glasses. An occasional snort of rum is the best way to stay healthy in this climate."

"No, thank you," Erika and Castellanos said together. Barnes took the bottle from Quarles, who seemed on the verge of dozing off, and poured a drink for himself. Barnes pulled his chair closer to Erika and fixed his beady eyes on her. He slapped his hand on the table. "Claus Boehm finally came down here to avoid paying the taxes he owed the American government. Pretty much like a foreigner. It's bad enough us Yanks have to fight the foreigners' wars for them."

Erika found herself trembling with rage. "We're both foreigners here!" she snapped. She was angry at herself for taking the fool seriously.

The small eyes narrowed. "Here, here, you have a tongue worthy of old Pancho Balam himself. Aren't you Madam Fi Fi, lounging in the tropics as if you were sitting under an umbrella in the Tuilleries. But I'll show you the kind of foreigner Boehm was. I was head of Meso-American studies in New Orleans when he plotted to have me ousted and sent back to botanical studies. I wanted to give the university the world's largest collection of pre-Columbian artifacts. But Boehm manipulated the trustees in favor of his interest in preserving the monuments and accused me of selling things to private collectors. He wanted to leave the temples the way he found them. But his refusal to compromise got him in the end. Ah, enough of that," Barnes's tone changed as he turned to Erika and smiled. "Let's drink to your beauty and refinements. I mean no offense. If you'll have dinner with me tonight, I'll prove to you that a Yankee can show a lady a good time. Let's forget the argument. It's not important."

"The argument is not important because you are not important," Erika said, getting up from the table. "If you will excuse me, Señor Castellanos, I'm going to my hotel to rest."

Barnes called something after her as she walked down the street, but it was drowned out by a sudden scream of terror.

Chapter Two

"*Dios—Misericordia!*"

The scream came from the mouth of Manuel Castellanos. A mule train had entered the town. One of the mules was led away from the train by a man beating it with a stick. Erika saw the animal, with its burden, approach the table she had just left. The mayor's shout had made her stop. He then emitted a deep groan that seemed to rise up from the pit of his stomach.

"Jesus!" Barnes exclaimed, his face frozen in horror. Erika was drawn back to the table, as if the horror that had transfixed the men was a magnet. In addition to the two *chicle* boxes strapped on either side of the mule, Erika saw a hanging vine bag that contained a large lump that she took at first to be a dried gourd. It swung back and forth with the animal's movements. Erika realized the lump in the bag had caused the mayor to cry out in horror. Even Quarles, stirring in his brandy haze, gasped.

"*Dios, mio*," Manuel moaned.

Through the mesh, Erika made out the features of a human head, its shape distorted in the process of decomposition. Then the scent of putrefaction reached her nostrils. The man guiding the mule stopped before the table and removed his hat.

Manuel Castellanos gasped, staring at the head. The mayor wept openly in sobs that spoke of outrage and sorrow. Erika turned away as the smell overpowered her.

Hadn't Germany hardened her against everything? But before she knew what she was doing, she was vomiting on a bed of deep red flowers. Looking at her green discharge, she felt ashamed. Then a new thought struck a nerve of fear. Had she looked upon the head of Claus Boehm himself?

"Do you recognize him, Señor Castellanos?" the man holding the reins of the mule said in a tone that suggested a reproach. "Do you see what happens now in the jungle? His other parts are in the bellies of vultures and in the tiny sacs of ants. But I have his heart in another bag. Look."

He held up another net bag in which a grey shapeless mass hung.

"The Lacandons!" Castellanos cried out, his voice shaking.

"The bastards!" Barnes said.

The mule driver glanced around the small group that had gathered. Even the sad, stoical faces of the town's Indians looked fearful.

"Yes, Mayor Castellanos. The Lacandons of the south. Those who hate Christ and serve the demons of the forest. Your friend had gone beyond El Zapote to find the ruins that the old stories say are near the Perlas River. Even the *chicleros* won't go there anymore."

"The bloody savages," Barnes put in. "I'd like to put the fear of Christ Almighty into them. I tell you, Castellanos, I'm your man. Just remember. Claus Boehm himself told us that the Lacandons had given up human sacrifice fifty years ago. If I know those barbarians, they ripped the heart out while it was still beating and decapitated him later. Give me a chance. I'll go in with alligator hunters as my field men. They're the only ones the Lacandons respect. You have to recommend me to the governor now."

Castellanos turned savagely to Barnes. "Do you want to eat my friend's head to give you strength?" Manuel lifted the head from the sack and held its grim visage before Barnes. Barnes did not flinch. "You should live with vultures, Señor Barnes!"

The mayor turned to the mule driver. "How did you find him?"

"We decided to look for him after he was gone from camp for a week. There was little sap in the zapote trees and we had little work. We knew we had gone in too early for *chicle*, but he had persuaded us to make the trip. We came to the Perlas River with fear in our hearts. There we found a dugout canoe—the kind the Lacandons make—half-hidden in some reeds. In it we found the head and the heart. As we collected them and started to leave that place, we heard a voice coming from high in the trees. It was one of them. We were surprised that there were those among them who had learned some Spanish. The voice said, 'We give back to you what you have given to our Lord Hachakyum.' We didn't know what it all meant." He turned to Barnes. "You are a *científico* of the forest. Who is Hachakyum?"

Barnes and Quarles exchanged puzzled glances. Barnes told the mule driver he didn't know.

Erika found her gaze drawn irresistibly to the head. The nausea came back. But she had to know if the remnant of a corpse was Claus Boehm.

She touched the mayor's arm. "Manuel, I'm sorry. The man who was killed, who was he?"

The mayor waited a long time before answering, as if to utter the name of the dead man were some sort of sacrilege.

"His name is Mateo," he said finally. "We grew up together. As boys, we dreamed of finding lost civilizations in the jungle. Mateo was a *chiclero* foreman but the archaeologists always learned from him. He went with Claus in the old days. Mateo was looking for ruins south of El Zapote. There have been stories by wandering *chicleros* over the years. But the only man I know who met the Lacandons south of the Perlas River and came back to talk about it was Claus Boehm himself."

The mule driver struck the side of the mule. "I am taking Mateo's remains to his family in the Tzeltal Indian colony of El Real. It is a long trek over a mountain and I want to get there before dark."

Chapter Three

Erika entered the mud-spattered courtyard. An emaciated flamingo and two plump vultures paraded about the stone enclosure of a well. She entered the hotel and climbed the stairs to her room.

Alone in the high-ceilinged room that had been darkened by closing the wooden shutters, Erika could not stop shaking. And now she felt the familiar gloom, hot and pressing against her chest. She removed her dress, but the feeling was still there. Erika turned on the frosted light bulb above her head and began to pace up and down.

Why had she come? No American periodical would be interested in a story built around a broken-down alcoholic. Even the war stories had to be inspirational. She had admired the young Claus Boehm whose personal accounts of his explorations in the twenties she had read. But now, her idea of writing about a man who had come to terms with himself in the rain forests of Middle America seemed doomed.

She looked at the shabby furnishings that were intended to create a European decor. It struck her that the owner of the Ocosingo Hotel had recreated a model of all the hiding places of her last ten years in Germany. Here was the same massive chest of drawers, the squat dressing table, the big warped mirror, the bed with the broken springs, the bidet in the bathroom, the high ceiling from which a frosted globe was suspended. It could be any of the rooms in which she had lived huddled with other members of the Party Against Fascism. They stayed in one until somebody got arrested and then they moved to another room. The thing the rooms had in common, she realized now, was that they looked as if they were designed for the storage of furniture rather than for any human habitation. Although the addresses changed, the rooms were always the same and the fear that came from knowing that you were being hunted always hung in the rooms and would not be wiped away with dust or washed away with the rains.

But as long as the fear was there, there was hope, hope that there would be news of Hans who had been arrested shortly after their marriage, hope that the madness of a civilization would subside, hope that rescue would come from across the ocean. When she was finally arrested, the fear left but so did the hope. And in the concentration camp, there was nothing but despair.

Erika opened the shutters and looked down at the straw figure of Judas which was hanging in the square. The boys had abandoned their baseball game and gone to join their families in siesta. The lifeless figure that was to be burned on Easter morning presided over the heat and the stillness and the sleeping drunks.

Was it right to have left Germany, to have abandoned all that responsibility? Of course, there had been no real choice. But she did not feel good about it. Still, the consul in Berne had been right. To have gone back would have been to face certain death. He had been able to use his diplomatic position to obtain her release from the camp because the Nazis, at least that early in the war, did not want a reputation for burning daughters, however wayward, of Swiss families of good German stock. Her father had been a doctor, a Lutheran, and they didn't know of her Jewish mother.

So she had been deprived of her martyrdom. Yet she was certain, even now, the perfection of Switzerland was no place for her. Her parents had died during her imprisonment, and she had despaired of ever gaining news of Hans. So she had taken the papers the consul had arranged for her and made her way to the port of Genoa and a ship to America. And now, on a lazy tropical afternoon, watching a Judas who was waiting to be burned, she felt more acutely than ever before, the pain of being alone and useless.

Erika was determined to shake off her mood and she came away from the window to sit before the dresser and comb her long, thick red hair which had matted in the moist air. As she pulled at the knots with her comb, she regarded her reflection with some satisfaction. Despite the telling lines of age around her eyes, she was, at thirty-nine, a compelling beauty with a figure that would make a school-girl proud. Her eyes shone with the brightness of a child's, and her skin, though it had lost the slick sheen of ripeness, glowed softly and was smooth. Her high cheekbones and broad features composed the beauty of her face. Her breasts, if they drooped lower than those of a younger woman, were full and would be ample treasures in the hands of any privileged lover. It had been a long time since she had been cradled in a man's arms, and Erika had almost forgotten the warm pleasure of skin against skin. But she thought of it now with a deep heave of her bosom. She had not wanted anyone after Hans had been taken away by the Nazis and here in Mexico her only potential lovers were nervous, giggly bureaucrats with fat wives. She did not want to increase her sense of alienation by being a Mexican's contraband mistress. Yet she knew that beauty's erosion had begun and her time, though prolonged by the grace of God, was running out on her.

Suddenly, Erika heard the whir of an engine coming from outside. Nowhere, in the last few days spent in Ocosingo, had she heard any sound faintly resembling it. Erika threw on her dress and ran out on the balcony. A flashing pinpoint of light swept across the sky. *Yes, it was a plane!*

She flew down the stairs and raced across the square in the direction of the cow field. The entire town of less than a thousand inhabitants, save for a few die-hard drunks, ran in the direction of the cow field. Erika ran with them. The plane circled as it descended. Indians drove cows and pigs out of the pasture. Then with the sound of the propeller roaring in exhilaration, the plane landed in skips on the bumpy field.

The crowd cheered. Children surrounded the plane. The pilot got out and went around to open the door on the other side. A handsome man stepped onto the field and Erika felt herself drawn to him instantly. There was a Danish cleanness in his features and in his sky blue eyes and salted, blonde hair. His body was lean and agile as he dropped gracefully to the ground. For all the presence of Scandinavian glitter, his attire of drill trousers, Chamula shirt and mahogany vine knapsack hanging over one shoulder, seemed natural to him. Then his eyes met hers, lifting her heart for one buoyant moment, assuring her that he commanded all within his purview, that he had come to perform some extraordinary deed. The admonitions of Castellanos and the Yankee were swept away.

"You are Erika Boeshure," he said to her in English. His voice was filled with chivalry which mixed deliciously with the sighs of the elephant ear plants that bordered the tropical cow pasture.

"And you are Claus Boehm." Her voice expressed the gladness she felt.

Chapter Four

A week later, Erika and Claus Boehm were sitting on the side of a mountain overlooking valley of Ocosingo. She felt more comfortable in the loose-fitting Chamula shirt he'd given her and the light skirt and sandals she'd borrowed from the maid at the hotel. He seemed perfectly at ease in his Indian clothes and high boots. They drank *posole* which Erika carried in a calabash. They both agreed that the Indian pick-me-up drink of cornmeal, chilis and water was best enjoyed with the addition of brown sugar.

But the agreement was one of the few they'd had. Claus had been chivalrous enough in their meetings, the perfect gentleman, courteous to a fault. When she'd accidentally sat on his field hat at their first meeting in Manuel's house, he'd joked it away, insisting he preferred the squashed shape she'd given it. He let her take as many pictures of him as she pleased. But during the interviews, his attitude changed. Whenever she asked some personal questions, he seemed offended, either choosing to ignore her or answering in a circumspect way. When she brought up some points she'd found in his writings, he was quick to correct her, or show impatience with her limited knowledge of Mexico and his profession.

"No, you can't say the oranges you're plucking from the trees are native to Mexico. Where did you get such an idea? All citrus fruit comes from the Old World," he snapped at her when she asked him to look at some notes. "Tomatoes are from the New World, yes, even the venerable potato. Corn, of course. Your vaunted Swiss chocolate is made from the cacao that grows in this jungle," he added impatiently.

"Swiss chocolate? Next you'll be telling me that Mexicans invented the Swiss watch."

But he was not amused and looked away from her. He seldom looked into her face and certainly not with the glint that shone in Manuel's eyes. A beam of lust in all that Scandinavian glitter would have made her feel a little human again. She knew Claus had a reputation for being a ladies' man but, she thought, with some regret, *he certainly isn't wasting his charms on me.* It was as if the very attributes of her body and mind, which had made countless dull men pant after her in the past, repulsed Claus. His eyes seemed to tell her that her Nordic brand of sexuality was obscene in the tropics, that despite her change in dress, she was still Lili Marlene sitting in a Berlin cafe with a veil over her hat and a tight fitting dress. If she was a sex idol to the Manuels and Barneses of the world, Claus had tired of sex idols long ago. If her mind struck other men as lucid and sharp, her intelligence was to him the essence of mediocrity—as boring as the neat, antiseptic streets of Copenhagen which he had abandoned years ago.

How could she interview him? She tried to see through her wounded vanity to find the true reason for his disapproval. Of course, the women he had known in New Orleans were parlor pillows: soft and frilly. They gossiped in whispers and pretended never to know the least bit about archaeology or what life in a rain forest was like except to marvel at his exploits when he chose to tell an entertaining story.

But Erika had the audacity to come to his special male preserve. She dared to ask him his secrets. Perhaps he believed she wanted to take him apart and put him back together again, rearranged. When she asked him about his life before coming to America, he was vague, saying only that he had not wanted to go into his father's machine manufacturing business in Copenhagen. He had roamed Europe, visiting castles and museums. He had wanted to be an artist, but he hadn't wanted to paint, not with a brush anyway. But he supposed she wouldn't understand that. She bit her tongue. Why had he agreed to be interviewed at all? Certainly, he was shrewd enough to know that he needed the publicity. But he obviously didn't like the price.

Around them, wild flowers displayed their blazing colors. The cluster of dull, red tile roofs nestled below. Claus had been speaking in a crisp, aggressive Spanish, but now he changed to English. It was the English of New Orleans and it floated easily through the moist, tropical air.

"That's as far as I dare go in Spanish as I learned most of the language from muleteers. I'm always afraid that some bits of profanity might creep in."

"Please speak as you wish," she pounced on the crumb of consideration. "I'm no boudoir flower although I was accused of being one the day you arrived."

"By Barnes. Yes. He has an eye for the ladies. If that sort of compliment is what you want."

She was sorry she had brought the matter up. Now she didn't know what to say at all. If a good reporter controlled an interview, she was a failure.

But she was a trained observer and had learned some things about her subject despite his oblique answers to her questions.

If Claus was an alcoholic, the jungle was more curative than all the spas of Bavaria. She had not seen him take a drink and she had to admit she was impressed with the casual way he dispensed medicine and treated the wounds of the townspeople of Ocosingo who approached him for help. When the women in the church had asked him to paint the places on the saints where pieces of plaster had peeled away, making the poor idols look as if they were covered with Band Aids, Claus had been happy to oblige, kneeling before the gaudy statues for hours with brush and paint, restoring the red of the blood that flowed through martyrs' wounds.

They sat in silence now, looking at the smoky hills across the valley. Erika felt she knew Claus Boehm best when she wasn't asking questions.

"I feel a great peace here," she said, as she let her surroundings take possession of her.

"We are only at the door of the jungle. There the peace is indescribable."

Whenever Claus spoke of the jungle, it was the way a man spoke of the home of a lost love, a home to which his mind continually returned.

"I can see the jungle is very important to you," Erika said.

Claus broke into a grin for the first time.

"No doubt about it. If Manuel wants an old mule skinner of Mexico and Central America to head his team, I'll be glad to oblige. No one knows better how to cuss a mule in Spanish, Nahuatl, Maya, Tzeltal, or Quiche. Show me a mule and an expense account and I'm on my way."

Erika took a deep breath and ventured a question.

"Is the expedition you're just coming from now the first since your trip of 1932?"

He looked at her as if she had struck him in the solar plexus. "This was a bread and butter mission. Is that what you want to write about? Looking for lost oil wells for a greedy oil company isn't the best kind of archaeology."

"You know it's my job to ask you questions. And I must make it clear to you that I'll write the truth as I see it," Erika said evenly.

He looked away as if he wanted to get as far from her as possible. "I'm aware of all that. I agreed to the interviews." He shook his head. "All right, let's go on and be done with it then."

She decided to set aside her need to be pleasing. She had come as a reporter and she was going to get her story, whether Claus Boehm liked it or not. She looked at her written list of questions.

"What does archaeology mean to you?" she asked.

A smile flickered over his face. He rested his head against the tree behind them and gazed up at some circling kites.

"Archaeology is the art of making dead men tell their tales," Claus said. She wanted to laugh at this inflated conception of his craft but she checked herself.

Erika looked down at her notes, "I've read about your famous expeditions in the twenties, your discoveries at Palenque and Uaxactun. And you've made the best maps of the jungle that exist. But tell me, do you think there's anything like Palenque in Chiapas that's never been found?" she asked.

Claus turned to her suddenly, gripping her hand in the manner of one who is about to reveal a secret that has been locked up in his heart for years.

"Yes." His voice trembled momentarily. "That's why I need Manuel's expedition! Most scholars think all the big ones have been found. But there's one more prize in there."

He gestured toward the dark shadows behind them and breathed deeply.

"Somewhere in that big jungle lie the ruins of a city that was built on a scale grander than Palenque and is perhaps just as beautiful. It's been known only to a few aborigines in this century and now, it may be lost even to them. Do you think I'm crazy?"

"Of course not." Erika found her heart beating rapidly in response to his excitement. "Tell me, why do you think it exists?"

"On my last expedition down the Jatate River in 1932, I met a Lacandon Indian, one of those aborigines who haunt the nether part of the woods. I'd befriended a group of Lacandons in the northern part of the forest in 1925. But the Lacandons of the south are another thing. They despise strangers. When I came upon this Lacandon, he had just missed hitting some flying macaws with his bow and arrow. He was an old man and his arrows had fallen short of their targets. He was so unhappy about losing the game that he wasn't surprised to see me and spoke freely about his failing powers. He said he was the chief of his people and that it would be taken as a bad sign for all of them if he did not come back with birds. I offered to help, but he got excited when I aimed my rifle at some curassow that appeared in the trees. He told me that if I fired at them I would only frighten all of the birds away from that place. We waited together another hour and in that time I brought down two macaws with his bow and arrow and we became friends. The old man was chief of some migrating Indians who were trying to escape invasions of lumbermen near their old lands on the Lacanja River. They carried few supplies with them other than sacks of corn and the little clay pots they burn incense in. He told me one of the pots came from the holy city of the gods. When I asked him where the city was, he became vague.

All he said was that it was in a part of the forest called Menche. He described a temple with painted walls, and a heroic-sized figure of the god of creation cut in stone. Well, I was coming to the end of an expedition when I met this chief. The mules were exhausted, and supplies were low. My muleteers were eager to get back to their cornfields. The chief was circumspect about giving me any information about the location of the site and I knew I couldn't bribe him. Yet I think there was a reason he told me about it, a reason he may have only dimly understood himself. But whatever his reason, such a discovery would be the greatest since the discovery of the Tomb of Ramses III in Egypt."

"Did you ever look for it?" Erika asked.

Claus shook his head ruefully.

"That's just it. When I returned from that expedition, I vowed to go back and find Menche. I didn't know I had just finished my last expedition as a professional archaeologist. Maybe it was my very confidence in the future that left me unguarded for what was to come."

Here he let his voice trail off. But he continued to talk in a half whisper, his eyes fixed straight ahead, as if he were addressing a ghost that had come to sit on a fallen log. "I never believed that things would get the best of me. I thought I could handle it all. Before I knew it, I was out of a job and a wife and my days as a hot shot explorer were over." He turned to Erika suddenly, as if just remembering she was there. "But, say, you can't end your story that way, can you?"

They sat in silence. Lights began to come on one by one in the valley below them. Erika saw smoke rise from pipe chimneys. Ocosingo seemed a world of comfort. She and Claus remained on a peak of tension, a mound of unfulfilled ambition where old dreams smouldered.

Erika turned to Claus. "I think you can organize an expedition and take it to the deepest parts of the jungle until you find those ruins," she said. "That's how I want to end my story."

Claus smiled at her.

"Thanks for your confidence. I know I can do it given half a chance. I need this expedition. Without a university connection, I can't get a grant anywhere. And let's face it, I'm not getting any younger. I know Manuel has decided to place the decision in the hands of the governor. That's the politics of it. There are two German teams that are bidding. You saw my old colleague, David Barnes hanging around town last week. He wants the commission as badly as I do. He didn't impress Manuel but he's gone to the governor to make his bid personally. Barnes's kind of archaeology is more to the governor's liking."

"Barnes is a swine," Erika said impulsively.

"I can't throw stones." Claus gave a short laugh.

A breeze came up and they listened to the trees moan as they rubbed together.

"Yes, I've thought about Menche for ten years. It's out there somewhere, waiting. The Lacandon Indians say the gods need people to worship them."

The valley below them had filled completely with shadow. Lights went on here and there until Ocosingo looked like a cluster of fireflies. On the mountains opposite them, the orange glow of the setting sun lingered.

Without another word, they rose together and clambered down the mountain.

Chapter Five

When Erika got back to the hotel, there was a cable waiting for her.

STORY OF LACANDON EXPEDITION SOUNDS GREAT CAN YOU ACCOMPANY EXPEDITION AND DO PHOTO ESSAY FOR SERIES WE CAN RUN IN THREE PARTS STOP BOOK POSSIBLE GET PICTURES OF THOSE SAVAGES EATING HEARTS STOP WILL CABLE 50000 PESOS ADVANCE TO TUXTLA BANK ON YOUR REPLY STOP
JOHN RAWLINS MEXICAN EDITOR COLLIER'S MAGAZINE

Erika was so excited, she took a bath to calm down. The warm caress of the water made her shiver with pleasure. She looked down at her shapely breasts and belly and thighs. Yes, she was beautiful, Mexico was beautiful, even old sour-puss Claus was beautiful. He had melted a little at the end of the interview. Maybe it was just that she had set his mind going on his dream. But just as she was enjoying an exuberant tingle that rippled over her skin, the doubts began to splash against her. Of course, she had failed to tell Rawlins in her cable, sent right after her first meeting with Claus, that it was far from certain that her chosen subject would get the commission. And now Barnes was in Tuxtla making his case to the governor personally. Wouldn't the governor see that Barnes was a fool? Maybe not. Perhaps it was irrelevant. But surely it was a matter of record that Barnes had sold the university's artifacts to private collectors. Of course, from the governor's point of view, the university shouldn't have had them in the first place. Mexico wasn't letting its archaeological treasures out of the country anymore.

Claus had visited the governor before going out on the oil well expedition. Did the governor know about Claus's alcoholic past? Who would have told him? Of course, Barnes was telling him right now. Claus said he never drank in the jungle and Erika believed him. But Barnes would lie about it. What a low form of life Barnes was. Of course she wasn't certain that Barnes was telling the governor. But he would. She certainly couldn't make a hero out of Barnes. She had been rooting for Pancho Balam all along even though he treated her like an old, sore-ridden mule.

The Mexican soap was not good at making suds and only succeeded in making the bath water cloudy. In the milky cloud, Erika saw the reflection of her biggest obstacle. Claus himself. Would he take her along? If her presence in Ocosingo was an intrusion, what would he think of her riding one of his mules through the jungle at his side? She had to convince him that she would be an asset. She was a professional photographer. She would pay her own way and save him money. Surely, he would see the logic of it.

Erika dried herself with the frayed towel that hung over the out-of-place bidet.

Suddenly, through the half open window that looked over the square, she recognized the driver who had brought in the corpse. He was adjusting a pack strapped to his mule. Goose pimples spread across her body. She saw the dismembered head in her mind, the matted hair streaming over the ghastly face. The dead man had been killed in the very lands Claus wanted to explore and by the very Indians Claus wanted to meet. Did she want to go to such places?

In the panic that seized her, Erika dressed hurriedly. She tried to remember the story of Claus bringing down birds for the old chief. Those Lacandons loved Claus, didn't they? Or was that romantic nonsense?

She put on the drill pants and boots she had bought in the market. The trousers were rather snug and she swam in the boots, but she would need them today. Claus had promised her a walk over the mountain.

Ach, could the jungle be more dangerous than the Europe she had just left? She had spent the last ten years with impending death. She thought about Manuel's reference to those who wanted to destroy the rain forest. Some instinct in her told her it would be a catastrophe greater than the destruction of Germany. Yes, she was a reporter and it was her job to get out the news. It could be the most important article she would ever write.

Chapter Six

Claus handed Erika a tortilla which he had wrapped around a fish.

"Manuel expects the governor's decision this afternoon," he said with a deep sigh that expressed his nervous excitement. "The Germans were eliminated yesterday."

"Then there's a good chance for you." Erika had to suppress a desire to touch his arm. "I'm excited for you, Claus." A cluster of flowers suddenly floated upward, causing her to realize they were butterflies. She wanted to go with them, the butterflies and Claus.

"It would have been politically awkward for Alvarez to have chosen the Germans," Claus went on. "Since the war, German citizens haven't been allowed residency in Mexico City. I suppose there's the feeling that they will establish a foothold for the fatherland wherever they go. Can you imagine Hitler addressing a throng of Indians on top of the Castillo at Chichen Itza?"

Erika found it hard to find anything about Hitler amusing. But it was good news. The choice was between Claus and Barnes. "I'm sure the governor will pick you over that fool."

"But he's not a fool. Even if I win, the money isn't enough to do what I want. If I'm lucky enough to be appointed, I'll need money for some first rate photographic equipment. Then I'll need a photographer and field men and enough money to buy supplies and hire a team of reliable muleteers."

"I know how you can get a photographer and a reliable muleteer free of charge," Erika said suddenly.

"Splendid," Claus looked up. "Tell me."

Erika took a deep breath before answering. "I'm a professional photographer and I have a natural talent for cussing mules," she said.

Claus jumped up as if he had heard a jaguar moving in the bush.

"See here, that's entirely out of the question. It has always been a cardinal rule for me never to take a woman on an expedition."

Erika's heart sank, but she pressed on. She had rehearsed her argument all morning.

"I don't fancy myself strolling through the jungle holding a silk parasol and trailing a gossamer gown with rustling petticoats underneath. I'm an excellent horsewoman, a trained observer, and a good nurse. And I was brought up hiking the Swiss Alps."

Claus was pacing about, and finally pounded his fist on the trunk of a banana tree. Erika remained seated on the grassy slope, struggling to maintain her composure.

"When it comes down to it, I'm convinced that a woman may be better suited biologically for the long trail than a man. But that's not the point. We once took a Tzeltal girl as a cook and within a week, one of our muleteers attacked another with a knife in a jealous fit."

"Do you think I will attempt to seduce your muleteers?" Erika said laughing.

"No, but, let's be frank. You're a woman and an attractive one. On a long expedition, as this one may be, complications will inevitably set in."

Erika felt her face burn. It was the first time he had complimented her for her beauty, but now she was annoyed at his reasons.

"What are you afraid of, Claus?"

"Having you on the expedition would simply be bad for discipline!" He brought his fist down hard on the bough of a nearby tree.

Erika almost laughed. "Believe me Claus, I'm the last person in the world you need fear will cause slack in discipline. There is a little Swiss canon at the very core of my being. You'll be sick to death of my disgusting efficiency. Your muleteers will tire of my badgering. Claus, from our walks together, and the stories you've told me, I feel the lure of the jungle and it's strong. You needn't feel any obligation to me no matter what happens along the way."

Claus sat down beside her. They listened to the silence together. Then Claus spoke. "The conversation of muleteers isn't always stimulating. One gets lonely for good talk. Look, I don't even have the expedition yet. But when the trip becomes my responsibility, I'll have to use my best professional judgment. And so I have to thank you for your offer and decline."

Erika wanted to tell him about the cablegram but surely, since he was such a disgusting man of principle, he would despise her for trying to entice him with that now. And she couldn't throw herself at his mercy, pleading her poverty, begging him to grant her the one opportunity she'd had in Mexico.

She bit her lip. Erika knew her eyes were wet with disappointment. She felt Claus's hand on her arm. His touch was gentle.

"I'm sorry. I really am," he said quietly.

They got up and began to climb down the mountain to Ocosingo.

Chapter Seven

As they approached the town square, they saw Manuel Castellanos sitting alone at a table. Erika knew he was waiting for them. Her heart leapt in anticipation. But as they got closer, she saw his face was glum. He rose from his table and placed his arms around his old friend's shoulders.

"Barnes got the expedition," he said straight off.

Claus stiffened, saying nothing, and sat down at the table. He stared straight ahead, kneading his hands together. His eyes focused on nothing. He was trying to maintain his composure, but Erika could see he was having a difficult time.

"Well, I rather expected it." He was breathing heavily.

Erika and Manuel sat down on either side of him. Erika did not know what to say.

"It really wasn't your kind of expedition," Manuel said consolingly. "The expedition didn't have the purist motives behind it. Barnes will botch it, anyway. You know he can't control a field team. To begin with, for muleteers, he'll hire the cheapest labor he can find in the saloons. The last expedition he led, a botanical study for Carnegie looking for wild rubber, the men wanted to kill him when he tried to cheat them out of their pay."

But Erika could see that the mayor's words were cold comfort to Claus.

"How much money did he get?" Claus asked wearily.

Manuel frowned. "Well, Barnes was very clever there. That's his knack. He got Alvarez to raise the figure considerably. I don't know the exact amount, but you'll hear him boasting about it."

"God!" Claus exclaimed. "I guess he promised to deliver everything Alvarez wanted."

"Yes, he even promised him a Mayan temple for his patio. And a Lacandon family for the Tuxtla zoo."

"The way they did in Guatemala," Claus said grimly. "Putting them on exhibition behind barbed wire at a fair." He strummed his fingers nervously on the table. Erika knew he would not be able to contain his unhappiness for long.

"Claus, I'm sorry," Manuel blurted out. "I should have insisted on you. I can see that now I listened to others. It was my cowardice."

Claus looked up at his old friend. "It's not your fault, Manuel."

The boy from the gaseoso stall came over to the table.

"Let's have a drink to cheer us up." Manuel looked up at the boy who held an empty tray. "Boy, bring us a bottle of brandy."

Erika shot Manuel an apprehensive look. Had he forgotten so soon that Claus was an alcoholic? A drink now could start him on a course of disaster. The expression on the face Manuel turned back to her told her that he realized he had made a mistake. They saw the boy return from the gaseoso stall with a tray on which stood a full bottle of brandy and three clear shot glasses. The boy poured the brandy. Erika heard only the sounds of the glasses filling and the distant night crickets.

Manuel raised his glass in a nervous toast. Erika did not pick up hers, and Claus, who had begun to raise his glass, set it back down on the table.

"Here, Manuel, drink mine for me. My stomach feels a bit uneasy. If you don't mind, I'd prefer some foaming chocolate."

Manuel nodded readily. "Excellent idea. I'll take this bottle home for medicinal use."

Erika drew a deep sigh of relief when Claus passed his brandy glass to Manuel.

The hot, foaming chocolate, spicy with chilis, came a few minutes later. Manuel made a feeble toast. "*Salud,*" he said in a low voice. Despite her sadness, Erika enjoyed the warm, bubbly drink.

When the big mugs were empty, Castellanos cleared his throat uneasily. "Since you two have—uh, only another day or so to spend in Ocosingo, I'll leave you to enjoy the simple evening pleasures of our town."

After the mayor left, Erika and Claus sat in silence. No gay marimba bands played in the square. Faint light bulbs flickered from strings above their heads. Erika felt touched by the melancholy of the world.

What happened to Claus was devastating. She would worry for herself later. There would be plenty of time for that. Claus was doomed to spend the rest of his life running errands for the oil companies. One day, he would be too old for that. She wanted to give him the consolation of human warmth. She reached across the rickety table and took his hand. He smiled weakly and muttered "Thank you." His hand was warm but she felt a tension in it.

They sat in silence, his hand in hers, listening to nothing more than the night crickets. But she felt the tension building up in Claus. His palm was sweating profusely now and he took his hand away.

Suddenly, Claus stood up.

"Will you excuse me?"

"Of course." She was surprised. "Where are you going? May I ask?"

"I'm going to get drunk."

Erika wanted to drag him back into his chair but she knew a scene would make matters worse. "I'm sorry," she said, helplessly.

"Don't worry. I won't drink in front of you. Do you want me to escort you to the hotel?"

"It's right behind us," she forced a laugh. "There's no need. Then she blurted out, "Claus, you were so brave when you passed the brandy."

"A mule skinner out of work can't afford to be brave," he cut her off. "Buenas noches." Erika watched him cross the square until he disappeared beyond a flicker of lights.

Somewhere, a phonograph record wobbled forlornly on a defective machine. The distorted voice of Bing Crosby, as ubiquitous as Coca Cola, crooned, "*Vaya con dios*, my darling." Then she heard the sound of rain as it began to fall on the orange trees above her and on the elephant earplants at the edge of the jungle.

Chapter Eight

The *mestizo* waited with the horse. Erika saw by the reddish patches of hair on its black coat and sagging underside, that the beast was very old. Anyone could see by its protruding ribs that it was underfed. Flies swarmed on open sores. Erika had estimated that it would take a healthy young stallion at least four days over the dirt roads that climbed the foothills of the San Cristobal mountains to reach Tuxtla. She knew of no other way to get there. It could be over a week before a plane came. When the rains got heavy, they wouldn't come at all. The *mestizo* said all the good horses had been sold to the coffee finca in El Real and the others were hired out to the *chicleros* who used them in place of mules. Luckily, she didn't have much luggage. Her camera equipment weighed more than everything else combined. Erika watched the horse switch its tail at the swarming flies in vain.

A light rain fell in Ocosingo. Soon the rains would be heavy and the die-hard sleepers she saw constantly in the square would all go into the jungle with their mule trains. The rainy season was the best time for collecting the sap.

She saw the boy coming from the hotel with her bags. There were two men with him. They were silhouettes in a swirl of fog, but when they got closer, Erika recognized Barnes's obscene grin. He tipped his sombrero.

"Madame Boeshure, if you please, we are driving to Tuxtla in my station wagon. You must come with us. You can't ride this disinterred carcass. We'll get you there in less than two days. I'll be buying some equipment and supplies in Tuxtla for my expedition. By the way, you and Quarles should have a lot to talk about."

Quarles tipped his field hat and bunched his jowls in a grin. "Doña Erika, I have read your news stories sent from Germany and admired them. You are brave but Señor Barnes is right, that beast cannot possibly make the trip to Tuxtla. Surely, as a horsewoman you realize—"

Erika thanked them for their concern, but declined. "I want to go by horse," she said.

"Nonsense," Barnes said. "We can't let you endanger your life. These hills are filled with bandits."

He signaled to the boy. He began to put her bags into the station wagon. "Excuse me! Those are my things. I really must go by horse!"

"I can't let you commit suicide. Besides, I have an offer to make you. The trip will give us a chance to discuss it." She felt the familiar acrid breath on her face. Quarles was holding open the door. The rain came down suddenly in strong gusts. Well, they were obnoxious but she had to admit that they were right. It was the only way she could get to Tuxtla and away from this town which she had no business coming to in the first place. Erika got into the car after her bags were loaded.

Barnes followed her and sat beside her in the back seat. She felt the pressure of his knee against hers through her cotton pants. Quarles began to drive along the square. The car bounced in the muddy street.

"This is an opportunity for both of us," Barnes said, putting his hand over her knee and grinning. "I know you have an offer to write a story about the Lacandon Expedition. Be thankful Claus didn't get it. I did and I invite you to join my team."

"I've really given up the idea," Erika said quickly.

"You'll be absolutely safe under my command. We're going to make some exciting discoveries too, and you'll be in on them. It may be the last great expedition in Middle America. We'll be getting rid of the stinking jungle and its savage inhabitants. I'm going to recommend some parkland preserves for recreation, of course. But the jungle is not immortal. It is only man who by his intellect—"

Barnes went on urgently. The car turned a corner of the square. Erika saw Claus Boehm standing in the doorway of the hotel.

"I'm sorry," she called to Quarles. "Please stop. I—I forgot something. I can't leave until tomorrow."

Quarles did not stop. Erika seized her bags and opened the door even as the car was in motion. Barnes clutched her around the waist.

"What kind of fool do you take me for?" he said savagely.

"Let go, Schweinhund!"

He tightened his grip. "Quarles, keep driving!" The car accelerated. Erika closed the door before it hit a lurching drunk. Barnes still held her. Leaving the square, the car had to stop for a mule train. Erika opened the door and threw her bags out of the car. She wrenched herself free of Barnes's grasp, and leapt into the street. Clutching a mud dripping bag in each hand, Erika ran to the hotel. But when she came to the entrance, Claus Boehm was gone.

Chapter Nine

The *servidora* said she hadn't been able to get into Pancho Balam's room to make it up all morning. When she came on duty at five to scrub the courtyard and help set up the kitchen she saw light under his door. She heard someone moving around behind the door and some occasional soft cursing. The cursing was in English most of the time. They were the only English words she knew. Sometimes the cursing behind the door was in a language she didn't recognize at all. But now the light under the door had gone out.

Erika had learned from the night clerk that Claus had not left his room the night before. He hadn't dined in the hotel restaurant and none of the waiters at the three gaseoso stalls had seen him. Nor had Erika who had waited until the cafe closed. When it did, she went to see Manuel Castellanos who assured her that Claus Boehm had locked himself up with a case of rum. Manuel urged her to go back to Mexico as soon as possible. A military plane would be coming in the morning or on the following day and he would get her on it.

It was now ten o'clock in the morning. Erika pressed some pesos in the *servidora's* hand and asked her to let her know as soon as there was any stirring in Pancho Balam's room. No, Erika said, she would not have breakfast in the hotel restaurant. She would like breakfast served at one of the tables on the square. The *servidora* agreed that the rain wouldn't begin until the afternoon.

Sitting in the square in her European dress with her eggs and chili sauce spread over a tortilla, Erika felt that all the signs were telling her to leave Ocosingo, once and for all. A man was asleep in the mud only a few feet away from her. His shining machete lay in the ooze. His hand had released its grip on the handle. Erika guessed that he was from an Indian colony in the hills, possibly El Real, and had come into town to buy the machete which looked brand new.

A perpendicular drunk lurched his way over to the machete, picked it up, and staggered off with it. Erika shouted at him but the man turned, laughing maliciously and waving the big knife at her.

If she had gone with Barnes, she'd be in Tuxtla now and away from these drunkards. What had prompted her to get out of the car? Did she really think she could do what she had been inspired to do when she saw Claus standing in the doorway? She found herself trying to make chains of reason. Hadn't she learned by now that they simply disintegrated here in the mud and the rum?

She knew her editor would have kissed the chains as though they'd been made of gold. *Collier's* magazine sets up grant to find lost Mayan city. Famous explorer heads expedition. As told and photographed by Erika Boeshure. Ach, was she crazy? She'd taken a wild gamble when she saw him from the car window, and made her mad dash across the square. But Manuel had told her only last night that the greatest danger to an expedition into the jungle led by Claus Boehm at this point was Claus himself. Still, Erika couldn't help remembering Claus saying that he never drank on an expedition. Maybe it wasn't as simple as all that. But she was determined to find out.

Erika stared at the door of the hotel. It was ten thirty and Claus hadn't come out. He had been in there twenty hours.

Erika finished her coffee. It was strong and she felt her blood quicken with it. Now, she was resolute. *All right, Panco Balam. So, you've crawled away to lick your wounds like a sick animal. Well, then, if balam means jaguar, I'm going to beard the jaguar in its den.*

Erika strode through the dimly lit lobby of the hotel and into the open court-yard. The vultures flew up in the wake of her brisk step. Without hesitation, she climbed swiftly up the stairs.

The *servidora* was mopping the balcony.

"*No, el no ha salido del cuarto,*" she said pointing to the door. The man had not come out of the room.

Erika went to the door and pounded firmly with her fist. There was no answer. She pounded again, harder this time. There was still no answer. Erika saw a machete leaning against the wall and picked it up. She banged on the door with the instrument.

She heard soft cursing inside. "*Deje me!* Go away!"

"Claus, it's Erika. I must speak to you. Open up."

There was silence on the other side of the door.

"I need to be left alone," he said finally.

"I missed an opportunity with Barnes to speak to you."

"Please. I can't help you. Or anybody. Go away."

"I won't go away. I thought you knew something about stubborn mules. Open the goddam door." She swung the machete with all her might and smote the door until it shook. The sound was like an explosion.

"Are you crazy?"

"You're crazy if you don't open that door. I'm breaking it down with a machete."

Erika heard him slide the latch on the other side of the door. She was admitted into a darkened room. The stale, fetid air sickened her instantly.

Claus gestured toward an armless, straight-backed chair and slumped on the bed. Erika dropped the machete, ran to the window and opened the shutters. The hot, white sun poured in, illuminating the huddled figure on the rumpled bed and the bottles of rum stacked on the floor. At least four of them were empty. The air was heavy with the odor of alcohol processed through sweat and fused with cigarette smoke. Crushed butts were piled high in a dish, like a plate of white beans.

Claus sat on the bed, shaking and rubbing his eyes.

She looked at his bent figure and sunken face. The man who sat hunched over on the bed was a far cry from the brave new Adam she had known a few days before. He looked about nervously, avoiding her eyes. He was unshaven. His clothes were wrinkled and soiled. She saw that his hands were shaking. His speech was random, and he left sentences hanging in mid-air.

"I'll be going on expeditions again, don't worry. Yes, I'm thinking of—" He broke off to stare out the window.

Erika noticed that his speech was slurred. He still had not looked at her directly. Claus picked up a bottle of rum and filled a small glass that was stained brown at the bottom.

"Yes, the rains will be coming, and, uh, what was I saying?"

There was an embarrassing silence as Claus brought the shot glass to his lips with a trembling hand. She listened painfully to the swallowing of the liquid and then they both stared at the empty glass shining on the small table. Claus filled the glass again. It was a cruel joke. Her impulse was to leave the room, run down the stairs and set off on the antique horse. But she stayed rooted to her chair. She had to have it out with Claus.

"There will be other opportunities," he said vaguely.

"Claus, you won't get any opportunities if you keep this up," she said sharply.

Claus passed his hands over his eyes and finally, in what seemed like a great effort, looked at her directly. There were veins of blood in his eyes that had been clear as a cloudless sky just a few days before.

"Listen, I didn't ask you to come here," he said.

She held him fast with her eyes, willing his to remain focused on hers. "I've come to tell you there is a way for you to go into the jungle, now, and do what you want."

He shook his head from side to side and slapped the side of the bed in a gesture of futility.

"I can't kid myself any longer," he said, putting the little stained glass down. "I'm sorry I drank in front of you. I promised myself I wouldn't. But you woke me up and I needed those drinks to stop shaking. Thanks for coming and cheerleading the losing team. But you're wasting your time. I have a reputation in civilized society for being a beaten man. That's why Alvarez turned me down."

"Barnes probably told him a pack of lies. You didn't drink on the expedition to the oil wells, did you?"

"No. Ah, I was counting on old Penelope Grey in New Orleans. She was my patroness in the old days. If I'd gotten the commission I might have convinced her to set up a fund. She won't give me a *centavo* now. As it is, she snubbed me on the street last time I saw her in Mexico City. Walked right by as if she hadn't seen me."

Erika remembered, from her background research, that Penelope Grey was a New Orleans patroness of the arts and sciences. Penelope Grey once wrote that being shown around Mexico City by Claus Boehm was like being shown around heaven.

"There are some people with faith and money," Erika said.

Claus laughed bitterly. Heaven's guide had fallen a long way to come to this dark corner of hell.

"Unfortunately, it's been the same with everyone I've met from the old days. You notice the signs of respect once accorded you have disappeared. Your jokes are not laughed at. There are no inquiries about your work. Your pithy comments go unheard. People interrupt your stories when they are reminded of stories of their own. You find yourself listening to the interesting lives of others."

Claus ran his hands over his eyes. Erika could see that he'd been struggling not to break down in front of her.

"Do you still think you can do it? The expedition I mean."

Claus gave her a wry smile. "I'm glad somebody believes that's still an open question. Oh, I'm going if it's just me and one stubborn old mule."

Erika was encouraged. Claus was staring at the bottle, but he hadn't touched it since he'd stopped shaking.

"Will you let me help you, Claus?"

"Please. Do whatever you can. Kick me, bash me over the head. That's the kind of help I need."

Erika summoned up her will.

"May I take this bottle away?"

Claus nodded. The bender was over. At least until the next time. No, he wouldn't drink if he went into the jungle now. Not until the journey was over. "Breaking a trail cures me of my suicidal tendencies."

Erika told him that Collier's was offering a fifty thousand peso advance for a story about an exploration of the unknown regions of the Lacandon Rain Forest. Claus looked at her in awe.

"Would the advance be enough to pay for the kind of expedition you had in mind?" Erika asked.

He continued to gaze at her dumbfounded. "Yes, of course, it wouldn't pay the salaries of professional field men for the length of time I believe the trip would take but it would pay for almost everything else. It wouldn't be as much money as Barnes is getting from the government, but it would do just fine. What are you talking about? I'm not a journalist. Who is getting the money?"

Erika swallowed hard. "The only catch is you have to put up with me. I've been assigned to write the article and take the pictures." She showed him the cablegram from Rawlins.

Claus got up and started to pace in the small, cramped room.

"You'd better give me the bottle back and get out of here," he said.

Erika tightened her grip on the bottle and didn't move. But the pacing frightened her. He glowered menacingly. She feared he would turn on her with physical violence as he swept back and forth. His voice trembled in rage and frustration. "Erika, you simply don't understand. I can't possibly take you into the jungle." He went over the dangers as he continued to pace. "The expedition will take months, and most of it in unexplored territory. If we run out of ammunition, we'll face dangers not only from jaguars and snakes, but we'll starve to death if we can't hunt for game. There is malaria in the jungle now. And the worst of the rains are coming. I'm not sure the Lacandons will be friendly. They'd learned to hate foreigners in the years since I last visited them. Besides, I'm the biggest risk. I'm a drunk."

"You've never taken a drink on the trail."

Claus looked at her wearily and sat down on the bed. Was his resistance crumbling? Or was he summoning the will to deliver the blow that would smash her case and send her away forever?

"When it comes right down to it, I couldn't be obligated to you like that. I can't go into the jungle tied to your apron strings."

She felt a cold fury surge in her blood. "Damn it, Claus, I don't want to hear any more of your prejudices against my sex. What's the difference if it's my money or Carnegie's or Collier's? I don't get a peso if there's no trip."

"Collier's is giving the money to you to write a story. I wouldn't feel like a man with you carrying the purse."

Erika felt the little click in her head that released a geyser of angry steam.

"A man? Is refusing to accept a woman as a partner in a business venture your idea of being a man? You were very much a man when you and I hiked the hills around here together. I never had such confidence in anybody. That's why I think you can lead us through the jungle and find that lost city of yours. But then you talk to me of women and apron strings! Do you want to prove that you have a Tarzan complex and you're lost without your vine to swing from?"

Claus looked at her in outrage. He raised his hand as if to strike her. "That's enough. I won't tolerate your insults."

His pronouncement left them with an oppressive silence that Erika found unbearable. It was stupid to have been insulting. The advantage of her momentum had collapsed and lay in a heap on the floor. And now, the silence told her that he was waiting for her to leave the room.

She breathed deeply and sat up straight in the armless chair.

"I'm sorry," she said. "You said you'd go into the jungle with one stubborn old mule. I'm a stubborn old mule."

He looked at her with wonder. "After all I've told you, why do you want to go?" he asked.

"If you really want to know, I need the job. Please hire me! I'm hard working, and contrary to the impression I've given you, I'm experienced at taking orders. I worked for the underground in Germany for years and had to take instructions that made no sense from people whose identities were only a password to me. All I ask of you is permission to write the story in my own way. You'll be completely in charge."

Claus drank from a glass of water that stood on the night table.

"I have to admit that what you suggest is the only thing that makes sense. I'm not sure I like it. The complications I spoke of earlier will still be there."

She felt a buzz of hope rise in the room. He was taking her seriously at last. "I don't doubt that the trip might—well, draw us close together and complicate things," she said.

"Or we might come to hate one another. That would complicate things even more."

She knew he was right. There were those endless days pent up in rooms with friends in Germany. The smallest faults became magnified. "I'm willing to gamble on that, Claus. Besides, I can't be the worst danger you'll have to face. The expedition needs both of us now."

Claus raised his hands in a gesture of resignation.

"Erika, you have the strongest will of anyone I've ever met. OK, OK, you're my lead field man."

Erika felt tears of joy spring to her eyes. "You mean, with my being a woman and everything?"

Claus laughed and his eyes lit up. "Field woman, I should say. There are no rules about gender in the jungle."

Erika leapt out of her straight-back chair and onto the bed to embrace Claus.

"Say, you'd better get out of my bed," Claus said when Erika kissed him on the cheek. "We have a long time ahead together in that jungle."

"I promise to behave," Erika said, obediently returning to her chair. "Just tell me what to pack."

PART II

LA SELVA LACANDONA

Chapter Ten

The Lacandon Rain Forest is bounded by its main rivers and contained by the uplands of Chiapas and Guatemala. From Ocosingo, the Jatate, Perlas, and Lacanja Rivers flow southeast. The Lacantun collects these waters and delivers them to the Usumacinta. This broad muddy river separates Mexico from Guatemala and flows northwest into the Gulf of Mexico. The Lacandon jungle flourishes in the great lumpy limestone basin defined by these rivers. Erika and Claus began their journey at the end of May, just as the rainy season was beginning. They'd spent two weeks preparing for the expedition before leaving Ocosingo.

The jungle collected fees at the frontier. The trip began with a strenuous climb up and down a parallel series of ridges. Erika soon came to know why few Sunday strollers ever achieve the heart of the wilderness. The muddy *chicle* trail led them up slippery hillsides and down through deep swampy gullies. Then they climbed into rocky pine country only to descend steeply into thick, dense jungle. They walked more often than they rode the beasts, including a horse whose main purpose was to keep the mules in line. Erika soon learned to use her machete against the thorny secondary growth that rose out of the old *chicle* trails. In her encounters with the tangles of vines and big, thorny plants, Erika held fast to the principle that it was just as important to prevent the mules from being scratched as to spare herself. A scratch on a mule was an open invitation to flies to lay eggs of parasitic worms. And the loss of a mule was the loss of indispensable transportation.

Erika did not know how long they would follow the old *chicle* trail. Claus had told her that the *chicleros* were a scourge to the jungle and its habitants. At the same time, they were best friends to the archaeologists. They made the only trails that were known in the jungle. Claus had often found a Mayan site near a *chicle* camp. What was a natural place for a *chiclero* to camp was also a natural place for the Mayans to build a temple.

Erika looked at Rogelio who rode one mule and led the two pack mules ahead of her. He looked serenely comfortable in his long white cotton shirt and his palm-laced hat tilted on his head. He had come here as a *chiclero* and had traveled with Claus years ago.

Rogelio had gone to the jungle in the worst of the rains. It was then that the sap flowed plentifully. He'd told her it was the job of *chicleros* to castrate the trees. Erika smiled to think of it now, although she hadn't dared do so at the time. It was the way they spoke of their work. Erika supposed that the thick white sap reminded them of a man's seed. At the height of the season, the *chicleros* brought hundreds of mules trekking back and forth over the trails. The mules brought malaria into the forest as the hooves of the animals formed pits of still water and the mosquitoes bred in the standing water. Claus told her that a drop of kerosene or salt in the water would prevent the mosquitos from breeding. But the *chicleros* didn't know this or else they didn't bother to take the precautions when Claus told them. The trail they were on hadn't been used for years and was heavily overgrown. But it was the route Claus wanted to take to the territory where he thought they'd find Menche.

Rogelio had recommended Jacinto, the young *chiclero* who had signed on as a trail cutter. Erika was surprised that either one of them had chosen to come on the expedition. It was a good season for *chicleros*. The sap would be flowing soon and Claus had estimated that the men could make over fifteen hundred pesos in the season. Even with the money from *Collier's*, the expedition wouldn't pay either of them that well.

"Fifteen hundred pesos for what?" Rogelio had said. "To buy clothes that are of no good quality, but for which I will be charged too much. With the extra money, I shall be tempted to celebrate with *comiteco*, a second cousin to nitro-glycerin. Last year, I woke up in the plaza robbed of all my eight months hard labor. Look my friend, here we are, the *chicleros*, working and sweating and getting sick months on end so that somebody can chew on a little piece of gum for a few minutes and then spit it out. No, I would rather look for the Mayan ruins with you. So would Jacinto. We will even go to that part of the jungle where no one goes except for the Lacandons. I do not know where they hide, but if we are lucky we will meet them. And if we are luckier, they will not kill us."

Erika could see Claus's gold-flecked head appearing and disappearing through the trees and thicket ahead. He was leading the bell mule, Amanda. Lazaro coaxed the mules behind her. The two young mule drivers from El Real, Jacinto and José, were somewhere behind him with more mules and the horse that was substituting for one.

Lazaro was the same age as Claus and had served with him in the famous expedition of 1925 when Oliver La Farge, the famous writer, had been the lead field man. Erika was giddy with the thought of the standard she had to live up to. She and Claus had gone to El Real to find Lazaro. He had been living in the Tzeltal colony next to Don Pépé Gambio's coffee finca. It was a day trip by mule from Ocosingo. Lazaro had a dark, wrinkled face which was a record of all the obstacles he had surmounted in his life. Claus said that he could trust Lazaro completely, that the Indian had more good sense and loyalty than any muleteer he'd ever known. The mules of *chicleros* living in El Real broke fences surrounding the cornfields of the Tzeltal community and ate their crops. The *chicleros* raped the Tzeltal women when their men were in the fields. There were too many marauding *chicleros* for the Tzeltal men to kill. It was the reason many of Lazaro's people were migrating to the jungle. Because Lazaro could no longer live off his cornfield, he'd ended up working for Don Pépé, who owned the nearby coffee finca. It made Lazaro a slave again, like his father in the lumber camps before the revolution.

Don Pépé released Lazaro from the coffee plantation at the request of Claus. He would never have done it as Lazaro always owed him money, but Don Pépé believed Claus still had influential friends in Mexico and might some day be a help to him. Don Pépé also released the two young mule drivers, Jacinto and José. Lazaro warned Claus about taking José. He said the youth was strong-minded and could not be disciplined once he got a foolish idea into his head. But Don Pépé said José was strong as an ox if stupid and Claus had found the boy's shy manners and good spirits likeable.

Erika knew that Lazaro didn't like the idea of her being on the expedition. She remembered the troubled look on his face when he had said to Claus, "The señora, will she ride with us?"

"She will ride with us," Claus had said.

"It will be as you say," Lazaro had said, shrugging in resignation.

The party entered a vale of giant trees and Erika felt as though she were part of a procession moving down the nave of an endless Gothic cathedral. Claus named the forest giants that soared above their heads—the mighty mahogany, the breadnut and fig trees, rising over a hundred and fifty feet. There was a lower canopy of woods made up of the palms and sapodilla trees from which the *chicleros* milked white sap in the rain. They walked across groping cables of gnarled roots that clutched the sides of the great centenary trees like flying buttresses rising out of the dark ages of man. Adjusting the light exposure on her Leica, Erika took pictures of the canopy and gnarled roots.

"Watch out for the roots, thorns, poisonous plants and above all, watch out for the *nahuyaca*, the deadly snake," Claus called out to her. Lizards, hanging by their tails from trees, were startled by the intruders and dropped into the mud.

Erika saw wild orchids growing in the forks of branches and on fallen logs, taking their nourishment from the thick, moist air. High in the treetops, she saw begonias and scarlet lily-like amaryllis flowers. Light drifted down from the canopy like motes descending from stained-glass windows. It seemed to Erika as if she always moved in a thin spray of light that illuminated one dark corner of the trail after the other and left the last in darkness again after the moment of her passing.

Claus let Erika go ahead for awhile so that she could feel the lace of gigantic spider webs that stretched across the trail. She enjoyed the tickling sensation of the webs breaking across her face.

From time to time, they saw monkeys above and ahead of them catapulting themselves from branch to branch like pole-vaulters. Hummingbirds whirred like tiny helicopters. The chattering of monkeys was like the clattering of plates but the voices of the birds were like the tinkling of crystals.

At one point, a pair of tapir crossed the trail. They were mammoth wild boars, with long snouts, hairy and obscene looking. They lumbered along disdainfully even as Lazaro and Rogelio cocked their rifles. Her eyes on the tapir, Erika hit her head against a branch hanging over the trail and gave a short cry of pain. The tapir went crashing into the concealment of the bush before the muleteers could get their rifles on them.

Erika was profuse in her apologies.

"It was the shift in the wind that chased them away," Rogelio said.

"They are too big to carry anyway," Claus said. "And it would take a while to butcher them here. We have a way to go before we camp. We'll find other food." But he didn't seem very interested in the lump on her head.

"They might have picked up the scent of the mules and other game might do the same thing," Lazaro said. "Pancho, perhaps some of us should go ahead on foot if we want fresh meat for supper."

Claus and Lazaro, carrying rifles and machetes, and Erika carrying her camera, formed the spearhead and soon outdistanced the rest of the party. They had allowed Erika to accompany them so she could take photos of the hunt, and, after all, she was the lead field woman.

After an hour they saw six pairs of bright red and gold pheasants streaking through the leafy roof above them. Claus raised his rifle instantly and fired several shots. Lazaro followed with a short burst before the birds were out of sight. Erika caught a falling pheasant in her camera. They found two slain birds in the bush. Erika helped Claus and Lazaro pluck the animals clean. Rogelio and the others arrived and put the plucked birds in mule packs.

They crossed a high ridge and the trail passed through swampy gullies on the other side. The mud sucked at Erika's boots with every step. In deep places, the mud spilled into her foot. She felt the mud, cold and clammy in her socks. But she was resolved not to complain about anything. She was part of a team and had to keep in mind the purpose shared by all.

They decided to rest on the banks of the broad Rio Santa Cruz. Claus took out a notebook and began writing in it. Erika was exhausted and sat down with relief. Then she roused herself to take some pictures of the river. Just as she was adjusting the lens, she heard a deafening whine and her head was engulfed in a black cloud. Legions of gnats descended upon her. They followed her with hot, stinging bites as she ran from one place to the next. They were in her hair, her mouth, her eyes. Looking up from his notebook, Claus laughed. "You'll have to smoke now." He lit a cigarette and offered it to her, then lit one for himself, as did Lazaro. "It's the only way to keep the gnats away." Lazaro looked at her gravely. Erika guessed his thoughts. *Just like a woman, is what he's thinking.*

A soft rain began to fall.

"We'll be camping soon," Claus said. It was the best news Erika had heard all afternoon. "We need to set up camp before dark. It will be easier and save us candles and kerosene." Erika could not believe that it could get darker than it already was.

They stopped at a clearing not far from a bubbling, crystal clear stream. It seemed strange that it was only four in the afternoon. But they had begun the day's march before dawn.

Erika thought about what Claus had said back in Ocosingo about the peace in the jungle being indescribable. But listening to the soft gush of the stream while the men unloaded the mules, she felt an aching loneliness. Erika found herself wishing she were back in the Hotel Ocosingo, sleeping away a lifetime.

Chapter Eleven

The men cut leaves for the mules to eat and built a fire. Erika shivered in her wet, muddy clothes when Rogelio presented her with a cup of coffee. While she drank the warming liquid, Claus cut four saplings and drove them into the ground so that they formed the limits of a rectangle. Erika watched him cross them with tree branches. Seeing what he was doing, she rose to help him thatch the branches with vines and palm leaves. The rain fell gently.

"Give me your hammock and we'll string it high under this roof so you'll be relatively dry when you sleep," Claus said.

"Let me put the hammock up myself. It's the best way for me to learn," Erika said.

Claus added some supporting poles to the open sides.

"There you are, my lady, your first hotel suite in the Lacandon Plaza. You can cover one side with an open blanket for privacy if you wish, or, at your bidding, we'll all just vanish into the bush. Now, the bathroom is down the hall. Just listen for your nearest murmuring arroyo. Here is a little bell. Ring it for room service." The patronizing tone in his voice disturbed her.

"Enough treating me as a guest. You'll spoil me. Let me do my share of the work."

"You needn't work. You're paying for the safari. We are all at your service."

"Claus! That's not the way it is."

He shrugged. "If you wish, you can help clean the pheasants while the others are taking care of the animals." Claus took the big pots to the stream to fill them with water. Erika sat next to the fire. While she and the young José washed and cleaned the pheasants, Rogelio tied the horse to a tree. Erika noticed that José couldn't take his eyes off her. Baggy as she felt in her jungle outfit, she was mildly flattered. But she had to keep in mind that Claus advised her not to become too friendly with the men for fear of distracting them, setting one against the other or provoking an outright sexual assault. She felt she could trust Rogelio and the others but it would be a mistake to encourage José.

"We won't have to worry about the mules with the horse tied up," Rogelio said, returning to the fire. "The mules will stay close to the horse." Rogelio filled leather baskets with water for the animals. Yes, Erika thought, Rogelio could be trusted. He was a professional, dedicated to the success of the mission.

Claus dressed the pheasants. Then he skewered them on a stick and stuck it in the ground next to the fire. They poured rice into one of the water-filled pots to which Claus added palm hearts. They put beans in another pot to soak overnight for breakfast. Claus set up his own hut a good distance from Erika's. She didn't know if he was trying to respect her privacy or if he wanted his own.

Erika gathered her machete, soap, and towel and undressed under a rubber sheet. As soon as she arrived at the stream, a black cloud of gnats formed over her. Erika tossed off the rubber sheet exposing her naked body to the microfiends of the tropics for an instant before leaping into the stream. The water moved swiftly and was clear with perfect pools for bathing. Erika was at peace as the currents caressed her.

Afterward, they all dined on rice and palm hearts stuffed with chunks of pheasant. Erika felt much better. She found the supper brought back memories of family meals in Switzerland. Erika had never dined on such fare as a child, but it struck her that what gave every new experience a ring of familiarity was that it invoked once again that lost sense of wonder that is at the heart of the experience of childhood. So here now with Claus, Lazaro, Rogelio, José and Jacinto sat her mother and father passing a serving bowl while a storm raged over the Alps.

If Erika had entertained fears of sexual assault, inspired by the savage lushness of the tropics, she now completely abandoned them. Except for the eyes of young José, she knew she was a shapeless mass in the eyes of Claus and the others. She laughed to think again of the warnings Claus had given her about sexual assault. Surely, if the men needed to give vent to their sexual longings, the mules were more enticing.

After supper, Claus went quietly to his lean-to. The men remained by the fire but Erika followed the Claus's example. She remembered his advice that the best way to get a comfortable night's sleep was to remove all her clothing and insulate herself inside the sleeping bag. Taking off her clothes would be insurance against bringing a world of insects into bed with her. And the sleeping bag would keep her dry and warm.

Erika undressed in the dark and hung her clothes from the crossbars of her lean-to. She was glad to be out of her clothes, not only to be free of their clinging wetness, but to feel the femininity of her body again. Erika climbed into her hammock and, holding a flashlight in one hand, fastened her mosquito netting to the hammock as Claus had instructed. The net had sleeves at either end through which the cords of the hammock passed, with drawstrings to close them. Erika slid into her sleeping bag and discovered the luxury of lying in a hammock. She loved the way it adapted itself to the natural position of her tired body, and she kept herself awake to enjoy it. Erika told herself that she must zip up the sleeping bag before falling asleep. Her body was warm now and she appreciated the cool air that was seeping through the opening.

Erika was surprised to see Claus sitting up in his hammock under a flashlight tied to a pole above his head. He was reading a book.

"What are you reading?" she called out over the forty yards that separated them.

"*Don Quixote.*"

"The jungle makes you literary."

"The only other reading matter I have is my own notes. I'm afraid Claus Boehm is too boring to read in large quantities."

Considering the well-used look of the book, Erika guessed that Claus brought Don Quixote with him on all his expeditions. He seemed to model himself on his hero. Indeed, Claus was a quester, lean and gaunt as he rode through the forest on mule back. His machete was his lance. The windmills fell all around.

"This hammock is wonderful." Erika exclaimed. Claus went back to his book. Erika had her own reading to do. First, she wrote in her journal of the events of the day, material she might use in drafting her article. Then she had her homework. Claus had begun teaching her Yucatec Mayan back in Ocosingo and had given her his notes to study. It was the language of the Lacandons and he was speaking their dialect to her and the others along the trail. After going over the notes, she settled down with a book he had given her about his early explorations. The book was hardly boring. Claus was a good writer.

Despite the aches and pains in her legs and back, Erika felt relaxed as she read and listened to the symphony of night noises around her. The cicadas established the beat while the night birds introduced themes, both mournful and compelling. Books and flashlight slipped away as Erika drifted into sleep.

It seemed she had not been asleep long before she was stirred to wakefulness by the nagging feeling that she had forgotten to do something. She felt cold air coming in from one side of the bag and then she remembered that she had forgotten to zip the lining of the bag up. She began to move when she realized that something was in the bag with her. There was a cold, slick pressure across her knees and along her side. All her senses awakened with a flash. There was a firm leathery presence curled around her legs and moving slowly.

Erika suppressed the impulse to scream, convinced that it would be certain death to do so. She did not know whether the snake was gathering himself in coils to strike, but she quickly decided that any movement on her part would be fatal. Erika lay perfectly still, breathing minimally. She lay limp as the tubular body of the snake, seemingly infinite in length and at least six inches in diameter, began its encirclement of her girth. Was it a constrictor? Claus had told her they lived in the rain forest.

The serpent slipped under her back, curled around her other side until she felt the triangular head slide over her abdomen. The serpent proceeded slowly but relentlessly, completing a coil around her waist. Erika felt beads of cold sweat form over her body and feared the effect of her perspiration upon the snake. She wished she could stop the pounding of her heart. She was so terrified, she knew she could not call out for help if she wanted to.

Claus had gone to sleep, his flashlight was out, but she could see the muleteers playing cards around the campfire fifty yards away.

"I have won again," she heard Lazaro say to his comrades. "Now if only any of you had money, I could come out of the jungle a rich man."

"Take some of my rum," Rogelio said passing a bottle.

"Let us play for the woman," she heard José say.

"No one plays for the woman," Lazaro said sternly.

"Her skin is like the snow on the mountains under the sun," the young José said.

"You know nothing. Have a drink and go to sleep."

Erika did not dare speak. Certainly, her skin and all inside it was now as cold as snow, she thought idly. *But keep your mind on this snake,* she told herself. Claus had warned her that a snake bite in the jungle was almost certain death, that victims died within an hour, and even if treated immediately, the wounds were vulnerable to fatal infections. She had heard stories of victims throwing up blood and turning blue as they succumbed to death.

The snake began another coil under her buttocks. Erika felt the serpent's head press under her thighs. She tried to hold her legs as tightly closed as she could but she was trembling and felt her strength ebb away. The serpent was insistent in the upward thrusts of its head, and Erika, fearing to offend the beast, allowed her legs to separate so that the snake was able to slip unimpeded between her warm inner thighs.

Even as she trembled with fright, Erika knew now how she would react if she were ever threatened by a rapist. Her only wish was to stay alive and let virtue be damned. Her virtues was precisely what the snake was taking. She felt the slick head press against her pubic mesh. She fully expected the hot fangs to strike deep into her vulvae at any moment.

Erika perspired freely in rivulets that slowly filled the non-porous bag. She did not know how long she had been lying entwined in the coils of terror, but she realized that the muleteers had turned in for the night. Moving her head slightly, she watched the abandoned fire flicker weakly.

Erika lay in the interminable darkness with the snake wrapped around her loins, trying to control her shaking and the wild beating of her heart. The snake had raised its head and crossed her belly to rest his chin on her navel. Now it ceased all movement and its neck lay limply across her body like a spent lover asleep on the soft belly of its mistress. Erika began to tremble uncontrollably. The snake was warm now but she realized that the heat had passed from her body to the reptile's.

Erika's teeth began to chatter and she wondered if she would have a heart attack or suffer a stroke. Time passed imperturbably and the snake slept on.

The sleeping bag was wet with her cold sweat and she shivered fitfully. *Why doesn't Claus wake up? Where is Don Quixote with his lance, rushing to the rescue? He'd probably be happy to see me strangled. Serve me right for intruding in his jungle. It's really best if he doesn't wake up. The snake mustn't hear movement of any kind. My best hope is that he will tire of me and just slide away. I wish I could stop shaking. Oh god, how long can I keep this up? What can I think of that will make him go away? What can I think of that will stop me from going berserk? I want to scream, that's what I want to do, I want to scream at the top of my lungs.*

Finally, in her emotional exhaustion, Erika drifted off into patches of sleep. In a dream, she rested on a mountain top. Then Claus held her in his arms. He wore a feathered headdress and she noticed that his body was snake-like and feathered. They flew above the forest. He confided to her that he was Quetzacoatl on a mission to return to his distressed people and bring them back their lost arts and sciences. Below them lay a Mayan city with shining white temples, each trimmed with bright colors.

Then she was awake and knew in an instant that she was still imprisoned in the coils of the snake. The sky had begun to lighten and Erika could see the night mists like pale ghosts departing with the onset of dawn. The fire was reduced to embers and she could see a thin line of bluish smoke mix with the forlorn wisps of fog. She lay in a bath of ice cold sweat.

The snake was stirring. Erika felt the coils unwind under her back and around her thighs. Then she saw the top of her sleeping bag rise and with a shrug of its diamond-shaped head, the snake tossed the top fold away. For the first time Erika saw the long neck and the bottle green eyes. The snake sat in double coils on her abdomen. The bottle green eyes were fixed on hers and she saw the fangs flash.

Erika screamed. The snake arched its body in the form of the striking S. The beady eyes became incandescent and now the snake emitted a strong musky odor that sickened her. Out of the corner of her eye, she saw Claus getting out of his hammock and advancing toward them. He held a revolver in his hand and was taking aim. But he was thirty yards away. Erika saw the fangs dart out and knew that the strike of the snake would be as swift as any bullet fired from thirty yards. But even as the thought coalesced in her mind, she heard the shot and saw the snake's head shatter and fall upon her bosom.

Claus was at her side in an instant, removing the head and body of the dead reptile. Erika sat up. Claus dragged the body of the snake to the fire. It was at least eight feet long. Then Claus went to his lean-to and got dressed. Erika heard the others getting up. She became conscious of her own nakedness and pulled a woolen shirt over her shoulders.

"Good grief, how big that snake was," Erika stammered through her shivers. "Claus, it stayed with me all night. I must have lost at least fifteen pounds."

Claus stood in his lean-to with his back to her. "Are you decent?" he asked.

"In a second." She slipped quickly into the woolen trousers.

When Claus came back to the fire, he gave her a savage look. With angry eyes and tousled hair, he looked like a wild man. Erika would not have been surprised if he struck her.

"You're going to have to get a few things straight!" His voice shook with rage. "We are not out on a walking tour of Alpine meadows. In order to survive here, you must be constantly aware of the possible consequences of everything you do. You can't make any assumptions. You told me you wanted to string up the hammock with the net yourself, but you managed to botch it. And how in the world did the snake get into the bag with you if you didn't leave it open? The jungle is not a tropical paradise where you can loll about in your hammock, naked as Eve!" Claus poked savagely at the fire with a stick until the flames began to shoot up. They rose with his fury. Erika muttered a series of *mea culpas* and waited for him to calm down.

"Thank you for saving my life," she said, when she had the chance. "But what did the snake want from me? Why didn't it strike me dead when it had the chance?"

Erika saw a smile flicker over Claus's face. The others were coming. They seemed surprised to see the long body of the snake.

"Well, I'll tell you," Claus said, his voice smoothing the edges of his anger.

"A norther came up last night and the weather got quite cold. The snake was only looking for a warm place to sleep. Your body, dry and warm inside the sleeping bag, was perfect. But when you produced all that cold sweat during the night, you made him uncomfortable. So, like a lover who doesn't want any painful breakfast scenes with his girl in the morning, he was slipping away when you started to scream. That, of course, spoiled everything and Mr. Snake was forced to take the bad end of a shotgun wedding."

Erika was relieved that the burst of anger was over but she had to admit she had been careless.

She changed to her rubber poncho and went to the stream to bathe. Thick white fog hung over the stream and clung to the vegetation on its banks like a giant spider web. Although she still shook with her fright, she almost felt sorry about the snake. Had she not screamed, the beast would have just slid away into the forest. The jungle was teaching her to respect all forms of life. She threw off her poncho and walked naked into the stream. Erika immersed herself in a deep pool of warm water that lifted her breasts like buoys. The imprinted feeling of the serpent's coils on her body gave way to that of the touch of her rescuer as he had lifted the dead animal from her bare breasts. Although she had not been conscious of it at the time, frozen with terror as she had been, she thought now of the lean naked figure leaning over her and the deft, gentle hands unburdening her of her nightmare.

Well, she owed him her life. It might make him feel better about having her on the trip, put him more surely in charge, despite her money. Would he see it that way? He'd taken the liberty to scold her. She admitted she preferred it to the silence of the day before. Was it a sign that he was beginning to like her? Or was he just starting to despise her? Of course, he was right. It would be a serious mistake if she and Claus became lovers. He had to treat each member of the expedition equally. She was a photographer and mule driver, no more important than the mule whose impatient braying she could hear coming from downstream.

When she dressed and returned to the fire, Rogelio greeted her with a steaming cup of coffee. Claus turned his back to her. The men were enjoying a breakfast of snake meat. Erika ate tortillas and beans.

Chapter Twelve

Shortly after noon Erika realized that the forest had gotten dark and the golden thread of light could no longer be seen through the treetops.

The rain came softly at first, like the whispered secrets of children in the last quarter hour before dark. The centenarian trees moaned as the wind rushed in and the rain came down. Soon, wind and rain came whining down the jungle canyons and raged in the leafy treetops. The argument between wind and rain was so loud that Erika could not hear what Claus was saying as he walked only a few yards ahead of her.

They all dismounted to lead the mules through marshy places. The water rose over the bellies of the mules. Back on the trail, such as it was, Erika had to be careful to avoid being scratched by the thorny growth that the mule pushed her against in its attempts to avoid the mud on the trail. Erika knew there was a trail only because of mud that had been churned up, a slimy testimonial to the former presence of *chicleros*. Then she stumbled and fell on an unseen root. Erika emerged blinded and encrusted with mud. Her misery was relieved only by the laughter of the muleteers. They scooped the mud from her body using big elephant ear plants as towels.

They waded across a shallow river and stopped on the other side for a lunch of cold *posole* which they drank from enamel cups. As they rested Erika could see that Claus was busy taking notes and drawing charts.

"Do you know where we are?"

"Where few people have been except for the *chicleros*. Right now, we're on the trail to the old *chicle* camp of El Zapote. I'd say we're running roughly parallel to the Jatate River which should be about ten kilometers to the southeast of us."

"Why don't we just take a sailing ship of some kind? Wouldn't it be easier than fighting for every foot of jungle?"

"The river can be nasty and difficult to navigate with a boatload of mules. Besides, El Zapote is closer to the source of the Perlas River. It is there that I met the Lacandons last time."

Erika felt the fear begin to gnaw at her as if a starving rat had invaded her bowels. Meeting the Lacandons had seemed a very remote idea in Ocosingo. The story about Claus and the old chief had a storybook quality that was reassuring. But it had happened ten years ago. Suppose the old chief was dead? Who would remember Claus then? She thought of what Manuel had told her about the Lacandons the night she'd waited in vain for Claus.

The Lacandons were sorcerers and Stone Age brutes, Manuel had said. They were the last aborigines in Mexico, and had waged successful guerilla warfare against her civilization for over four hundred years. They crouched in treetops with drawn bows ready to release poisoned arrows.

She was beginning to understand what Manuel meant when he said the Lacandons could send the demons of the night against you. For here, in the trackless forest, it was easy to believe in the demons. And when it rained, it was always night.

"The Lacandons may have moved on," Claus said when Erika asked him if they would meet them soon. "El Zapote was established after my last trip. I don't think this tribe would maintain a settlement so close to a *chicle* camp. They may have retreated deeper into the forest. Now they might go there to trade. The most seasoned traders leave dogs or machetes on the banks of the river at night and in the morning find them gone and replaced by tobacco or chilis or cotton materials. Don't forget, the Lacandons we may meet have split off from the group on the Lacanja River on the other side of the jungle north of here. The Lacanja group has become almost tame as a result of conversions by Baptist missionaries. The old chief I met ten years ago had refused to buckle under and was leading the remaining heathens into more remote parts of the forest. They seldom allow themselves to be seen."

The demons were still with Erika and she knew that Claus sensed her growing fear.

The rain bombarded the canopy above them and dripped down to the limestone floor in rivulets. Erika thought of the dead Mateo. "Do you think we'll see the Lacandons?" she said, her voice wavering to betray her fear.

"You know I'm counting on meeting them for vital information," Claus said shortly.

"Of course, you want to see the old chief again. But the ruins Mateo was looking for, the ones reported to be just south of this *chicle* camp you speak of, do you think they are the ruins of Menche?"

Claus packed his maps into a canvas bag and wrapped it in a rubber sheet.

"It sounds too good to be true," he said with some impatience. "Whatever they are, the ruins the *chicleros* spoke about and Mateo went hunting for are surely worth investigating."

"How long do you think it will take to get there?"

"The trail is tougher than I'd supposed. It hasn't been used in years which is why it's so impassible. We should reach El Zapote in five days. We can hold up there a few days and dry out our things. If we don't find Menche in that area, we'll strike out for uncharted territory." He turned quickly to Erika and gave her a hard stare. "I hope you're not having any misgivings at this stage of the game."

"Of course not. I have no more cares than the mules."

Claus arched his brow and sighed in exasperation. "You'd better be absolutely sure before we go any farther. It's your money. If you want to call it off, say so now while there's still time to go back."

Erika refused to answer. A seething anger was building up in her. It wasn't only that he had brought up the money. She resented Claus for being so intolerant of any sign of weakness. She hadn't complained anywhere along the trail. Certainly, her fears were normal. If he'd only said that he too sometimes got scared thinking about what lay ahead. Maybe he never did. If the jungle was strewn with corpses, severed heads and hearts beating away by themselves, he would happily seize upon them as trail markers pointing the way to his goal. Of course, it was all clear now. What she had taken to be dedication to an ideal, was in reality a mad obsession. The more she seethed, the more she was convinced she was right. He had no real interest in others. Of course, he had saved her life, but he would have saved that of a mule for the same reason. They all existed just so he could chase his crazy dream. It had seemed so romantic back in Ocosingo. Now she saw the truth. His monomania had made him selfish and completely indifferent to the feelings of others. She'd been the victim of a schoolgirl crush. Here she was, a hard-boiled journalist who'd resisted the Nazis, acting and feeling like a teenager. Well, there's no fool like an old fool. But he wasn't going to fool her any longer. From now on, it was going to be strictly business. But wasn't that what he had been telling her all along? Erika was confused and it made her even angrier.

Without speaking further, they washed their cups in the stream. The others had started on the trail. Claus told her they would have to hurry to catch up.

"I haven't slowed you down, have I?" she asked sharply.

He didn't answer.

Erika brooded. She was angry at herself for giving in to her terror and getting so upset about Claus. It didn't matter what he thought of her or what she thought of him. She was here to do a job. Her one concern had to be the story, nothing else. With that in mind, she trained her Leica on the madman walking ahead of her.

Chapter Thirteen

The night brought no relief from the rain. Even though Erika covered her hammock with a blanket, she could not keep from getting wet. Morning came mercifully. Lazaro rose first, built a fire, and heated coffee.

The rain had eased up a little and rolling mists seemed to stick to the vegetation around them like cotton. Erika was miserably wet. To add to her distress, her feet had become water-burned. She didn't want to tell Claus about it, but when she tried to walk, she felt as if she were walking over a bed of hot coals.

Claus saw that she was unsteady on her feet and asked her to sit down. He inspected her feet, scratched his head, and set to work. He filled a plastic container with water and ground up pieces of mahogany bark in it.

"Just soak your feet in this jungle remedy. By the time we've broken camp, you'll be able to light out on the trail like a frightened deer."

She forced a brave smile. "My feet feel as if I've been walking on fire." But she enjoyed the tingling sensation of the bark bath.

"The jungle has a cure for all the ills it gives you," he laughed playfully as he massaged her feet. Erika could see that José was watching them with great interest.

"That feels much better. Thank you, Claus."

"We can only move as fast as the slowest of us. But you have well made feet. Like those of a Lacandon woman."

Erika knew she couldn't control the blush that had rushed to her face. All her rancor of the day before flew out of her. When she finally lifted her feet out of the bark solution, she was ready to run through the forest just as Claus had said.

But during the ensuing days of pounding rain, mud and stubborn roots, her spirits lowered with each gully and crag. The party clambered up punishing mountains only to slide perilously down their other slippery sides. In wet gullies, they had to unload and reload the mules several times to keep the boxes from being thoroughly soaked.

They waded across another river. On the trail again, she looked at Claus hacking at the bush resolutely with his machete. He was in his element, getting on with the task at hand. She needed to get on with hers. When they stopped to get their bearings, she took photos and made some notes.

The rain abated that night. Instead of the unending clamor of water, Erika heard lugubrious screams emanating from somewhere on the other side of the fire. Whatever they were, they were wonderful imitations of the cries of the dead. Then the screams seemed to be directly overhead.

"Claus, those sounds seem to be coming from the pit of hell," she called from her hammock.

"Those are howler monkeys," he said.

"They certainly live up to their name. I've never heard such shrieking beasts. Are they angry about something?"

"You may be sleeping under their favorite tree. Pull your rubber blanket over your head, quick!"

Fortunately, Erika did as advised without asking for an explanation. As she pulled the sheet up, a strong-smelling liquid splattered her rubber shield. Some slid off the sheet, hot and dripping down over her head. The howls filled the night. Erika wanted to cry.

The message was clear. All the voices of the jungle, the driving rain, the sucking mud, the stinging gnats, roiling river, rattling snakes, thwacking thorns and moaning trees were warning her. Claus had been saying it with his silences. And now finally, the clear voice of the jungle's consciousness was speaking to her, howling at her and sending down streams of piss: 'Get out of the jungle! We don't want you here. You don't belong!'

In the morning, everything in the camp was in disarray. A bag of flour had been torn open and the flour was strewn about like snow.

"The monkeys were imitating us last night and decided to play house with our things," Claus said. But the disorder was not the worst of it. Mold had rotted through stitches of some of the canvas bags. The monkeys had gotten to the contents of some of them.

After having breakfast and taking inventory, a look of concern crossed Claus's face. "No need to fear," he said gamely. "We ought to reach the old *chicle* camp of El Zapote near the Perlas River in a day or two. And we should run into Lacandons soon."

"Will they be friendly, Pancho Balam?" Rogelio asked.

"They'll just have to be," he said grimly.

Back on the trail, they had to be particularly careful that the mules did not fall, as the boxes on their sides tended to hit against outstretched branches. Erika was also careful that branches in her line of vision did not collide with her head as her mule was only concerned with those branches just above his own eye level.

Late in the afternoon, one of the mules collapsed.

"He can't go any farther," Rogelio said, after much coaxing and prodding of the mule.

"Then put him out of his misery," Claus said.

Erika turned away when Lazaro loaded his gun. She jumped when she heard the shot and the mule's sudden cry of surprise, pain and anger. There was a second shot and she heard the deep groan of death.

Chapter Fourteen

They arrived at El Zapote in the rain and dragged themselves into the remains of the abandoned *chicle* center. It was a large thatched roofed hut with double plank walls on all sides. Squealing bats poured out from under the roof as they entered with flashlights.

"At least we won't have to build our shelter tonight," Claus said with a sigh of relief.

Erika saw long columns of crickets and roaches marching up and down the walls.

"I think I'd rather sleep outside in the rain," she said.

"It won't be so bad once we clear it out. We'll have to suspend everything from the ceiling and leave our boxes wrapped in rubber sheets outside. But with a good fire going, we'll be able to dry our clothes."

There was a pail of coagulated *chicle* sap in one corner, some unopened cans of condensed milk, a sack of flour that had been broken through, its contents almost gone, and a pile of salt that had spilled out of a sack and was held together by moisture. They also found a bundle of tobacco leaves and a sealed container of lard.

"They were trading with the Lacandons," Rogelio said, sifting flour through his fingers. "They gave the Lacandons salt, perhaps some cloth and some rifle shells. This tobacco they got from the Lacandons."

"How long ago do you think?" Claus asked.

"As you know, *chicleros* castrate the zapote trees in a territory until they have drained all the sap and then they do not come back for five years when the trees are full with milk again. It has been at least five years since anyone was here."

"What about Mateo?" Erika asked.

"We know he was here, but he left nothing."

Lazaro found an old kerosene lamp and lit it. The floor was swarming with fleas.

"Ach, those fleas are thrilled to see us," she said. "They must be starved."

Erika was especially careful to seal herself in her hammock that night. As she lay listening to mice running up and down the walls, she thought of the *chicle* camp inhabited by *chicleros* at the height of the season, coming into the rat-infested hotel after spending the day climbing trees in the rain like telephone linesmen, stabbing the trees until their lifeblood flowed into buckets below. She imagined the men in the big room at night, boiling the sap, drinking homemade corn liquor, getting crazy drunk, and attacking one another with machetes until human blood flowed with the *chicle* sap. She imagined them succumbing to the malaria that rose from the mud churned up by their mules. Did man ever live in harmony with nature? What of the Lacandons? How had they survived in the forest for the last four hundred years and who knows how long before that? Certainly, theirs could only be a society of savagery and the worship of death. And in all this, man once built beautiful cities. Erika listened to the rats squealing as they ran up and down the walls.

And what of Claus? Was he prepared to endure anything, go anywhere in this jungle, driven as was he by his ambition? Was it all just so that the birds in those far-off academic groves would sing for him once again, and powerful men and women who had repudiated him, yield to him as before?

Erika realized now that she believed this only when she thought the worst of him. She'd known another Claus, the man who moved through the jungle as if he were a part of it, the otter serenely putting twigs in place in the rain. Claus had told her that all of life on land came out of the jungle, that human intelligence itself was a response to its complex demands. And yet all of her experience had taught Erika that her kind lived separated from nature, and, in fact, was pitted against it. Was Claus driven by a passion to resolve the riddle of man in the world?

Lying awake in the darkness, she tried to understand it. In this forest, man himself was the glory of nature, he knew his connection to it and was its most wondrous manifestation. Perhaps that was it. Claus was looking for his and all of humanity's missing link to creation. Erika was beginning to feel her own bond to the jungle in her blood. For as cruel and deceptive as the jungle was, she had never felt so intensely alive, so conscious of all the things around her.

Somewhere in this big forest that was so dense you couldn't hear a shout ten feet away, lay the end of Claus's quest. Maybe it was just a few hours away, perhaps many more weeks, but it was out there, somewhere. Erika knew because she felt its pull, and it was strong. Was it now her quest too?

In the morning, Claus suggested that they use the *chicle* center as a base camp while they searched for the ruins. It was decided that he and Rogelio and Erika would set out on foot with backpacks while the others stayed in camp, mending luggage and taking an inventory of supplies that were running low.

"How are we going to restock our supplies if we don't find the ruins soon?" Rogelio asked as they began to cut a trail.

"That is where the Lacandons come in. I think this is one of their trails. Or was."

"Pancho Balam, I ask you how we are to survive in hell and you tell me that the devil will provide for us."

On the second day of searching, they came upon a level hill near a spring.

"Look at those chechen trees. They are often found near Mayan sites," Claus said. "The Mayans tended to build on hills with lovely views. Like the Greeks, they wanted to be close to the gods. There was a practical reason too. They were good drainage engineers. Now, if this hill were cleared, I think we'd have a magnificent view."

Erika noticed something. Her heart beat excitedly. Before her eyes stood a stone structure that seemed to have been made by human hands.

"Claus, I've found something."

Claus came running to the heap of stones she'd found. There were others rising on the hillside. They seemed to be a series of disconnected walls. And there were shards of pottery.

The stones were swarming with ants.

"Are they Mayan?" Erika asked as Claus examined them.

"Yes, they're Mayan." But Claus was absorbed in his observations. Erika took some pictures and followed him as he roamed the area of the walls. Then he sat on a dislodged stone and shook his head in disappointment. The gnats seemed thicker here than anywhere else except for the pools.

"All we have here are some land retention walls," Claus said finally. "This broken pottery is from Lacandon incense burners, probably left here when they evacuated. Poor Mateo was probably murdered for taking them, but they are not Mayan treasures. Ah, these walls are all over the jungle, as plentiful as the stone fences in New England. And as interesting to archaeology." Erika could see the disappointment in the sag of his shoulders. Unexpectedly, she found herself bursting into tears.

Claus got up and marched to the nearby river. Erika watched him dive headon and fully clothed, into the water. Had he gone mad? Or was he finally sick of her altogether? She watched him swim to the far side of the river. There he plucked an orchid that was growing out of a fallen mahogany branch. Claus swam back and presented the orchid to Erika.

"You see, the jungle has some advantages. This flower would cost you many dollars in New York."

Erika cried happily this time. A laugh broke through her sobs and slapped back at the whining rain.

When they returned to the *chicle* camp, Rogelio told them he'd found something they'd missed the night before. He showed them an open fireplace off to the side of the building. There was a horseshoe arrangement of stones, charred chunks of mahogany, and some empty tins that were a little rusted.

"Do you think Mateo was here? "Erika asked.

"By the looks of those cans, someone was here a week ago, two weeks at the most, wouldn't you say Rogelio?" Claus said.

"Yes, the cans are not very rusted," Rogelio agreed. "I looked more carefully inside the hut and found this. We must have been very tired last night."

Rogelio produced a weathered American Armed Forces paperback edition of *She*, a novel by Ryder Haggard.

Claus took it in his hands. A look of recognition came over his face.

"Yes, I should have known. Ryder Haggard is David Barnes's favorite author. He'd always dreamed about being a Haggard hero as a boy, finding diamond mines and coming out of the jungle a rich man. I remember his telling me that the Haggard books influenced him to choose the profession he did."

A folded sheet of notepaper fell out of the book. Erika picked it up and saw that there was a message scratched on it.

"Good heavens, Claus, there's a message for you."

Claus read it and then let her see it. It was written in English.

"Greeting old Colleague. Welcome to the bush. Castellanos told me of your pick-up expedition before I left Ocosingo. I'm afraid your Mayan city is just pyramids in the fog. It's certainly nowhere around here. Ryder Haggard stuff. I've learned to look for lost treasure in books and not in real life. Am leaving you this book so you may do the same. Nothing around here but old retaining walls. I don't think they're so old at that, probably not even pre-Columbian. Good luck finding your fantasy temples. I envy you your lovely companion. They say those Kraut ladies know how to satisfy a man. As for me, I'm sticking to the business of the government, mapping the unexplored country south of here and then west of El Cedro.

By the way, I wouldn't enter the unknown territory if I were you unless I had a team of good riflemen and plenty of ammunition. What happened to Mateo and the others won't happen to me. In addition to some crack *cientificos*, I've brought along a dozen well-armed alligator hunters. They're the meanest men to go into the jungle with and they'll take no shit from the Lacandons. Good pay keeps them loyal to me. It's the only way to get through this lousy, shit hole of a jungle. The Americans got rid of their forests. It's time the Spics wised up. Love and kisses old colleague.

Dave Barnes."

Erika read the letter with disgust. She remembered the molesting hand of Barnes on her thigh in the station wagon. "What an absolutely despicable human being!" she exclaimed.

"But a good explorer," Claus said, with admiration and no trace of envy in his voice. "He's way ahead of us. If only he loved the jungle, he could do great things."

But Erika made a keen resolve. She would not waste any more time for the expedition making silly mistakes or brooding about Claus's reactions to her. She'd become hardened to the rigors of the trail and was learning to deal with everyday problems. The expedition would move ahead faster. All the anger that the jungle had unleashed fixed on Barnes.

Writing her notes at the end of the day, Erika thought about it all. She could not believe Barnes did not want to find Menche. Why did he bring a professional photographer along with him and why was he taking the route Claus felt would ultimately lead to the discovery? It just wouldn't do to have Barnes find Menche. Megalomaniac or not, Pancho Balam had to be the hero of her story.

PART III

JATATE

Chapter Fifteen

Somewhere, before the plain of San Quintin reaches the Jatate River, the great limestone shelf that forms the lumpy bed of the rain forest begins. The limestone enriches the thin topsoil out of which the giants rise majestically, lifting their stunning crowns to heaven. The mighty ceiba, mahogany, and wild fig trees so monopolize the sun that all smaller forms of vegetation must creep about in shadows for stray crumbs of light. Even the noble sapodilla and Spanish cedar fall over one another to keep their heads in the sun. But when a sceptered monarch falls, the members of his court dance over his body while the masses rise up in rebellion. The continual tumult produces more varieties of species than any other realm among the kingdoms of the earth.

It was into this rich, teeming, anarchistic world that the Lacandon expeditionary force traveled. This time there were no *chicle* trails to guide them. The territory they set out for showed as white areas on the maps Claus had made and studied.

They proceeded southeast. The path lay over a mountain. Man and mules struggled to reach the top of the steep muddy incline. Mules toppled, some turning somersaults as they fell backward down the mountain. Boxes became dislodged and some broke open against rocks and branches. Fifteen times the pack animals rolled down the side of the trail. Fifteen times they were gotten to their feet and reloaded. The horse, though far from being a steeple-chase champion, was sure-footed. Of course, he didn't carry the loads of the mules although, on more even ground, he was often ridden by Erika or Claus.

The growth became dense again as they descended into wet gullies. They had to use machetes constantly and it took many hours to advance one mile. Surely, the scramble of growth was inhospitable to the purposes of man. Erika found it hard to believe that Mayan cities had once flourished in such a setting.

Camp brought little relief. It was impossible to find level ground. Sleeping bags were soaked and they slept in their wet clothes to keep them from getting mildewed. Even the note paper on which Claus made his nightly entries was damp and soft.

In the morning, they took to the trail in a downpour. Game became harder to find in the turmoil of weather. That afternoon, Claus sighted a herd of wild pigs. They gave off a foul odor that Claus said came from a white musk gland on their shoulders.

"The smell is disgusting," Erika said.

"But the taste is delicious," Claus replied raising his rifle to his shoulder. He pulled the trigger, but the rifle almost exploded in his hands. The shells were rain-soaked.

A few days later—(Erika had lost count of the days unless she looked in her journal), she ran to the assistance of Lazaro and Rogelio who were repacking a stuck mule. A cake of sugar fell to the ground. Rogelio pounced upon it and retrieved it just as it began to sink into the mud.

Patiently and with keen interest, Rogelio washed it off in a pool and scraped the dirt off carefully with a stick. He was about to pop the cleansed cube into his mouth when his eyes fell on Erika and Lazaro who watched him with envy and longing. He offered to share it and the three famished explorers took eager bites of the sugar cube. Erika decided it was the most delicious sweet of her life. She savored the taste until they made camp. When she told Claus of the incident, he frowned.

"You falling on that piece of sugar is the first sign of hunger," he said.

That night, Lazaro, who had taken on cooking responsibilities, presented his trail mates with roasted palm hearts stuffed with rice.

"Are there no tortillas?" Claus asked.

"We have run out. We will have to use palm hearts in place of bread from now on."

"Our kerosene is out, too," Jacinto added.

"We only have a few flashlight batteries left," Claus said. "Well, we'll be getting to bed early these nights. How are we doing with the rice?"

"Enough for a few days if we ration it carefully," Lazaro said.

"We'll have to do some heavy shooting," Claus mulled. "We must have some dry shells left."

"Not many," Lazaro shrugged.

"How far do we have to go before we meet the Lacandons?" Rogelio asked.

Claus sighed deeply. "Well, you know we are in uncharted territory. That means we should meet them soon, but I can't promise—"

Just then, Jacinto, who had spoken very little the past few days, and had only groused and looked sullen, spoke up. "Why are we such in a hurry to meet the

Lacandons? From everything we've heard, they are savages who may want to kill us."

"Jacinto, we have to believe in something. The Lacandons are all we have left to believe in," Lazaro said, laughing.

"Yes," Rogelio said. "They will lead us to the city of the gods where we will find more gold than all the conquistadors in history."

"Pancho Balam tells us the Mayans adorned themselves with jade." Lazaro put in. "We will sell it to the museums. I will buy my own plantation and the Indians who work for me will get their rightful share of the labor."

"I will go to Mexico City and study at the university," Rogelio said.

"I will buy pretty clothes for my women," Lazaro went on.

"I will be happy to get out of here alive," Jacinto said.

"As will I," José said. Erika was aware that José no longer ogled her. He seemed preoccupied with the dangers that lay ahead. Well, he was young and the dangers were real.

In the morning, Claus called the group together. "Our staples will last us ten to fifteen days if we ration them strictly," he said. "As I said, I can't promise you, but we should meet the Lacandons soon, maybe over the next mountain."

The climb up the next mountain was punishing. On the other side the explorers were dumbfounded by what they saw. Across a river of violent rapids, a sheer wall of limestone towered about four hundred feet above them. The rain had stopped and a rainbow was reflected off the great white mass that stretched as far as the eye could see. As much as it was a beautiful subject for photography, it was all the more forbidding. The wall was sheer and impenetrable. From where they stood, the explorers saw no way to surmount it.

The next day, they set out to look for a pass but with no success. The crew broke into two groups. Claus, Erika and Rogelio went in a southerly direction while the others went north. But they could not find a pass. The sun shone with bright intensity. After hours of staring at the high, white cliffs across the rapids, Erika began to see spots in front of her eyes. But no declivity in the formations or ravine or cave could be discerned.

Then Rogelio cut his foot with his machete trying to open a nest of white ants to extract some honey and was little use in the search for the pass. He spent his time in camp fishing, but it was not a good time for fish. After another week, there was no meat in camp and they were very dependent on Rogelio's fishing. Everyone else spent all their days searching for a way around the pass.

Each night they gazed at the white escarpment under the light of the moon and their spirits dropped lower each time.

Claus tried to be cheerful over the supper of palm hearts and the fish Rogelio had caught. "We won't starve as long as there are fish in the river and game and palm hearts in the forest," he said.

Erika could see that the others did not share his optimism.

"This fish is delicious," Claus went on in high spirits. "Not enough for six people to be sure. I'll go fishing with you tomorrow, Rogelio."

"It is impossible, Pancho Balam," Rogelio said.

"Impossible? Why do you say that?"

"There are no more fish hooks. I lost the last one, trying to catch the brother of this fish."

"Well, well, and the gun shells, Lazaro, how do we stand there?"

"There are sixty shells left and half of them are too wet to be of any use," Lazaro said glumly.

Claus looked up at the white wall that was magnificent in its solitude and unassailability.

"Yes, it's pretty serious," Claus admitted finally. I've been bullheaded. You've all indulged me too much. There's a village called Margaritas back in the charted territory, the other side of the Perlas River. It's just a few days from our *chicle* camp at El Zapote. We'll go there to resupply and head on home. I can't take any more chances with your lives."

"Pancho Balam, it's just as dangerous to turn back. We will find a pass," Rogelio said.

"We'll find food," Erika said. "There's fruit in the forest."

"It's the wrong season for most fruit," Claus said quickly.

"I want to stay and look for a pass," Lazaro said.

"I'm too lame to go anywhere," Rogelio said, shrugging and smiling.

"I have an idea," Jacinto said, looking about nervously. "José and I will go to Margaritas. I think I can find it. If all goes well, we will come back with help and supplies."

"Go, if you must, and God be with you," Claus said.

When she watched Jacinto and José vanish into the thicket, Erika was sure she would never see them again. The others shook their heads and sighed deeply. Erika knew they were thinking the same thing. Now there were only four humans, three mules, one horse, and miles of sheer white wall. Erika thought with irony that the wall was composed of the very stuff out of which the Mayans carved their cities. Looking at the blinding whiteness, she imagined she saw carved reliefs of jaguars strutting, and Mayan nobles feasting and cavorting.

Weary with searching and hunger, she began to see a vision of history parading across the wall that stretched endlessly.

Chapter Sixteen

White, falling moonlight streamed through the trees and covered the forest carpet of leaves. Erika and Claus sat on a knoll that was clear enough on one side to afford a view of the soaring escarpment and the water rushing below. In the moonlight, the pale, beetle-browed cliffs brooded. Erika could almost believe that the earth had thrown up this limestone fortress as a final defense of the jungle against human invaders. The sepulchral wall offered a silent promise of death to those who sought to prevail over it.

As Erika and Claus gazed speechlessly at the cold white mystery before them, the forest fell silent. From afar, an owl hooted unanswered. Somewhere there was a brief thrashing sound, a stifled cry. A jaguar had made his kill. Then silence fell again, save for the distant thrum of crickets. Erika, sitting next to Claus, could hear the beating of her heart. They had left the rest of the party wordlessly to find the stillness together, and had taken their places on a fallen log, like lovers keeping an undeclared tryst on a park bench.

There had been no decision to come here, away from the others. Erika thought again that she often understood Claus better when they didn't speak. She thought about what Claus had told her about the cycle of nature in the forest, how the fallen leaves built layers of leaf mold to nourish the earth from which the trees drew sustenance, how falling branches replaced lost roots, how the moisture in the roots moved up to the leafy tops which then filled the air with wetness so that more rain would fall. The leafy curtain protected the life on the forest floor from dying of exposure to the hard tropical sun. But when a tree fell, ferns and orchids sprang up on its vanquished branches and were fed by the air itself. It was a perpetual cycle of growth and death and renewed fertility. In her comprehension of it, Erika felt her own connectedness with nature and the man who sat silently at her side.

The mournful sound of rubbing trees spoke for her suppressed longing for love. She was weak and giddy after her near-starvation diet of palm hearts and breadnuts, and she felt her inhibitions slide away. She wondered if Claus was aware of the unevenness of her breathing and the trembling of her thighs. Erika felt embarrassed for her mildewed garments, her stringy hair and lusterless middle-aged skin. The air was perfumed with the scent of rotting leaves.

Without knowing who had made the advance, her hand was in his. Fingers kneaded palms, following the rhythms of the moaning trees.

Yet, even as her body shook against his, Claus did not put his arms around her, nor did he kiss her. Why did he cling to his resistance? Did it make any sense now to say that a physical intimacy was bad for the expedition? The cold stones that looked down at them might become the only tombstones they would have. Why not take the consolation of love?

Well, it wasn't love. Erika couldn't trust her emotions anymore. Not too long ago, she hated Claus. But the jungle had dissolved their differences and she was in the power of the jungle. They were as Adam and Eve. Didn't he feel it, the whole of creation sucking the vacuum between them, drawing them together?

Claus stirred, sighing deeply. "Being out here makes one feel so … insignificant," he said softly.

"And lonely," Erika said.

Claus placed his arm around her shoulder. Erika realized that he too was shaking all over.

"Yes. Sometimes lonely," he said gravely.

Erika turned to face him just as he turned to face her and they kissed. Erika opened her mouth and Claus sought out her tongue.

Then he abruptly withdrew and turned away from her. Now the quiet was agonizing. Finding it unbearable, Erika said, "I'm sorry, Claus."

"No, I'm the one who should be sorry. I had no right to drag you out here and then try to compromise you."

"That's not what I'm sorry about." Certainly he must have understood the signals of her body and the look with which she held his gaze now.

She felt the space between them coming back. He had summoned it. Had he kissed her just to be polite? Maybe she just wasn't attractive to him. Another man would be delighted to take her on this soft, primeval floor. Ach, what was wrong with him?

"Do you want me, Claus?"

"Of course. You're a damn fine looking woman. There are times on the trail when I can't take my eyes off you. But my days as a lover are over."

Erika gave him an uncomprehending look. "Why do you say that? Don't tell me about the rules. What difference does all that make now? Claus, why are you shaking?"

Claus pulled at a hanging liana and began to chew it, spitting out the fiber in quick, nervous spurts as he did. "Erika, suppose we do get out of here alive. I can't promise you a future. I'm an old mule skinner married to the bush."

"Promise me a future? You don't have to marry me, Claus."

His jaw dropped and he gaped at her.

"You mean you would just …?"

"Claus, this is not the time to talk about the future. Yes, I would just—"

He turned to her with a smile that was tender, and at the same time, was the smile of resignation. Erika brushed his arm with her cheek, wanting him to hug her. He sighed deeply. Then his arm was around her.

"Why did I come back here and take you to this awful graveyard?" he said.

Erika gazed up at him and smiled steadily. "I guess we're here because we have no place else to go. But I've never known a place so beautiful."

She was happy in the crook of his arm and leaned her head against his shoulder. It was strong and sure, a shoulder to carry a world.

"You're beautiful and brave," he said at last. "I wish I'd met you another time. It's too late for me to love anybody now."

Erika tugged at the pocket flap of his shirt with her lips.

"Claus, make love to me. We'll leave loving for another world."

Erika felt his hand moving along her waist. It started the sap of desire coursing through her spleen. He touched her lips lightly with his own and paused. His smile was tender and a twinkle of delight lit up his eyes.

"Will you undo your hair for me?" he asked her.

She was happy to take her hair out of its tight, protective bun and shake loose her glory for him. She hadn't cut it since she was a young girl. She removed the pins deftly and quickly and the long red tresses streamed down below her waist. She smiled at Claus expectantly.

His face was close to hers and she watched him behold her tumbling crown. She almost swooned under the proximity of his clear eyes, incandescently blue in the moonlight. His face was masculine, but even so close, the features were fine and sensitive. She enjoyed the touch of his hands as they gently traced the sweep of her hair, following the fallen tresses down her back and searching out the crook of her spine. He lifted her blouse out of her trousers so that his fingers kneaded the contour of her back and prodded the declivity between her buttocks. His gaze on her was steadfast. She saw her eyes in his and waited for his kiss. It was upon her like a soft, slick pressure. She parted her lips begging for his tongue which fluttered into her mouth. Together, their tongues performed a kind of butterfly dance. It was all new, yet familiar. Again the experience of wonder that is at the heart of childhood returned: the first taste of chocolate, the first feel of snow, the first kiss like honey sliding down her lips, and it was all honey now. It flowed in her mouth and deep inside her sexual center, lubricating her sexual vault.

Erika felt her thighs shudder in anticipation. She placed her hands under Claus's shirt and ran her fingers up his back until she came in contact with the strong, elegant blades of his shoulders.

Together, they removed her blouse. While Claus took off his shirt, Erika unhooked her brassier and her breasts fell out like overripe fruit. Half-naked, she looked up shyly at Claus and saw the wonder in his eyes as he gazed at her stunning bosom, pale and proud as the unyielding palisades above them. But her breasts were the shapes of life, inviting him with the supple movements of her breathing. Her nipples stood up like the stamen of flowers, almost insistent in their demand that he take their honey. Claus caressed them eagerly, his fingers kneading the buds that became hard and big under his molding. Then laughing, Erika pressed his head to her bosom and shook at the joyous tickle of his mouth.

Just then, Erika felt an object strike her head. It was a breadnut. There was a chattering of monkeys above. A rain of breadnuts fell. As they sat up, Erika felt something wet on her breasts. Her naked bosom heaved in a sigh of vexation.

"Claus, I think they're peeing on us."

Consumed with passion, Claus sunk his head into her bosom.

"Claus!"

"Hmm? Oh, that." He looked up at last. "Those are the spider monkeys. They're not as ornery as the howlers. We must be sitting under their home. They just came back from hunting or a movie or something."

"Different monkeys but the same—"

Claus was kissing her nipples when Erika felt a splatter of hot liquid on her head. It was strong smelling and fell in rivulets down her shoulders and into Claus's hair. Erika wanted to scream. The rain of urine continued while they gathered their clothes and fled back to the campsite.

Chapter Seventeen

The next day, they found a crossing where the banks sloped gently and the current in the river was not very strong. Claus coaxed the bell mule into the water with him and coming to the pass, tried to get her to climb. But as Claus ascended, following the reluctant mule, the grade got steeper. Finally, Amanda slipped, bringing man and beast down the pass. Both were bruised and bleeding and Rogelio and Lazaro had to help them back across the river.

That night, the crippled band shared a can of slightly sour milk and a block of bitter chocolate.

"I have a special treat," Lazaro said. "I found some wild honey that will make the chocolate taste as it does in your Switzerland," he said to Erika.

"It's delicious," Erika said, wrapping the chocolate in pieces of honeycomb and biting into it.

"This is a royal feast to top off a perfect day," Claus said. "Tell me, Rogelio, what are we having for breakfast?"

"Palm hearts."

"And?"

He shrugged. "Perhaps we can shoot one of the mules."

"We'll need all the mules for the trip back to Margaritas," Claus snapped.

He left the fire and walked in the direction of the river. Sensing he wanted to be alone, Erika did not follow him. But when she went to the river for her bath, wrapped in her rubber sheet, she saw Claus standing a little way downstream gazing up at the great white wall. He was a dark silhouette against the bright moonlight. Erika wanted to go to him, but something told her that he had come out here to be alone with his failing dream. He stretched out his arms and held them up to the escarpment. Was it a gesture of surrender? Claus raised his arms a second time and then Erika lost sight of him as he retreated into the darkness of the bush.

In the morning, Claus announced that they would break camp the next day and begin the return to Margaritas. The others agreed reluctantly. Rogelio would have the day to recover from his wound while Claus would rest his bruised leg. The others would gather breadnuts and palm hearts for the trip.

Later in the morning, Erika found Claus sitting on a great root that hugged the bank of the river. She sat beside him and watched the bottle green water under the sun throw shimmering shadows on the chalk white wall.

"If it was just you and one stubborn old mule, you'd keep looking for a pass, wouldn't you," she said. She wanted to take his hand, but in the strong light at the river's edge, the night of the white falling moonlight seemed like another rejected dream.

"No point in discussing that. We should have turned back two weeks ago. I have no right to expose you all to this kind of danger. I knew things were bad all along. But I wouldn't admit it, even to myself. It's the same crazy optimism that ruined me in New Orleans. It was only my crazy obsession that made me refuse to face it until now. It may be too late. We're in serious trouble and it's my fault."

"I think the men would give it another try."

"We're in more danger than even they know."

"You were the one who told me that if Christopher Columbus, on his last voyage, had turned east instead of west along the coast of Yucatan, he would have discovered cities more fabulous than any he might have found in India."

"Christopher Columbus was an old man at the time and should have retired long before that voyage," Claus said with bitterness in his voice.

Erika felt a surge of compassion for Claus. It welled up, an unbidden torrent of love. She recognized its force. Yes, she had fallen in love with this silly, single-minded, brave and magnificent human being. She wanted to tell him about it, wanted to comfort him with the love she felt. But she held her tongue. Surely, he would be embarrassed by a declaration of love he didn't want. His eyes were on the haughty palisades. His soul's craving lay beyond them. She might as well love the unfeeling stones. But it didn't matter. Her love was unconditional, it struck no bargains, demanded no terms. Like the river before them, caressing the indifferent stones, it needed only to flow. She reached out to touch him but he shifted his position away from her. His eyes were on his lost dream.

Chapter Eighteen

The sun was high and its eye was fierce. Perspiration was dripping from Erika's forehead and the salt stung her eyes. Through her blurred vision, she thought she saw angels. Appearing to stand on the water, they had long silky hair and white flowing robes. She wasn't sure whether she saw wings. They glided miraculously toward them over the sparkling water, parting it with long staffs. Claus did not seem to see them. Erika began to believe she was experiencing a jungle mirage or a vision induced by her lack of nutrition. And if what she was seeing was real, why didn't Claus bestir himself? The angels kept skimming along toward them. Then she saw that they had round human heads and were floating along in three long canoes.

"Claus—"

"Don't move until they get closer. We don't want to frighten them away," he whispered.

A lone figure stood in the first canoe. The other two canoes each carried two standing oarsmen and a seated woman. Then the canoes turned away from them and went to the opposite shore. There, an excited discussion seemed underway.

"Will they come back?"

"Wait."

The lone man in the lead canoe poled off from the far bank and crossed over to them.

The prow of his canoe cut through the tall grass at the river's edge and nestled in a tangle of roots that gripped the shore. He set down his oar and stepped barefoot onto the shore.

The man appeared to be young. He was a little over five feet tall. His dress consisted of no more than a white knee length smock of sorts. But by his startling face and crowning locks of long rich, dark hair, Erika knew she was in the presence of royalty. His head was round, flat on top and exquisitely framed by his long silken hair. His face was broad and his large caramel eyes fixed her with the penetration and frankness of the inscrutable cats of her childhood.

Carefully and nonchalantly, Claus placed himself between the Indian and his canoe.

"We can't let this fellow get away," Claus said softly.

Almost as if he understood Claus's concern, the Indian laughed and said, "Utxim Pusical."

Smiling, Claus answered, "Ne Tsoy."

"What's all that about?" Erika asked. For all her learning of Yucatec Maya from Claus, she knew she needed more practice in conversation with these native speakers.

"He said his heart is good and all I said was, 'That's fine.'"

Erika blushed as the stranger made a candid surveillance of her body. Then the Indian stared at Claus and broke into a broad grin.

"Hair the color of corn, eyes the color of sky," he said in broken Spanish. After a pause, he repeated his description of Claus, apparently for his own benefit. It seemed to have some special meaning for him that he was not going to reveal.

All the while, his manner was proud, almost lofty. Erika didn't know whether rescue was at hand or whether she and her friends were going to be murdered in a matter of minutes. The Indians in the other canoes along the wall took arrows from sheaves on their backs and fixed them to long bows. Erika's throat became dry at the thought that she and her half-starved band were totally defenseless. She searched the proud Indian's eyes for a clue to his intentions, her own eyes almost begging, but he looked back at her implacably.

The princely figure turned to his fellows along the wall, and held up one arm. Erika had never seen anyone whose slightest movement was so full of grace and beauty. The Indians on the other shore put their bows in their canoes. They came over in the boats. Now a half dozen Indians stood before Erika andClaus. If nothing else, the curiosity that prevailed on both sides stretched wires of tension around the silence.

The leader spoke to Claus again. Erika was able to make out that his name was Bor. He was the son of one Bolon Kin who was the Tohil, a chief of sorts, in the land beyond the escarpment, and that Claus and his party were to be taken over a pass to his settlement which was called a caribal. Erika could not determine whether this was an offer of hospitality or an order given a band of captives. Claus, answering with alacrity, said that he and his friends would be happy to visit the caribal of the great Tohil.

Lazaro and Rogelio came out of the bush. Upon seeing them, the Indians spoke excitedly among themselves. The muleteers stroked the empty revolvers in their sashes but it made no impression on their hosts/captors. One of the Lacandons wanted Rogelio's shirt. Rogelio gave it to him before it was all but torn from his back. For his pains, he was given a homemade cigar which he choked on.

The Indians tied the three canoes together with lianas and loaded the *chicle* boxes. Erika watched the improvised ferry, poled by two Lacandons, disappear downstream.

"Are we prisoners or royal guests?" Erika asked Claus while they waited.

"It's hard to tell. But wherever they take us, we're safer than we are here. Bolon Kin is the old chief I met ten years ago. He's still alive! That's wonderful news. He was rather ancient at the time."

Bor was not happy to see the mules and insisted that they be left on the west side of the river. Claus explained that they had to be fed at regular intervals.

"Ne Tamacchi," Bor said angrily. "Ne Tamacchi!"

Erika could see the loathing in Bor's eyes at the sight of the unnatural beasts. What ships and muskets must have meant to his ancestors, these squat, useless animals represented to Bor. Erika could read the mixture of contempt and fear in his face. The mule brought the mosquito—the source of malaria—to the jungle. And the mule brought the parasites that lived in the Indian's body and gave him the fever that burned him alive.

Bor's nostrils quivered nervously as if the mules were not merely domesticated servants of the foreigners but of a separate order of being, evil instruments of some dark apocalypse, beyond the power of the gods themselves.

"Perhaps we shouldn't antagonize him. Why can't we leave the mules here?" Erika whispered to Claus in English.

"We'll need the mules on the other side of the pass," Claus said. Erika looked at him in astonishment. Then Claus told Bor that if they could get the mules over the pass, he would tie the horse to a tree and the mules would remain there throughout the visit to the settlement. Bor instructed Claus to have the animals led downstream where the Lacandons would show the muleteers a crossing. Lazaro and Rogelio set off with the beasts.

Two canoes returned for the rest of the human cargo. Erika and Claus were asked to sit at the bottom of what was a canoe carved out of a mahogany log. Two Lacandons stood at either end of the canoe and poled away from the shore with their long oars. Bor manned the other canoe alone. The river was smooth for long stretches and the sun turned the water the color of rose wine. They met rapids and the long canoes surged confidently over them. The Lacandons paddled with intense choppy strokes. Long hair and loose robes billowed in the wind. Erika looked up to see a fleet of twenty scarlet macaws flying in pairs. Their plumage was ablaze against the pink glow of the sun that stained the underbellies of the clouds and brushed the white cliffs. Erika's head was reeling with the thought that she was being led back thousands of years in time. She wanted to take pictures but was afraid their escorts might find it offensive.

After an hour or so, the canoes turned into a hidden inlet. They rowed silently between the sheer white walls that towered over them for hundreds of feet. The hidden creek took winding turns. After several hundred meters, Erika saw the mules, the horse, and the *chicle* boxes waiting on a ledge. Then the party went by foot up a pass that climbed gently to accommodate man and beast.

They made camp at the top of the limestone mountain and the Lacandons provided the famished explorers with a marvelous supper of deer meat and wild rice. They set out for Bor's caribal in the morning. The mesh of leaf above Erika's head afforded few glimpses of upper spaces. There was little secondary growth here, only that which struggled out of an occasional fallen branch. What color there was could only be seen in the rich variety of flowers occasionally sighted high up beyond the dense layers of fan leaves. Here was the real big jungle where no *chicle* trails had ever been cut, a primeval forest such as might have first confronted Mayan eyes before they built their pyramids.

The trail followed a green, sulfurous stream until it led them to a cluster of thatched-roofed wooden huts that were widely separated. The roofs reminded Erika of Chinese hats. Erika saw no people, only some thin, sleeping dogs and restless chickens. She recognized the voices of women and small children coming from inside the huts. When the party came to a large hut, Erika thought they would be ushered inside as it looked like the home of the chief. The bearers set the luggage before it but did not stop there. Bor led them past the house, beyond some smaller huts and soon they were out of the settlement altogether.

"I don't like the looks of this," Erika said. "Why didn't we stop back there? What are they doing with our things?"

Claus sighed. "We'd better go along with them. In the shape we're in, we don't stand much of a chance if they try something nasty. I'll ask to see the chief."

They came upon another clearing. Before them stood a row of wooden cages. They were large enough to contain a jaguar. *Or a man*, Erika thought with a shock that splashed across her face like ice water.

"Claus, tell me—"

Rogelio and Lazaro paled, but quickly turned to their captors and drew their empty revolvers. The Lacandons were unimpressed.

"Pancho Balam," Rogelio said excitedly, "Those are the jails—"

Erika saw Claus's jaw drop as if it were independent of the rest of his face, like a ventriloquist's doll.

"I can't believe it! This is precisely what Maudslay and Maler wrote about!"

The cages were about four feet high and just as wide. Beyond them, at the edge of the clearing, Erika saw a large hut. Rows of small bowls were set on planks inside. Before the hut lay a dark-stained limestone slab. Bor went over to the cages and raised lids that opened from the top. The trail back to the settlement was blocked by the eight or so Lacandons who had accompanied them. Dense impassable bush bordered the square. Erika felt fear sweep through her like cold ether.

Claus said something to Bor in the special dialect of Mayan they had used before. Erika knew he was asking to see the chief. Bor looked at him, his arms folded across his chest, his face implacable. His answer was short. Claus spoke again, more insistently this time. Bor nodded to the other Lacandons.

Claus motioned to Lazaro and Rogelio. "We'll have to make a run at them," Claus said in English. Before the Indians could draw their bows, Claus, Rogelio and Lazaro rushed at them. Rogelio struck a Lacandon over the head with the butt of his revolver and Lazaro kicked savagely with his booted feet at two attackers. The Lacandons moved in pairs toward each explorer. Another pair stood at the entrance to the trail and drew bows. Claus swung his rifle like a machete and held off the two Lacandons who appeared to be assigned to him. Rogelio fell and Erika remembered that he had only one good foot. His attackers dragged him off to one of the cages. Lazaro and Claus still resisted capture, Lazaro slashing the air with the buckle of his belt and wielding his revolver with his other hand. One of the Lacandons, who had been guarding the entrance, came up behind Claus and managed to fasten his arms behind his back while the other two tried to hold his kicking legs.

No one approached Erika. She looked about frantically for something to use as a weapon.

Erika picked up a clay pot she'd spotted on the ground and smashed it over the head of the Indian who held Claus. As the Indian fell, Erika saw two Lacandons lift Rogelio into the air and drop him into a cage. They slammed the lid over him and a Lacandon jumped on top of it.

Claus struck out at the men who were hitting him. Suddenly, more Lacandons dropped from the trees that enclosed the clearing. One of them landed on Claus's shoulders and subdued him with a quick jab of a stone axe. Erika felt a heavy blow on her own head and lost consciousness.

Erika awoke in the dark. She was curled up in a ball. She was aware of having a splitting headache. Erika rubbed her head and discovered a large lump on her forehead. She was surrounded by the wooden bars of her cage. There was a bowl of *posole* and some tortillas filled with scrambled eggs at the bottom of the cage.

She fell on the food like an animal. Afterward, Erika looked up to see the shadow of a Lacandon sitting on top of the lid. The cage was not high enough for her to stand up or long enough to stretch out and she crouched, looking up at her captor. Through the mesh she could see his genitals hanging freely under his smock. He chanted softly and patted a small drum.

There was enough moonlight to make out the other cages, each with a guard on top. They were all chanting and beating small drums. Erika could see the silhouettes of her friends slumped in the cages. She could see the ragged edge of the forest and above it, a clear, starry night.

"Claus!" she called out.

He answered out of the darkness. "Are you all right?" he said.

"As well as can be expected. And you?"

"Fit as a fiddle. But my head feels like the worst hangover I've ever had."

"Do you think we can escape these wooden cages?"

"It's impossible. I've tried. They've taken away all cutting instruments. And there's no way to push your way out. Our guards are firmly implanted over our heads, and they're armed with flint-tipped spears."

She called to Rogelio and Lazaro. They answered glumly. Rogelio said he felt like a rooster waiting to be butchered in the morning. "Except the roosters don't know what is going to happen to them and are happy making love to the hens."

Erika couldn't believe that it would happen, that they would really be sacrificed. Maybe if they could talk to somebody, explain that there was some mistake. The guards continued their singing and thumping and didn't seem to mind the conversation of the prisoners. She could smell incense and see a red glow over the pots in the open hut. The slab underneath was slightly illuminated and looked like a grey coffin in the moonlight. Erika wondered if it was an ancient Mayan sacrificial altar. But she refused to accept the finality of such a fate.

"Claus, what happened when you asked them about the old chief?"

"Bor told me that his father was away on a pilgrimage to the shrine of the rain god. He will come back after so many rivers and hills and lakes. I told Bor that his father would be angry if he came back and found me dead, but Bor told me he would go to the God House for dream divination and the gods would tell him what to do with us."

"Doña Erika, you can't look death in the face," Lazaro said.

But Erika was succumbing to the terror again. She felt the need to light her way down the black abyss into which she was sinking, no matter what horrors were revealed.

"I have a right to know," she pleaded. "It's bad enough without being left out of your secrets. It's too late to protect me. If I have to die, I want to die with the rest of you, knowing what you know."

She heard Claus sigh again. "The truth is, I don't know. These people have been isolated for a long time and we don't know their customs. The Mayans ripped the hearts out of living victims. They wanted the hearts fresh and beating away when they pressed them against the lips of their stone idols. The victims were often volunteers. Dying for the gods was an honor and left your survivors prosperous. Later, the victims were prisoners. They sometimes beheaded prisoners of high rank but what we've seen along the way seems to have a special meaning for these people at this time in their history. I don't know what it is."

Erika was impressed that under the threat of imminent death, Claus maintained a detached curiosity about the manner in which his annihilation would be carried out. She asked him when he thought they would be taken out of the cages.

"Well, if you really want to know, the Aztecs believed that the sun god, as he traveled through the underworld, needed the hearts of men for strength in his battle against the demons of the night who were trying to prevent him from rising in the morning. I don't know if these people inherited any of that mythology but we might expect something to happen just before dawn."

There was a sound of footfalls at the beginning of the trail. Erika saw Bor advancing toward them, his tunic a silver robe in the moonlight. The high grass whistled as he moved effortlessly through it. Despite the simplicity of his dress, he would be taken for a prince anywhere. His lower lip brooded and the moonlight caught its wetness. As he came closer, she saw that his face, in the wan light, was grave. He said something to the men sitting on top of the cages and then walked away. Claus called after him but Bor disappeared down the trail without answering.

"What did he say to the men?" Erika asked Claus as soon as Bor was gone. With her scant knowledge of Yucatec Maya, she had recognized some of the words Bor used, but she had missed the sense of the message.

"He said he is going to the God House to pray to the corn god but in his dream Sukunkyum asked for us."

"Who is Sukunkyum?" Erika asked. The very name sounded filthy and obscene. "What do you think the gods will say to Bor?"

"Maybe the gods will give us a break." She heard him sigh in the darkness.

"Claus, I've already imagined the worst. You know that. Just spell it out for me."

He was squatting and Erika could make out the shape of his head as it touched the lid of his prison.

"Yes, these cages are what you think. They are precisely what Maudslay and Maler wrote about in the nineteenth century. They claimed the Lacandons kept victims in wooden cages before sacrificing them to their gods."

Erika thought of the twisted face of Mateo in Ocosingo. Then a thought came crashing through her headache like a jackhammer.

"Claus, do they rip out the hearts first and then remove the heads?"

"You really don't want to know that," Claus said.

Erika heard Rogelio and Lazaro groan on the other side of Claus.

"Who is Sukunkyum?" Erika asked again. "Tell me."

"Sukunkyum is the dead sun," Claus said.

"What would he want with us?" Erika asked.

"Sukunkyum judges the souls of men when they die."

Erika found herself pulling hysterically at the poles of her cage. She was not going to die like this. She would rather be a witch burned at the stake than a sacrificial lamb. The cage rocked with her pulling and banging. She shouted up to her captor who began to giggle. Erika found a loose stick on the ground and shoved it through the lid at her keeper's bare genitals. He did not cry out but giggled more and showered Erika with a stream of piss.

Chapter Nineteen

Erika fell asleep out of exhaustion just as a pre-dawn fog rolled in. Then she was being awakened by hands that reached under her arms. The lid was drawn back and two Lacandons were lifting her out of the cage. The fog was thick and she could see only dark shapes moving around her. She knew she hadn't slept long as the sun had not risen. She was taken to join the others. Each prisoner was escorted by two Lacandons bearing long spears. Others followed with torches. Claus greeted her with a strained "Buenos dias." So did Rogelio and Lazaro. They all looked sleepless, wan, and resigned to the worst.

They were led down the trail by which they had come. Erika thought they were going back to the settlement until they were guided down a path that took them to a quiet stream. The sky was just beginning to get light. Couldn't the sun rise without their blood as it did on all the other days? One of the guards holding a torch said something to Claus.

"He wants us to bathe," Claus said.

So we can be clean for the sacrifice, Erika thought.

A woman joined them and led Erika around a bend in the stream. The woman wore the same tunic as the men with the addition of a necklace and a pink skirt that seemed to serve as a petticoat. Erika was struck by the woman's beauty. Her face was ageless. Erika marveled at the woman's clear skin, limpid eyes and soft curves. Her long brown hair was miraculously straight and full-bodied. Erika knew it would take hours in a Paris beauty salon for her to achieve that effect. The woman smiled and gestured toward the stream.

Then she left Erika to bathe in privacy. Erika knew there was no point running away. She might as well take her chances with the Lacandons as with the impenetrable bush. In any case, she couldn't leave without Claus and the others.

The water was warm and the air was filled with sweet smells. When Erika came out of the stream, the woman reappeared and presented her with a coral-colored skirt like the one the woman wore under her tunic. Erika's skin tingled with hope. Was she being accepted by the Lacandons after all? They wanted her to be dressed like one of them. Perhaps the terrifying night was a rite of initiation and she had passed.

The woman smiled but her eyes were solemn. Erika wrapped the skirt around her waist and the woman helped her fasten it with a cord. Erika looked at her reflection in the stream. With her hair falling in wild cataracts over her shoulders and breasts, her Lacandon skirt hugging her hips and her face frozen in a startled look, she saw herself as a creature of the forest for the first time. Her heart skipped like a little girl released from school. She couldn't wait to try on the tunic and turned to the woman eagerly. The woman didn't move and an expression of regret came over her face. Erika realized that the woman had no other garment for her.

Somewhere nearby, a parrot screeched. Erika's heart skipped again, this time with fright. She pointed to the woman's smock and gave her a questioning look. The woman only nodded sorrowfully and pointed to the path. Erika ran to the tree on which she had hung her clothes. They were gone. She ran back to the woman.

"I want my clothes!" Erika demanded. The woman smiled thinly and gestured toward the path. Erika was not going back down the trail dressed only in a wrap-around skirt that was obviously insufficient attire even for a Lacandon woman. Why did they want her to return bare-breasted? The answer came in a flash. They wanted her bare-breasted because they were going to split her bosom open with an axe.

Erika turned to face the stream. She would take her chances with the vultures and the jaguars. She heard a shriek and spied a huge howler monkey looking lugubriously down at her from a branch that stretched over the water.

Death by the forces of the jungle would be more horrible than a swift execution. And she couldn't leave Claus and the others to an unknown fate. Another thought struck her. Perhaps one sacrifice was enough and she was chosen because of her sex. Didn't the Mayans sacrifice young virgins? She was hardly such a one but perhaps she would do.

It would all be funny if only she could stop the shaking fit that suddenly came over her. She tried to compose herself as she returned to the woman who stood motionless and silent. A new thought struck Erika. Perhaps she had read the signals all wrong. Wraparound skirts were the proper attire for guests and tunics were restricted only to natives. She was being taken to an elaborate breakfast.

Erika knew she was grasping for straws. There were goose pimples over her naked breasts that bounced in the semi-dark as she followed the woman. They turned on the main trail and Erika realized she was being taken back to the clearing with the cages.

The others were already there. Their hands were tied behind their backs with vines. But they were still dressed in their clothes and were not bare breasted. Erika looked down at her naked breasts and then looked up at Claus. The sorrow in his eyes removed any doubt she had. She was to be the sacrificial victim. She felt as if the earth had suddenly dropped a few feet out from under her. Erika and Claus searched each other's eyes but couldn't speak. Lazaro and Rogelio wept openly but turned their heads away.

"Erika, I wanted it to be me," Claus said, sobbing. She wanted to run to him but two attendants were at her side holding her arms. It started her knees knocking. The attendants tugged gently at her arms, leading her to the altar. She found herself walking slowly toward it without their prodding. Bor sat cross-legged on the plank platform above it. Around him a dozen or so strapping young men stood. Two waved singed palm leaves over Bor's head. Others held aloft pine pitch torches. There were daubs of red and blue paint on their bodies and clothes. The bluish smoke that rose from the incense in the bowls mixed with the dark fog.

The men around Bor began to chant. Those with drums began to beat them. It all seemed like a dream. Then someone blew on a conch shell and the sound penetrated Erika's heart. The Lacandons stopped singing and beating the drums. Then a Lacandon came forward and stood at one end of the altar. He was carrying a stone axe which he held at attention like a soldier with a rifle. Erika wanted to look away but she found her eyes riveted to the large double edge flint blade. The conch shell sounded again. Erika felt her blood drain from her face. She felt her legs give under her and then she fainted. But she was awake in seconds. The Indians knelt beside her and helped her to sit with her head lowered until the blood returned to her face. She heard Claus struggling against his captors and shouting. When she looked up again, she saw Rogelio biting the arm of one of the men who held him. Erika gasped for the moist air around her and listened to her doomed heart beating against her chest. She knew there was no use resisting. She would walk to the altar and get it over with. She got up and began to walk, trembling but unaided, toward the grey slab and the Lacandons who waited for her. Her attendants followed behind. She was alone now. They knew she had accepted her part. The woman rushed forward and pressed a bunch of begonias into her bosom. Erika almost smiled. The flowers made her feel less naked. It was as if she were a bride. Maybe that's the way they saw it. A sacrificial victim was a bride of a god. The Lacandons looked at her solemnly. There was no cruelty in their eyes. They were all of them taking part in a holy rite. If she could only be sure that Claus and the others would live. She still couldn't control her breathing or the fast beating of her heart. Nature rebelled even as Erika's mind accepted the end.

She was going to raise the sun. That's why she was going to die. She didn't want to think of it any other way. Reality was no help in the face of death. All right, she might save the lives of Claus and her friends. That was real. Maybe. She only hoped the Lacandons wouldn't rape her, that they would take her with dignity. But they were going to cleave her chest in two, she was sure now.

She trembled as she walked the last few paces to the altar. The executioner continued to stand at attention with his axe. She looked into Bor's eyes. They looked back, troubled, as if trying to penetrate some dark mystery locked in her heart. Nothing would be locked in her heart for long. She felt it banging rebelliously. Behind her she could hear Claus shouting, a counterpoint to the knocking in her chest. She wished he would stop. It was all too late and just increased her fright. Erika turned to look at Claus for the last time. She wanted to tell him that she loved him. But love seemed far away now. One died alone.

She turned her head back to face the altar. The drums stopped beating. The palms were stilled. All eyes fell on her as she stood clutching the flowers against her bosom. Bor stood up and bowed to her. Perhaps one who was about to give blood to the sun was due a final show of respect. The executioner remained motionless with his axe. Bor waved a hand as a sign for Erika to lie back on the altar. She froze.

No, she couldn't submit like a lamb. She turned away and began to run to where Claus stood. They seized her in an instant. Erika felt a hand grip the long tresses of her hair. In a flash, she was pulled backward over the altar so that her eyes and breasts pointed up to the hanging lianas. She felt the flowers being crushed under her back. Her hair was wound in a braid and tied to some stone projection behind her. She felt the cold stone against the calves of her legs as her feet were strapped into a niche. With some painful tugging at her hair, she could move her head from side to side. Erika rolled her eyes back and saw the executioner standing at the head of the slab with his axe.

Claus was sending out a verbal torrent. Erika wished he would stop shouting. What could he hope to accomplish? She wanted it done with. Claus boomed on. Erika could turn her head freely from side to side and now she saw the troubled look in Bor's face deepen. Erika didn't know what Claus was telling him, but pieced together something about angry gods. Bor's features recomposed into resolve. He took a deep breath and gestured to the executioner. Erika could see the axe raised high above her head. A grey light showed above the dark silhouettes of trees. Claus continued to shout. The axe was lowered slightly for position and

Erika could see the first rosy hues of dawn reflected in the smooth blade. She closed her eyes. Claus cried out a final time and stopped.

Erika heard a thump. It was not a drum. At first, she thought it came from the last desperate beatings of her heart. Then she realized the thump was outside of her. And still her chest had not been cracked open. She dared not open her eyes. Erika heard a shout in the distance. It was not Claus. Someone ran down the trail toward them. Erika opened her eyes and gaped at a young Lacandon who was running, out of breath, toward her. In an instant he was standing before the altar and speaking excitedly to Bor. By his looks, it was clear that the newcomer was Bor's brother. Erika could feel the heat of their argument on her breasts.

Then the axe was gone and she felt hands untie her hair and feet. When she knew she was free, she ran as fast as she could into the arms of Claus. He was also unbound. They embraced warmly. Erika began to sob convulsively as she buried her head in his chest.

"Claus, I was going to die," she said over and over. "They were going to break open my chest and pull out my heart. Can you feel it beating? Is it still there?"

"Yes, I can feel it. It's still there and it's very strong."

"Is it really?"

"Yes, it's a strong, very brave heart and has every reason to be proud."

Erika looked up into his face. Claus was smiling at her. Whatever his shouting had been about, it had helped to save her. She believed now that she would never die in the jungle as long as she was with him.

"What were you telling them? What did you say to Bor?"

"I was stalling for time, telling Bor that only his father had the true power of dream divination. Of course, I knew he was testing his priestly powers while the old man was away. But I kept telling him the gods would punish his whole tribe if he took your life by mistaking their signs. He was trying to show his resolve in front of the others but I had him scared. In the meantime, I was hoping the sun would rise without the help of your blood and therefore make the sacrifice pointless. Now Bor's brother has brought the news that the old chief has returned from his trip. He wants to see us."

The woman returned with Erika's clothes folded in a neat pile. She dressed behind a tree. Just as they were leaving the clearing to take the trail to the settlement, Erika saw the sun, a blood-red ball, climb out of the dark trees.

Chapter Twenty

A young girl, ripe with life, admitted Erika and Claus into the house of the chief. Bolon Kin lay in his hammock like a heap of fallen vines. Upon seeing his guests, he disentangled himself and sat up. The old man seemed to be composed of nothing but age itself. But his eyes shone as bright and immortal as stars. "Kulem," Bor said, waving the visitors to small mahogany benches that stood beside the doorway.

"Yes, it is Pancho Balam with hair the color of corn and eyes the color of the sky," the old man said not looking directly at them.

"How could you have known I was coming? It has been over ten milpas, old priest. Your settlement was in another place, many days from here."

"You have little faith in the Lacandon powers of dream divination," he shook his head and emitted a childish giggle. "In my dream I met a jaguar in the milpa. This is a sign of visitors coming from far away. Then I dreamt of water flooding the forest which told me that visitors would come where rivers are high. Now, I know the jaguar is the animal with whom you share your spirit, Pancho Balam. All signs pointed to your coming. So I left the holy cave of Metzabok and came home. My son Bor had the same dream and went to meet you. But he did not know the jaguar was a friend. He still has things to learn about dream divination."

"And to think Sigmund Freud congratulated himself for having solved the riddle of the Sphinx," Erika said in awe when Claus translated what Bolon Kin had said.

Bolon Kin then lay back in his hammock and curled up into a ball.

Bor squatted on his haunches in front of his father's hammock. He seemed to be consumed with his humiliation, but when his father turned his back to them, Bor's princely demeanor came back.

Bolon Kin will rest now," he said softly. "He is very old and is tired from his journey. He is also tired from the many days of fasting which he did before making his pilgrimage to the cave of the god. Two of our people had to carry him back in a hammock strung between two poles."

A silence followed. It was as if there had been an unspoken agreement not to interrupt Bolon Kin's rest. Erika saw two women seated cross-legged around two fires while the girl who had let them in to see the chief sat before a cold hearth. Erika recognized one of the women as her escort of the morning. Their smocks were daubed with color and they all wore necklaces. Soft brown hair streamed over their shoulders. Bor introduced them in a quiet voice. The two women were wives of Bolon Kin. The young girl was his daughter, Koh. Chan Bol was the oldest wife though she did not look as old as Bolon Kin. Nakin was the wife Erika had met. She was able to see Nakin's features more clearly in the firelight. She was a great beauty by any standards. Erika envied her smooth glossy skin and round voluptuous curves. Her face was the mold of beauty itself. She was the mother of Koh, who was neither child nor woman but at least one part forest sprite.

Koh was a radiant crystal. She rose to fetch a hanging gourd. Koh moved with such nimbleness that Erika thought of Claus's stories of Indian maidens capable to running days on end with children on their backs. She sat again before her hearth and rolled a stick vigorously between her fingers into one of a row of holes that lined a reed resting on a stone slab. She blew on it from time to time while everybody watched. Suddenly, a spark flared up. The girl seemed as surprised as everybody else. The spark was fed to a pith. She blew it into a flame and then had her own fire. The other women applauded the feat with a burst of song. But the young lady appeared glum in the face of her achievement.

"Why didn't they just give her an ember from one of their fires?" Erika asked Claus who was accepting a cigar that Bor had just rolled from tobacco leaves.

"I think she is learning to make a fire from scratch," Claus said.

Erika declined the offer of a cigar but she accepted the bowl of *posole* given by Nakin.

"Koh is promised to Chankin of Sakrum who has no wives," Bor explained in fractured Spanish. "He wants to marry her and is ready to do his bride service in my father's milpa. But she keeps telling him to wait. She says she must learn more things from her mother before she can become a wife. It is true that Bolon Kin does not want to give his daughter away until she has learned all the things that a woman must know to feed a man and keep a house. But she continues to delay her wedding, being slow to learn from her mother when we know she is as quick as a bird. Indeed, she is quick to remind her mother when she forgets to teach her something. She could have learned to build a fire long ago. You saw how unhappy she was with her success. She wants her mother to teach her to weave hammocks before she marries."

They sat in silence again. Erika looked up at the parrot feathers, gourds, and fiber bark bags that hung from rafters. She recognized limes, onions, and root plants in the bags. There were also strips of dried tobacco. Erika saw basket traps for catching fish, long bows, and rows of arrows, some with chipped flint heads and others with blunt wooden tips, "to stun birds," Bor explained.

When the cigar was finished, Bor said he would take Claus and Erika to the hut where they would spend the night.

"Yes, Bolon Kin is very old and does not hunt anymore," Bor said as they left his father's house. "But he is the only one who knows the ways of the gods. He can tell us which gods are angry when a child is sick or when the corn does not grow high. He alone knows the way of counting of the ancestors. Because of this, only my father knows when it is time to plant the corn."

"What will happen when he dies? Will he teach you this knowledge?" Erika asked.

After a pause, he said, "My father has taught me many things. Come, I will show you where you will sleep."

Lazaro and Rogelio reappeared after repairing some damaged *chicle* boxes and Bor showed them huts where they would stay.

On the way, they passed an open-sided shelter. A woman and a girl child were kneeling on the ground surrounded by prancing turkeys, chickens and sleeping dogs. They were grinding corn on stone slabs which Bor called *metates*. On seeing the visitors, both the woman and the girl ran into the adjacent closed hut.

Bor laughed. "It is my wife, Juana Nabor and her daughter Akan. Akan is her daughter from her marriage to Baats who died by the bite of a snake. We are not accustomed to visitors here."

He led the muleteers to one hut and showed Claus and Erika to another, not asking the nature of their relationship.

The guest hut was similar to the others Erika had seen, though each hut had its own distinctive decoration. There were two huge clay pots filled with water in which corn and lime that had been crushed from snail shells soaked in water. Erika soon became aware that it was cooler inside the wall enclosure than it was outside. The roof shielded them from the sun. The spaces between the slats provided ventilation and kept the heat out. The earthen floor was cool. Net bags of vegetables hung here too. Erika saw little bowls of ashes under the bed frames that were made of vine-tied bamboo sticks.

"In the night you will want to put ashes from the fire into the pots to warm you when the winds come from the north," Bor explained.

Then he left his visitors alone.

"Claus, I can't make it out. Are we still prisoners?" Erika asked when Bor left.

"I think that's an academic point. But Bolon Kin wants us alive, at least for the time being. We may find out why later tonight. Lacandons only discuss their intentions with guests after all the formalities of eating, drinking and smoking are done with."

Erika and Claus stretched out on their separate bamboo beds. She reached out and their hands touched. Within seconds, Erika fell into a dreamless sleep.

Shortly before dark, Bor returned to take them to the hut of Bolon Kin. The visitors were offered mahogany stools to sit on. Bolon Kin sat in his hammock. His sons sat on their haunches near him. The women, including the family of Bor, squatted around the fires getting the food ready. The guests were presented with tortillas and invited to fill them with food from a big vessel in the center of the room. There were slices of roasted *cojolte* which tasted like sweet, tender turkey, roasted bananas stuffed with beans, and flower squash that had been dipped in a batter of egg and corn. After several weeks of hunger, Erika had not enjoyed a meal so much, and kept repeating the phrase "Ne T'soy," or it is good, to her hosts and hostesses. She was catching on to the Yucatec dialect and was pleased that her talent for languages had not deserted her.

A coffee sweet with sugar was served next and the traditional cigars came out again.

It was now dark. Erika and Claus gazed at the fires and the faces reflected in them. As best she could, Erika joined in the conversation. As obscure as the language was, she found herself picking up its rhythms.

"The dinner was superb but what do you suppose they intend to do with us?" Erika whispered to Claus.

"We'll find out soon enough," Claus said.

Bor led his visitors to a cool, bubbling arroyo which he identified in Spanish as *el lavia*. Then he pointed to a path that led deep into the woods to a fallen log for those guests who needed to evacuate their bowels.

Coming back from the distant latrine, Erika walked across the clearing to where Claus stood. Above the dark ragged silhouette of the jungle, the night was full of stars.

Bolon Kin, supported by his two wives, came out of his hut and gazed up at the heavens. "Our Lord Hachakayum has cast seeds of corn to mark a trail across the sky," he said.

Then Bolon Kin turned his luminous eyes on his guests. Erika felt her heart beat quicken. Something told her that the mind behind the eyes had made a decision and the fate of the lost, crippled team of explorers, was about to be revealed.

The old man's voice was as audible as the chorus of crickets that sang in the darkness. "It is time to drink the *balché*. We will speak of why you have come and what you must do."

Chapter Twenty-One

Erika and Claus followed the old chief to his hut. Koh was sitting by a fire outside a lean-to, her head covered with a blue shawl. Nakin, her mother, whispered something to her in a tone that Erika took to be reproachful. The young girl did not answer and gazed impassively into the night. She was beautiful wrapped in her blue shroud and the moonlight falling on her face.

Inside the hut, Bolon Kin squatted before the fire, rolled some tobacco leaves, and tied them together with elastic vines. He lit them from a stick he poked into the fire, and passed this homemade cigar to his guests.

His wives, on the other side of the hut, talked quietly together.

Bolon Kin arranged some pellets of incense on a board that had rows of nipple-like projections. Erika watched the ancient face reflected in the firelight.

"It is necessary to burn incense to help the gods who must get the sun through the underworld. There was a time when the sun needed the blood of men. But the creator sent Akinchob, the corn god, to protect all men. Now only those who defile the places of the gods can be sacrificed. My son Bor needs more training in dream divination," Bolon Kin said.

The old man's voice took on a confidential tone. "I will tell you something that your people, the T'sul, do not know but was taught to me by my father. He learned it from his father. Whenever a tree falls in the jungle, a star falls from the sky. The T'sul do not know this for there are places in the forest where they have cut down so many trees, none can grow again. And if the forest dies, then surely the sky will become empty of stars."

"What else did your father teach you about the stars?" Claus asked eagerly.

"My father taught me many things. When I became old enough to understand, he taught me the secret counting of the true people of long ago. It is only by the counting that the ways of the sun and moon and stars can be revealed to man. And it is only through the ancient knowledge of counting that the true people of today can know when to plant corn in the milpa. Without this knowledge, the planting cannot be fulfilled and the people will die." He paused for a moment and his face became sorrowful. "It is because of this that I must pass on the knowledge of the counting to my son." He shook his head and Erika could see that for some reason the thought of passing on the knowledge was painful to the old man. But why had he waited so long? He had two sons. Which son did he mean? Bor was the oldest.

There was a gloomy silence and they waited for the old man to speak again.

"The gods must be worshiped properly," Bolon Kin said finally. He sighed deeply and his young wife brought a bowl containing a yellowish liquid. The chief dipped his fingers into the bowl and flecked drops of the liquid into the air.

"This is the wine of the gods. It is called *balché*. This wine is made from the bark of the *balché* tree crushed with sugar cane inside a *cayuco* filled with water. There we let it sit until it becomes holy. I must serve the gods first. Then we will purify ourselves for the task ahead." He flecked more drops into the air and his wife brought another bowl. He passed the bowl to Claus.

"Must I drink?" Claus asked.

"Absolutely. It is necessary to drink to become holy."

"Claus, you can't drink it," Erika said in English, unable to suppress her concern any longer.

"Erika, I agree with you that it could be a disaster, but what can we do? To refuse would be an insult to their gods, and I doubt that we can do that and escape with our lives."

"Then pass the bowl to me."

"But women aren't allowed."

"Pass me the bowl, Claus."

A look of apprehension crossed the old man's face as Erika took the bowl from the hands of Claus. The women sitting next to the other fire gasped when they saw it.

"Señorita, it is forbidden of women to drink the *balché*."

"Why is that, great Tohil? Cannot women worship the gods?"

"Let me explain. It is forbidden of men to make the food of the gods. Only women can do that. But only men may pray to the gods. Drinking *balché* is an act of prayer and is the duty of men."

"But great wise one, would you not agree that we must worship our own gods in our own way? In our land, it is forbidden of Pancho Balam to drink the wine of Jesus Christ but I am permitted to drink it in his place."

"Then so be it. Since you are not a woman of the true people, no harm can come of it. Let us drink."

The chief drained away his bowl and Erika followed suit. The drink tasted like a slightly alcoholic ginger beer. When she finished, Nakin refilled her bowl from a big clay vase.

Erika saw a twinkle in the chief's eyes or else she saw her own lightheartedness reflected in them.

"Why did you leave Lacanja years ago?" Claus asked. "Was it not your true home?"

Bolon Kin nodded gravely.

"It was because of the Kah who came to the jungle to cut the trees that I led my people from the caribals on the Lacantun River. The killers of trees came first and then came the planters of coffee when the fields were cleared away. In time, they took our cornfields. First, we climbed trees and sent poisoned arrows against them while they murdered the forest. It is against the way of the true people to wage war but we could not sit back and watch the destruction of the earth and the heavens. We hope the gods will forgive us.

"But there were too many of them. Things became worse. I saw that they were destroying the forest and the souls of our young people as well. The Kah traded whiskey in bottles to them for tobacco. Doña Erika, the *balché* you are drinking will rid you of all the poisons in your body and soul. You shall discover this when the morning comes."

Nakin filled the bowls again. Erika was experiencing a floating sensation and was enjoying herself so thoroughly that she was sorry that Claus could not share the pleasure with her.

"This is not so with the whiskey in the bottles of the Kah," Bolon Kin went on. "The whiskey takes away thoughts. With their thoughts gone, many Lacandons traded their land away to the tree cutters for more whiskey. I could see that our people would become like other Indians, the Tzeltales in the north and the Tzoltsil in the mountains who have become slaves of the foreigners. With the coffee planters came the *evangelistas*, the priests of Jesus Christ. So I decided to lead those Lacandons who wanted to worship the true gods of the jungle away from Lacanja."

Claus, who was listening intently, interrupted to ask, "How long ago did you leave?"

"It is more than a generation's time by the old counting. My children here were born along the way. It is more than a katun and five milpas."

"That's twenty-five years," Claus said excitedly to Erika. "A katun in the classic Mayan count is twenty years! This man still uses it!'"

Bolon Kin's face was a wrinkled moon in the firelight. He continued his story.

"It took us two moons of climbing mountains and marching through swamps to get to the Jatate River. We settled in a place to the north of here. But the *chicleros* came riding mules. Some of them took our women while we were away in our fields. They left fever and disease and many of our women and children died. So we moved deeper into the forest until we came to this place. Here we will stay. We cannot go back to Lacanja. From Lacanja comes news of many Lacandons hunting with guns and following the ways of Jesus Christ."

He sighed, took a deep quaff of *balché* and relit his cigar from the fire.

"I try to teach the young what I remember from my father of the old ways, but many do not listen. My youngest son, Kayum, has gone north to Capulin and traded with the Kah, leaving tobacco at the edge of the jungle at night. Now he hunts with a shotgun and the young follow him wherever he goes. They no longer listen to Bor who hunts with the bow. Bor is my oldest son and follows my teachings. He and Koh are my children by Nakin. But Kayum is my son from my oldest wife and it is to him that the old teaching says I must give the secret of the counting. But how can I do this when he has committed the gravest sin against the gods?"

"Is hunting with a shotgun a sin against the gods?" Erika and Claus asked almost in chorus.

"No, it is not a sin in itself. Neither the Kah nor their things can make us sin. Kayum's sin cannot be spoken of. Ech Tamacchi!" The old man threw down his bowl and the *balché* sizzled in the fire.

He looked at them now with suffering, almost pleading in his eyes. "What if the gods should tire of us and leave the jungle altogether? What then?" he asked. "What does Jesus Christ know about growing corn? What do you think Pancho Balam?"

"The gods will not leave the jungle," Claus said.

Nakin brought another bowl. Bolon Kin took more *balché* and his voice rose. "Pancho Balam, you know that the gods need people to worship them. You have told me of gods across the great waters who have no one to worship them. You spoke of big cat gods who sit in front of pyramids where there are no trees or flowers as far as the eye can see. Travelers come to see them but no one burns incense to them. Is it still so?"

"It is still so."

"And what of the gods whose stone idols are cut in human form and who live in the god houses in the cities?"

"Their houses are called museums. Many people come to see them and marvel at their beauty but no one burns incense."

The old man shook his head in a helpless gesture.

"And so it must be with the gods in Menche. But does anyone come to see them? I don't believe so."

"Tell us about Menche," Claus said, unable to keep a quavering out of his voice.

Bolon Kin spoke in a whisper now. "My old wife Chan Bol has told me in the night that it was wrong to bring my people here and that we should go back to Lacanja. She believes that the terrible things that have befallen our children would not have happened had I not taken us so far from the home of the gods. Our sons have never seen it and do not know in which part of the jungle the gods have hidden it. It is impossible to go back to Lacanja now. Even the people of Lacanja no longer go to Menche. There is no one living among them who has ever been there. They have given up their incense burners for the flashlights of Jesus Christ. I brought my people here to save them from the evil ways of the T'sul and the Kah. But in doing so, I took them even farther away from the true home of the gods."

The old man called for another bowl of *balché*. Erika read the excited look in Claus's eyes. Wherever Menche was, it was not here in the Jatate River Basin. It was in another part of the forest altogether.

"Where is Koh?" Bolon Kin asked Nakin when she poured fresh *balché* into the bowls.

"You know where she goes in the night."

"And you do not prevent it?"

"We can't treat her like the daughters of the Kah. Only the gods can judge her. You told me that yourself, my husband."

"Where is Kayum?"

"Do not think of it. You know it is only necessary that we worship the gods."

"But how can we? Of course, you are right, as usual."

Bolon Kin turned to his guests. "My wife is very wise. Although it is my job to speak to the gods, she prepares their food and reminds me to serve them properly. But I cannot truly serve them any longer. Which brings us to our business together. I know why it is that you have come. But I must warn you both that the gods demand sacrifice."

Erika knew her cheeks had turned red. She felt like a little girl whose father had found her playing with her private parts. The old chief had lived so long she feared he could see through her sin-sopped soul even in the dark. What did he mean by sacrifice? She thought of the cages.

"Tell us what sacrifice is required," Claus said quietly.

The chief drank deeply as did Erika. "I went to the God House for dream divination and read the signs that were given to me. In my dream, I walked in a cornfield under a blue sky. I saw a tapir blowing water from his snout in a wind that came from the north. Then I saw two macaws perched on a limb in the forest. Tell me Pancho Balam, why do you search for Menche Tinamit?"

Erika heard Claus gasp in the darkness. "You are very wise, Bolon Kin, far wiser than I," he said. "When I began, I had many reasons for finding Menche. I no longer know what they are. I only know that I must find it."

"You are looking for Menche because the gods will it," Bolon Kin said.

"How did you know our purpose?" Claus asked excitedly.

"Menche will be found by someone who comes from far away. That is what the tapir in my dream blowing water in the wind from the north means. And there was sky and corn in my dream. Your hair is the color of corn and your eyes the color of the sky. So, you see, my dream tells that you will find the holy city."

"Then Menche is lost to you, too," Claus said in surprise.

The old man stood up, taking a long time. "Pancho Balam, you helped me years ago when I lost the ability to hunt. You can help me now. I want you to burn incense for me at Menche. I will give you an incense burner to take with you."

They waited in silence for the chief to sit down again. He sat down like a tangle of lianas falling.

"I will burn the incense," Claus said. "Can you tell us where to look?"

The old man shrugged, raising his arms slowly. "Ech, that is the hard part." He went on to tell them that when he was a boy his father had taken him to Menche. There, they burned copal incense before the statue of Hachakyum, the creator of mankind. They took a stone from his temple to place in the god pot dedicated to Hachakyum in their God House in Lacanja. His father told him the sacred stone would bring the blessings of Hachakyum to their caribal. But on the way back his father had a dream. In the dream, he saw woodcutters cutting off the head of the creator. He said it was a sign that the jungle would be destroyed if the gods were not worshiped properly. Before he died, Bolon Kin's father asked his son to make another pilgrimage to Menche. But when Bolon Kin became the Tohil, the troubles came and he led his people from Lacanja. He did not lead his people in the direction of Menche because the lands that way were filled with lumbermen.

Some years later, after they had settled in Jatate and while Bolon Kin still had running in his legs, he went to make his pilgrimage. But he lost the way. Bolon Kin went beyond Lacanja and took the trails of his father, but the city was not in the place where his father had taken him. He wondered if the gods had destroyed it or had taken it up to heaven. Bolon Kin went back to Lacanja and asked the Lacandons there but few worshiped the gods any longer, either in caves or in the

God House, and no living person among them had ever made a pilgrimage to Menche. He came away in great sorrow. Chan Bol was right. It was because they had lost the way that so many of their women had died in coming to this place. Now evil lived in the souls of Bolon Kin's children.

But though he told his story with great sadness, Bolon Kin looked into the eyes of his guests when it was finished and Erika could see a new hope in the age-less eyes of the old man.

"With your help, we will find Menche," Claus said.

Bolon Kin called for more *balché*. Erika knew she was drunk and was waiting for the room to spin. No matter what Bolon Kin had said, she knew she would have a hangover in the morning. But a look of concern now came over the old man.

"I must tell you what the two macaws in my dream mean. They are the red candles that are placed on a grave. They tell of a funeral in Menche. It may be yours or your friends'. Or it may be the funeral of others who will come at the same time. But two will die. However, the gods have opened their buried treasure to you in the past, Pancho Balam. I can see by your continued youth and the beautiful señorita at your side that you are favored by them."

Bolon Kin emitted a deep sigh of satisfaction and offered Erika another bowl. She hoped it would be the last as she was on the verge of slipping into oblivion. She wanted to kiss Claus and Bolon Kin and she knew she was drunk. Bolon Kin had a sacred well in his stomach, she decided, as she watched him drain away another bowl. Chan Bol had fallen asleep by her fire. Koh had returned and was talking to her mother in whispers.

Then Erika was assisted by Claus who held her close to him as they made their way unsteadily to their hut. She stumbled many times and found herself giggling at Claus's attempts to keep her from falling to the ground.

When they got back to the guest hut, Erika collapsed upon her bamboo bed. Claus was pacing up and down in a frenzy of excitement.

"Did you notice the old man's head?" he asked.

"Looks very old. Yes, very old man. Nice man though."

"Yes, but the head, did you notice the peculiarities of the head?"

"I admit I had a lot to drink but I saw only one head at a time."

"I hadn't noticed it before, but his head is elongated like those of the Mayans in the frescoes. The Mayan nobility bound the heads of their children at birth."

"Why would they do a thing like that? Claus, must you pace? The room is spinning enough as it is."

"I'm sorry. I don't know why the Mayans bound their heads. My guess is that it was a badge of class. The young Lacandons don't have elongated heads."

"I like them with flat heads. Tell me, Claus, will you burn the old man's incense for him?" she yawned.

"Yes, but I'll be doing it to find out how fast it burns inside a temple and how precious it was to the ancient Mayans. Erika, are you asleep?"

"No. Are you undressed?"

"I undressed in the dark. And you?"

"Too tired—drunk, I'll just sleep the way I am."

"Erika, there are gnats in your clothing. You should get out of your clothes and into your sleeping bag."

"Balche will take care of the gnats."

"Nonsense. Here's my flashlight. I'll look the other way. They must have thought we were married to put us in this hut together. Maybe they think we're pagans with no morals."

"It's hard to drink *balché* and have morals. Claus, I dropped the flashlight and I don't know where it is."

Claus was standing over her. She could feel his warm breath and barely make out his naked silhouette in the dark.

"Here, I'll help you unbutton your shirt. Excuse my indecency."

Erika enjoyed having Claus's hands move over her body as he loosened her clothing. He removed her shirt easily, but he had trouble with the trousers. They agreed that the fallen flashlight would have to be put to use for a brief moment.

As he pulled her trousers down with one hand, the other holding the light, she felt the trouser tugging hand tremble against her skin. Suddenly he cried out, "Astonishing!"

"What's so astonishing about me, Claus?"

"I'm sorry. It's just that Maudslay and Maler were wrong."

"Maudslay and Maler. They never saw my body."

"No, I don't mean that. They were wrong about the Lacandons. They are not savage brutes. I'm convinced now that they are the physical and cultural descendants of the Mayans. And Bolon Kin is the last Mayan priest. To be sure, they've lost the art of writing and the knowledge of building with stone and mortar. Now into the sleeping bag with you. But think of it, Erika. The Mayan calendar is spinning in Bolon Kin's head. Just think of what else may be in there!"

Erika couldn't follow what Claus was saying. His voice faded in and out and she found herself unable to pay attention. She was only mindful of his hand grazing her waist.

"Now get all the way into the sleeping bag and zip it up." The hand was guiding her into the bag. It was warm and confident and she didn't want him to take it away. She could barely make out his naked form behind the light. But she knew he could see most of her erogenous features as the light played on the reddish moss of her triangle and highlighted her taut, moist nipples.

"Claus, don't you think we left some business unfinished in those palisades?"

"Erika, please, into the bag. You're drunk."

"That's not an answer to my question."

He was kneeling beside her, his arms around her shoulders as he slid her down into the cotton sheath. Claus had set the flashlight on end on the floor, and it cast a light strong enough to reveal the outline of his male organ. Erika could see that it was erect.

"Erika, you've really had too much to drink. We were facing death then. It's all changed now and the old reasons still apply. We can't let what happened that night happen again. You'll regret it in the morning."

Her feet touched the bottom of the bag and Claus took his hands away. But the folds of the bag were open and she knew that her nude body, faintly visible to him, held his attention.

"Claus, isn't there a statue of limitations on those old reasons? I can't find the zipper anyway. Drunk, as you say. You'll have to find it for me. Do you think you can do that, Claus?"

Claus groaned deeply. He stood over her, anguish on his face. Then, in a sudden movement, he forcibly zipped up the bag. "I won't take advantage of a drunken woman," he said, returning to his bed with the flashlight in his hand. "Remember, we have a mission and we can't afford to get sidetracked. Goodnight!"

"Goodnight, and thank you, Claus. You are the perfect hero for my story. But why do you have to be so damn noble."

Chapter Twenty-Two

Erika woke up alone on the bamboo bed. Bolon Kin had been right about the *balché*. She was surprised that she was clearheaded. In a flash, she remembered what had happened with Claus. She looked around quickly to see him sleeping in a heap in a hammock strung between two poles of the hut. As she saw him, Erika suffered deep pangs of shame. She had been drunk, of course, but that was no excuse for provoking him as she had. And he was right. They were on a mission and under no circumstances could they afford the complications that having sex would inevitably bring. Hadn't she promised, from the beginning, to make no more demands than the mules? Yes, Claus was noble and, yes, she had fallen in love with him. It was an impossible love, of course, yet she enjoyed the warm glow that swept over her when she wrapped herself in a rubber sheet and set out for her bath.

Erika felt born anew as she bathed in the sulfurous stream with Chan Bol, Nakin and Koh. Even the aging Chan Bol, whose skin was wrinkled only in discrete places, was lovely to behold. Erika felt she had earned the right to bathe with such beauties. Her body had found its own beauty during the long weeks on the trail.

When she returned to the hut, Claus was up and dressed. He smiled at her, made no mention of the events of the night before, and gallantly asked, "Are you ready for breakfast?"

"I'm starving," Erika said, a thrill in her voice.

After a meal of tortillas, mangos and turkey eggs, families from all the surrounding caribals assembled in front of Bolon Kin's hut. There were five caribals in all. Some families, such as those of Sakrum, came from several hours away. Each caribal consisted of thirty or so adults and children. Close to a hundred and fifty people gathered to meet the guests brought by the north wind. They traded gifts. The visitors offered salt, sugar, machetes, metal cooking pots, and blankets. The Lacandons gave yucca roots, sweet potatoes, pineapples, bananas, tobacco, and clay dolls.

Bolon Kin's wives, Chan Bol and Nakin, were pleased with the enamel pots, as was Koh. Young Kayum sulked throughout the proceedings, turning over swirls of dust with a stick and muttering to himself like a man gone mad.

Erika was surprised that Bor's wife, Juana, lacked the courtliness of her husband. She flirted unabashedly with Claus and fingered Erika as if she were corn dough for making tortillas. Liking Erika's colorful blouse, Juana demanded that she have it. "Give shirt. Give belt. Can your breasts still fill with milk? Do you wear anything under your pants?" Erika strained to control her annoyance. She gave her one of her blouses but that was as far as she was willing to go. The memory of her sacrificial nudity was all too fresh.

Claus was busy taking notes. So preoccupied was he with his work, that he seemed to ignore her altogether. And he disappeared soon after the trading families left. Ostensibly, he had gone to explore the surroundings. Erika wondered if he was avoiding her. She told herself she would stop trying to guess his thoughts. What had happened between them didn't change anything as far as the expedition went. Claus was out doing his job and she would do hers.

Most of the men of Jatate had gone to the milpa. Rogelio and Lazaro lay about the settlement in hammocks eating fruit that was constantly being brought to them by the Lacandon children.

Erika visited the women of Bolon Kin in their open sided kitchen hut. While they spent the long afternoon grinding the dry corn on their stone *metates* and rolling the soft dough from the soaking pots with pestles, she learned their songs and taught them some of her favorites. Perhaps the world's most unusual rendition of "Deutschland Uber Alles" was performed by a dozen or so female Lacandon choristers and one Swiss band leader on that steaming afternoon for an audience of sleeping turkeys, dogs and small children.

Inside the big, ventilated hut, Erika painted the women's lips with lipstick and they painted her garments with juice from red and purple berries. Erika gave Nakin eyeshadow. They all put macaw feathers in their hair and blue *rebosos* over their shoulders. With her western cosmetics, Nakin looked like a Paris boulevardier's dream. The Lacandon women did not object to having their pictures taken and loved to pose.

Chapter Twenty-Three

The next morning, Nakin waited outside the guest hut with a present for Erika—a Lacandon tunic with a necklace and a toucan feather. Nakin presented the gift and ran away giggling. Erika was thrilled and put it on at once.

"It's the supreme gift," Claus said when he saw it. "It's amazing how the Lacandons have taken to you, Erika."

"I've become inordinately fond of them all," Erika said, fixing the feather in her hair.

"Then I hope what I have in mind will meet with your approval."

"You're going to abandon me here." She said it lightly, but a feeling of alarm stirred in her.

"For a short while, only if you consent."

"If you really want to go on without me, I'll be all right here," she said, feeling the burn of rejection.

"Let me explain. A small group of Lacandon men are going on a hunting trip that could take three to four days. I think it would be a good idea if Lazaro, Rogelio and I went with them. We owe these people something. Game is becoming scarce throughout the rain forest even here. There is an alpenglow of deer that have sought this place as a refuge, just as the Lacandons have. But they are hard to hunt in the jungle. I sympathize with Bolon Kin's warnings about western ways. But, I'm afraid the bow and arrow is becoming obsolete in the competition for game that is certainly in store for these people in the future."

"But won't Bolon Kin be angry if you use guns? Besides, we have no ammunition." Erika imagined the reproachful gaze of the old man.

"Kayum has given me all his shells. He was to be the leader of the hunt. But now he has refused to go. I am told that he does nothing but sulk although no one seems to want to tell us why. Some disagreement with the old man is my guess. Anyway, Bolon Kin can't disapprove of our using our own guns and we can enrich our hosts' food supply while providing for ourselves."

Erika was beginning to feel better about the whole thing.

"Do you think you'll find any clues as to the whereabouts of Menche?" she asked.

"I doubt it, but we may find some mounds or other things. I think we have a lot more traveling ahead of us." She felt her heart lifting with the thought. "From what I got out of Bolon Kin, Menche is north of here, possibly in the unexplored region east of El Cedro. But we need more clues."

"Claus, the end may be weeks away."

"Are you still for it?"

"Of course I am."

"But the hunting trip. How do you feel about it?"

"Claus, you're leaving me stranded in paradise."

Chapter Twenty-Four

Watching Claus vanish into the bush with Rogelio, Lazaro and the four young Lacandons, Erika felt a deep sadness. It wasn't that she was losing him. She would miss him, of course. But she felt sorry for Claus. She wasn't sure why. Perhaps she'd come to feel the loneliness of his quest. Fame. How important was it to Claus? The last infirmity of the noble mind, Milton called it. Claus had told Bolon Kin that he didn't know why he searched for Menche, that he knew only that he had to find it. And he'd said the same to her. What was it then? She listened to the chattering of birds in the canopy above her head. Erika tried to catch the thoughts that tumbled through her mind like ripe fruit. Yes, the answer had to do with the jungle after all, the rich teeming surge of life that was taking possession of her consciousness more and more each day. She had been looking for causes in his background to explain Claus. But all that was occidental logic, as alien to the jungle and its inhabitants as paved streets and machines. No, the cause was ahead of them, pulling them toward some appointment. Perhaps the appointment was in Menche. But the cause was the jungle.

Erika felt dazed with her thoughts. She listened to the moan of the great ceibas. The jungle had invaded her soul just as it had taken complete possession of Claus. Yes, it overwhelmed her, affected every breath, every emotion, every thought. The ferns and creepers grew riotously inside the vacuum of her spirit. And just as the emptiness was being filled, she recognized for the first time that there had been a gaping hole in her soul ever since she'd abandoned Berlin.

She thought of the times when she had been happy in her life. Her childhood in Switzerland was happy. Her father had taught her to love the world. She was happy in Berlin when she got her first reporter's job and Hans courted her under the linden trees. It was because of her love for the bright, good life of Berlin that she'd gone into hiding with Hans to prepare the fight against the pestilence that had infected the city and disfigured its face. She went to the underground rathskellers to compound a remedy, and, like her father, tried to become a doctor only to find that the patient didn't want to be cured. Now the world that her father had taught her to love lay dying. And her love for it was long dead.

Instead, she felt the jungle growing in the thin, impoverished soil of her spirit. And no matter how far away from her he ran, Claus was a part of the new scramble of life that coursed through her veins. Because of him, long dormant feelings of pain and beauty opened like flowers. He had brought her here. Erika was convinced she would survive and flourish as well as the orchids that grew on fallen branches. Now she was looking forward to spending some days with the Lacandons whom she was learning to love.

Returning to the caribal, she saw Bor sitting outside his hut. Little Akan was with him. Erika went over to them. Bor was beating a strip of bark over a stone with a pestle. Erika could see the bark softening to form the material from which the Lacandon tunics were made. Little Akan, the daughter of Bor's wife by her first husband, watched her stepfather as intently as did Erika.

"Who taught you the things you need to know to live in the forest?" Erika asked Bor.

"My father."

"Did your father teach you everything?"

"My father taught me all the things that are of the greatest importance to my life and serving my people."

"What are these things?" She smiled at him.

"My father has taught me the names of all the gods he knows. The names of the animal spirits were told to me walking back from the milpa with him when I was a child. He told me there is an animal spirit in heaven for each person on earth. But there is one thing my father has not taught me. My father is the only one among my people who knows the way of counting of the ancestors. Because of this, only my father knows when it is time to plant the corn. It was taught to him by his father. But even now that he is old, he has not taught me the counting. Nor has he given the teaching to my younger brother, Kayum."

"Your father is an old man. What will happen when he dies?"

"We do not know. The people of Jatate cannot exist without the knowledge of the corn. I am Bolon Kin's oldest son and the one who follows his teachings, even if I make a mistake once in awhile." He looked at her sheepishly. "But my brother Kayum is his son by Chan Bol, who is his oldest living wife. The old teaching says that my father must pass the wisdom on to him. My father does not know what to do because Kayum does not follow all the ways of the gods. And he has committed a sin I am forbidden to speak of." Bor fell silent and beat the bark with increased vigor.

It was all complicated but Erika was catching on to the language and the culture.

"Can you speak of it to no one?" she asked finally.

"My father forbids that I speak of it with him. I cannot speak with my brother as it is not my place to do so. I can only speak to the gods. Yet it should be spoken of because to speak of an evil thing can prevent the worst from happening. This too is a teaching of Bolon Kin."

Bor went back to pounding the bark. Erika and Little Akan watched him in silence. The incessant thud resounded in the forest and was answered somewhere by a lonely woodpecker.

Sweat poured from Bor's face. Then he put his pestle aside and turned to Erika. "I will speak to you, Doña Erika. You are a friend and it must be spoken of with someone. My brother is the only one of the true people who has tread his sister."

Bor gazed at the stream and paused before continuing his story.

"It is not good to tread one's sister as it makes the gods angry. When he dies, Kisin will burn Kayum as long as it takes to punish him for his sins. Then Kisin will turn him into a mule so that he can serve the lord of death forever. My brother tread his sister because she is beautiful and he cannot find a wife. Many girl children died on the way here from Lacanja.

"I cannot judge my brother or prevent him from doing what he does. Only the gods will punish him. I pray to Akinchob to help my brother. The young Lacandons like Kayum. He has traded with the Kah in the north for flashlights, and now he has traded for shotguns. All the young men of Jatate use the Kah's machetes because of Kayum. But the Kah have also brought fever and more of our women have died. Bolon Kin says this is because the gods are angry at us for not following the old teachings."

Juana Nabor came shuffling across the clearing toward them. She was the most aggressive of the Lacandons and Erika found it hard to warm up to her. Bor's wife spoke with a continual sense of urgency. She always seemed to be the bearer of bad tidings. This occasion was no exception.

"What I warned you about has come to pass. It is as in my dream."

"Juana, I told you to speak of your dream to Bolon Kin. Only he can tell us how to avoid bad things that are foretold in dreams."

"Your father will not discuss dreams about his daughter. But why do you speak harshly to me? I haven't disobeyed the gods. Your sister has, and now she is being punished."

"Juana, please do not speak badly of my sister. Just tell me what happened."

"The fever has got her. The god Kak has brought sickness and she lies in her father's house burning and raving. Kisin will take her soon."

Bor looked glumly at the long bark in front of him.

"It is a terrible thing."

"Maybe it is a good thing that she dies. Then the gods will come back to us again."

"They never left us, Juana!"

"I left my father's home in Sakrum to live here. Before we came to Jatate, husbands lived in the homes of their wives. It is still that way in Sakrum. But I came to your caribal because your father was a great Tohil, or so they said. But how great is he that so many Lacandon women have died and you cannot get another wife to help me in my work. I should have insisted that we stay in the house of my father after you finished your bride service to him in Sakrum. This is the way it was done in the old days. It is only because my husband Baats died that I married you and brought my only daughter here."

"Juana, enough!"

"And she follows wherever you go. I know how you look at her, even though she is too young to do wifely things. Ech, only evil comes out of the house of Bolon Kin. He led us away from the gods and has angered them. Our maidens go to early graves and evil itself licks the womb of the princess. And don't think I don't know what goes on in the God House, even though it is not my place to go inside. Bolon Kin tells us the gods are there even as they are in Menche. Well, I know something about our religion too. Only those pots that have stones from their homes have gods in them. And what if the pot of our creator, Hachakyum, is empty?"

"Juana, you don't know what you're talking about!"

The woman was working herself up to a rage. Erika fully expected her to beat on her husband's head at any moment.

"All right then, my husband. We'll change the subject. Why hasn't your father taught you the way of the counting? He's an old man and can die in the night. How will we plant the corn without the knowledge that he is holding back? Is he afraid to give up his power? He sees his soul draining away. He is old and afraid to die."

"Juana, my father is a great Tohil. Only he preserves the old teaching."

"The old teaching! I'm tired of his old teaching. My mother in Lacanja told me years ago that the gods have left us. In Lacanja, my sister was given fine things by the *evangelistas* of Jesus Christ. Her husband had to tell his other wife to leave the house in order to please the *evangelistas*. She was much older than my sister but the *evangelistas* said Jesus would be angry if he had more than one wife. So they gave him a cooking machine to make the work of my sister easier."

Bor turned to Erika. "You have met the wife who was sent away. She is Chan Bol, Bolon Kin's oldest wife. He found her wandering the jungle, afraid and dying of hunger. He brought her to his home and made her his senior wife."

"It sounds to me as if Bolon Kin is more a follower of Jesus Christ than are those *evangelistas*," Erika said.

Juana looked at Erika hotly but Bor smiled, nodding his head as if he understood.

Juana would not let up. She glared at Erika.

"Has Bor told you that a band of alligator hunters passed through here this past moon and killed our pigs? He hasn't told you because none of the brave young Lacandons stopped them. Bolon Kin said it was better to let them go their way than to make war. Are the alligator hunters friends of yours, Doña Erika? Yes, there are those who say you are a sorceress. You have cast a spell over the family of Bolon Kin. When will someone pray to Kak to bring courage back to the men of Jatate?" *Alligator hunters!* Erika thought to herself. *Were they the field team hired by Barnes?* What were they doing here? Were she and Claus going to be dogged by Barnes throughout their quest? Would they meet in this jungle? She shuddered to think of it.

Juana spun on her heels, her long hair and tunic twirling, and disappeared down the path that led to the stream.

Chapter Twenty-Five

Erika received permission from Koh's father to take her to the guest hut. Bolon Kin allowed Erika to give his daughter quinine and wrap her in blankets. But he insisted that it was the god Kak who brought the fever, and only Kak could take it away.

While Koh was delirious, Kayum came to the hut and told Erika he would go to the God House to burn incense to Akinchob for his sister and await dream divination.

"My father will not burn incense for us because he knows the gods are angry at us for what we have done," he said.

Erika thought of how handsome the boy looked in his sadness and with what reverence he approached the God House. It stood only fifty yards away from Erika's hut. The God House was the largest edifice in the settlement.

Koh moaned and thrashed her way through the feverish night. Erika, placing her bamboo bed close by, got up from time to time to pull the falling blankets over the sick girl, and to give her water when she woke.

Erika was up with the first thin light of morning. She stepped outside the hut to be greeted by a sea of thick white fog. Then she saw the silhouette of a bent figure shambling toward her. It was Kayum. His long hair was twisted and matted. His face was lined with sleeplessness and he looked sadder than he had the night before.

"Did you sleep?" Erika asked him.

"I slept long enough for dreams to come. But in my dreams I saw a macaw perched on a limb." He shook his head. "Ne Tamacchi! Ne Tamacchi!" His hair swirled from side to side with his shaking. "It is a bad omen. I will mourn my sister. A macaw in a dream means the red candle that is placed beside the head of one who is dead."

"Do you believe that what you see in a dream will come to pass no matter what anyone does?"

"No." He looked up at her. "A dream is a warning. Only the dream prophecies of my father come true. Sometimes, if you tell someone of a bad dream, it won't come true. A bad prophecy takes shame, but my shame is greater than any other, and no one, not even my father, will speak of it."

Erika placed her hand on the young man's shoulder. She tried to assure him that the fever had passed and that the girl slept soundly.

Kayum smiled weakly. "My father says your medicine is good only if the gods permit it to work. I thank you for staying close to my sister in her soul wandering."

He smiled wearily and gazed off sadly into the mist. "I have heard my father say that when I die I will stay with Kisin who lives under the earth and serve him forever. It is a dark unhappy place that all souls must pass through to be punished for their sins before they can take the trail to the sky. But I will never take that trail. I will never see the city on the moon where the souls of my ancestors live.

"Maybe the gods have punished you enough, and will forgive you," Erika said.

"How can I truly want forgiveness?" the young man beat his breast. "I know that when the feeling comes back strong in my blood, I will once again tread my sister in the fields or in the woods. And now the sin is hers. For if I avoid her, she comes to my hut in the night."

Erika listened as Kayum told of his obsession for his sister. Koh and Kayum were alone together for many days in their father's milpa. Bolon Kin sent them to clear the field of weeds while others hunted. Kayum cut the weeds with the iron machete that he had traded for in the north and Koh gathered the weeds into piles. Kayum was reaching his manhood and was green as new corn with his need. With each passing day, he became more aware of the beauty of his sister. Kayum fell under the spell of her movements in the cornfield, the smell of her person as she came close by. He was under the spell of the light in her eyes and the drop of dew that always seemed to form on her bottom lip. Her skin was as ripe as chayetes in the time of harvest. Kayum prayed to T'upp, the god of the sun, to help him, but every time the god set his light to fall against her tunic, Kayum could see the wonderful shape of her body underneath. He felt the weakness in his limbs and the rising of his staff under his own tunic. Each time she turned to him to tease him for daydreaming in the field and not working, her laughter made him dream all the more. So taken was Kayum by her movements coming toward him and going away that he felt drunk the way he did when he first drank the *balché* that his father and Bor had made in the *cayuco* at his *meek chahal*, his initiation.

Finally, a day came in the milpa when Koh swatted Kayum playfully as she ran past. The god Kak sent a roaring fire that swept from Kayum's chest to his lower parts. Even as T'upp watched, his eye hard on them in the field, Kayum caught his sister around the waist. They tumbled together against the bundle of weeds he had cut and she had gathered into a pile. But when Kayum fell upon her, she did not laugh anymore. She looked up at him gravely, helpless as he was in their love.

Kayum finished his story and spat upon the ground. He was a mournful figure in the half-morning light and moving banks of fog.

Erika had been boiling water over a fire. She gave him a bowl of instant coffee which he drank in big gulps. Erika smiled kindly at him. But he was still in a state of distress.

Erika placed her hand on the young man's shoulder. "Look, your sister rises from her bed. Perhaps the gods have taken away their anger."

Koh had come to the door of the hut. Her face was pale and wan. But her eyes were tragically beautiful as she gazed upon her brother. Seeing her, Kayum rose and strode off swiftly in the direction of the God House.

Chapter Twenty-Six

Six days had passed, and there was no sign of Claus or the hunting party. Erika had begun to worry after the fourth day. The Lacandons were not alarmed, but she knew they did not share her sense of time and that an ingrained fatalism hung over all their expectations. Claus had said he'd be gone four days and it was the morning of the sixth. Erika could not keep herself from brooding.

She walked along the sulfur stream to shake off her mood. Then she came back to the caribal to sit with Bor outside his hut.

She had become fond of her death-sentencer. It was hard to believe that he had once wanted to pull her heart out of her chest. But he had held nothing personal against her even then, though she was a creature of Jesus, the destroyer god. Indeed, as a sacrificial candidate, Erika was sacred to Bor, god-like herself in that she had been chosen to become one with the sun.

But Bor had read the signs wrong and it had hurt his standing with his people. His error might yet cost him his jungle chieftainship and deliver his people to a terrible fate. Worst of all, the day when Bolon Kin would teach one of his sons the counting was postponed again. Perhaps Kayum would become the heir after all. That didn't matter. Bor loved Kayum. But someone had to be taught the counting before the old man died or all the people in Jatate would perish. Yet Bor took new hope. He had made two successful dream prophecies. Last night he dreamt of Maäx killing an opossum. When Bor woke up, he told his father that Maäx would suffer from diarrhea. And sure enough, right after breakfast, Maäx complained bitterly of the condition. Bolon Kin was impressed when he saw Maäx running back and forth to the *lavia*. The chief told his son that he was finally becoming expert in dream divination. Bor laughed about it now with Erika.

But as amusing as Bor was, Erika found it hard to rid herself of her anxiety about Claus. She gazed at the God House that stood thirty yards away. Because of the gods of the Lacandons, no missionary had won their pagan souls, no Spaniard or his heir had ever subdued them. She found her heart beating fast. What a marvel if she could penetrate the inner sanctum. What things she could then tell Claus.

Bor was whittling a wooden doll with a flint knife for little Akan who sat watching at his side. A dog lazed in the sun. Next to them sat a big clay pot in which corn soaked. The soft scraping of the flint on the wood and the distant crow of a cock were the only sounds heard on that clear, sunlit morning.

"Who are the gods?" she asked Bor.

"They are in the God House."

"Can I see the gods?"

"Only the men of the Hach Winik are allowed inside. It is not permitted for a woman to enter."

"What can women do for the gods?"

"Women make tortillas and *posole* for the gods. Without these, it is impossible for men to worship the gods. And men do not know how to make tortillas or *posole*. Can you make tortillas?"

"No."

"You would be useless here. Your husband would not be able to eat or worship the gods," he laughed.

"Who are the Hach Winik?"

"They are the true people, the Lacandons. We are the people created by Hachakyum. The T'sul and the Kah and their things were made by his brother Akyantho. The Kah are the ladinos, the *chicleros* and your friends who ride the mules. Kah means people who live mashed together. The T'sul are people from far away. T'sul means one who can read and write on paper. That is why you are of the T'sul."

"Is it a bad thing to read and write on paper?"

"It would be a bad thing for the Hach Winik to do, but you have your own god to answer to. Akyantho made Jesus Christ as he made you."

"When are you going to eat the corn you grow in the milpa?" Erika asked.

"We eat only after the gods have eaten."

"How do gods eat?"

Bor put down his flint tool. Akan inspected the unfinished doll. Bor shrugged and smiled at Erika.

"It is hard to say no to you, Doña Erika. Even my father has given you the sacred *balché*."

"Come. I will show you the gods."

And so they entered the thatched chapel. Clay whistles and conch shells hung from the rafters. Erika beheld a long wooden plank shelf on which stood a row of clay pots painted with white zinc, some with designs drawn with charcoal or red berries. From the side of each pot, a ghastly head jutted out. Each pot contained ashes and a blackened stone. Erika felt that she was being confronted with a row of stern jurors from the nether world.

Bor spoke softly. "Hachakyum made the jungle and the gods who dwell in it, as well as the true people. He rules over the other gods. Hachakyum's real home is in Menche. But the gods are everywhere. They will rest in any place where there is the smallest piece taken from their true home. In the beginning Hachakyum's house was in Palenque. The sky above Palenque is the heart of heaven. It was there that Hachakyum made our gods out of spring flowers and later made men out of mud. The most beautiful god was Akinchob, the corn god. One day Hachakyum asked Akinchob to build a new home for the gods."

"Why did he do that?"

"Because he wanted to get away from the gods of the T'sul. The gods of the true people caught disease from the gods of the T'sul by taking salt from them. Because the true gods had no medicine, they died. They did not truly die. They faked their deaths so they would not have to come in contact with the gods of the T'sul again. The souls of the true gods reappeared on earth and hid in rocks. They left their earthly bones in caves. Then, after time passed, I don't know how much, as I don't know how to count time, Hachakyum asked Akinchob to build a new house for the gods at Menche. It was a place unknown to the T'sul. Since that time, Hachakyum has dwelt in a great stone statue in front of his temple in Menche. But Bolon Kin believes that one day the Kah who cut the trees came and cut off the god's head." Bor shrugged, his face sad, and pulled something out of the mouth of one of the god pots. "Here is the jade stone from the lake of Aky- antho. He created you and all the people who are not Lacandon. He also created all your things; guns and bottle whiskey and the iron birds we have seen flying over the jungle. We need to burn incense to him too.

"Here is a stone from the lake of Akinchob who protects the world."

"This is Kisin who lives under the earth. Whenever the earth trembles or fire comes out of the mountains, we know Kisin is taking the earth as his wife."

"Here is Sukunkyum, the dead sun, who resides in the underworld with Kisin and judges the souls of men. It was to help him lift the living sun that you were taken to the altar for sacrifice."

Erika stared at the sight of the stern, wrathful face whose countenance betrayed no trace of mercy. Bor went on. "Okna is the moon and the wife of the sun god T'upp. We have seen Okna rise in the day and cover the face of T'upp. Then we know she is angry. Only Bolon Kin can foretell when this will happen."

"These two gods look especially angry," Erika said. Two ghastly human images jutted out of the pots like leaping jaguars. She was dying to take pictures but she knew that to take pictures of the gods in the god house would be considered very sacrilegious and she didn't want to take advantage of her privilege.

"Yes, they are the forest gods who punish. This is Kak who brings fever. You know of him. Hachakyum never brings fever but he sends Kak to punish men."

"And who is the other sour looking fellow?"

"He is Metzabok, the god of rain and thunder. He can shake the sky and make the lakes and rivers run wild and spill over. He throws spears of fire into the jungle. But without his rain, there would be no forest. He lives in many places but his real home is in the cave at the end of his sacred lake. He took a T'sul woman for a wife from their village of Dolores that is now named after her. He is the only god who ever consorted with a T'sul. When you came, I thought that after the dead sun took your blood, we would give you to Metzabok as a new wife. I was going to take your head to his cave on his sacred lake, as was done by the Lacandons of long ago."

"Thanks for fixing me up, old friend." Erika gave Bor an amused smile she knew he wouldn't understand.

Erika was about to inspect a huge pot that stood on a high shelf when Bor clasped her arm.

"Doña Erika, come away. We must not make the gods more angry than they are!"

"But this large pot. Who lives here? I don't see a stone in it. Yet it is the largest vase of all."

The face that projected from the vase was large and loving, its features softened by gentle curves as in the Olmec heads she had seen in the museum in Mexico City.

"Doña Erika, we will both be punished. Maäx warned me not to talk too much to you."

Erika had sensed that Maäx suspected her of being a witch and was spreading suspicion among the others. Bor had taken her into his confidence but now she could see the terror in his eyes. Still, her curiosity about the pot was too great to ignore.

"Bor, you haven't told me. Who lives in this god jar?"

Bor's lips trembled. "Doña Erika, it is time for us to leave."

"The face is so big and it is the only face that looks peaceful."

"Do not look into the face!" Bor gripped Erika's arm to turn her away but she continued to stare at the image.

"Is it the god of the sun?"

"There is no god in the jar." Bor was shaking and covered his eyes with his hands.

"Who is the god who is not in the jar?" Erika insisted.

The young prince looked at her in anger and embarrassment. "Bolon Kin told me not to tell you. He is ashamed. We have no stone from the home of Hachakyum, our true lord, the god of creation. Bolon Kin lost it on the way from Lacanja. Doña Erika, why do you make me talk so much?"

"Maybe I can help you."

"No one can help us. Without creation there is only death. Our wives are barren and so many children have died. Hachakyum has abandoned us because we do not have a stone from his home in Menche to put inside his vase."

"But you have stones for most of the other gods. Did the stones come from Menche?"

"Many of the gods who have homes in Menche also live in lakes and caves in this part of the forest. They've lived here since olden days. We have stones from these places. But we do not have a stone from the home of our true lord. My brother was born on the trail the day after the stone was lost and my father said that his newborn son would grow up to bring another stone from Menche. But my father speaks of it no longer."

Erika looked at the rows of heads that sprang out at her from the sides of the pots. They were the objectifications of spirits wronged and fatally wounded, their divine powers distilled into a divine wrath. Her gods had driven them into the far reaches of the wilderness where they licked their wounds and blew sparks of rage throughout the jungle, as they waited, in cold fury, to destroy those who came to hunt them out of their final shrines. The eyes looked at Erika with suffering and hate. Only the visage of Hachakyum looked serene and gazed beyond her into eternity where all things are reconciled. Yet, he had been the most violated of all.

"Come, let us leave," Bor said.

Erika needed no urging this time. Yet, when she sat outside her guest hut writing in her notebook, she was filled with excitement about her privileged glimpse of the religion of the Lacandon Maya.

Chapter Twenty-Seven

The next day, Claus returned with the hunting party. They carried deer and tapir on long poles that rested on their shoulders.

Claus looked wonderful. Erika had forgotten how bright his eyes were. They were as bright as Christmas morning, and she felt as gay as a little girl bounding out of bed on that day. She ran carelessly to him and threw her arms around him. She found herself crying, burying her head against his chest.

"There, there," he patted her back. "What's happened? Are you all right?"

"I'm just so happy to see you. Is that against the rules?"

He was smiling broadly. He held her tear-strewn face in his hands and kissed her on both cheeks. Then he adroitly slipped out of her embrace and went straight to a discussion of the hunting trip. Her heart dropped a little, but Erika refused to feel rejected. The important thing was that he was safe and well.

All the caribals shared in the feast after the hunters returned. It was also a send-off for the explorers. Claus explained that the hunting had been poor for the first few days and then they had tarried near some mounds Claus wanted to study for clues to ancient habitation in the area.

Claus chomped happily on a big piece of roasted venison. "We will find Menche, old Tohil!" he called to Bolon Kin. "All your children will live to be as old and wise as you."

Bolon Kin smiled thinly. "I may be gone long before you find it."

Kayum, who had been brooding silently, suddenly addressed his father. Murmurs spread throughout the gathering. It had been known throughout the Jatate region that the young son had not spoken to his father or been spoken to by him since Kayum's affair with his sister had become known.

"Father, I went to the God House for dream divination and dreams were given me for your interpretation."

The old man turned away. Everyone at the feast had stopped talking. Then Bolon Kin spoke, still looking away. "My son speaks of dream divination. When a man is in a state of sin, devils take his thoughts and he is lost in the confused images of his dreams."

"But Father, that is why I submit my dream to you. I want your interpretation."

"Do you speak of evil things?"

"Tell me if I do. In my dream, a north wind came. I walked into it. I came upon a jaguar drinking from a stream. Then I came upon a deer that was running toward the sunrise. I did not hunt the deer but followed it until it stopped at a river bank where the sun shone on many flowers."

Erika saw the face of the old man suddenly break out in a smile of child-like wonder.

"My son. So you wish to go with the T'sul who have come to us like the wind from the north. You would follow Pancho Balam, the jaguar, to the east where Kak, whose emblem is a deer, appears as the morning star that pulls the sun up from the underworld. There you will find the home of Hachakyum who made gods out of flowers and men out of mud."

Kayum could not suppress a smile on his side. Erika saw tears of joy forming in his eyes.

"Yes, Father. Thanks to your teaching, it is also my interpretation of the dream. I will help our friends find Menche. Then I will bring a sacred stone back to Jatate. When I was a little boy, you told me it was my destiny. Have you forgotten Father?"

"I have not forgotten."

"I will bring the stone back here. Then I will go to live with the Lacandons in the north. Let Bor be the Tohil here when you leave. Teach him the counting."

"Do you hear what my son says, Pancho Balam?" Bolon Kin said, giving up the effort to keep the lines of his face from twisting into a joyous grin. "Do you think the gods will allow a sinner to enter their home?"

"I think they will, old chief, for your son gives you a great opportunity. He has solved the riddle of who should receive your power."

"Father, it is the best solution for all of us," Kayum said, manifestly happy to be speaking to his father again. "You know I can't continue to live here in Jatate. I am the son that the old teaching says should receive your priestly office when you die. But even though the young men like to hunt with me, the people of Jatate will never accept me as their priest. If I go, you can give the secrets of the priesthood to Bor and feel you have done right by the gods."

Bor came forward, his face troubled. "My brother, I always loved you. I am the one who should leave."

Kayum was proud and confident now. "No, Bor. It is better for you to stay. Help our father and keep the old ways. I have been too much spoiled by the traders in the north. And I have the guns and machetes Pancho Balam will need to travel through lands where there will be *chicleros* and *bandidos*. Pancho, with all our wisdoms together, Menche will be found."

The ragged chicken skin of the old man's face stretched into a beatific smile. He reached out a palsied hand, and placed it gently on Kayum's shoulder. "My son, only Hachakyum can deliver you from Kisin. May he also deliver us. Go with my blessing."

PART IV
EL CAPULIN

Chapter Twenty-Eight

An unseen goddess stitched together the canopy of trees above them with a golden thread of the sun. The explorers followed the thread, patiently, resolutely in their continued search through the labyrinth of the forest. Erika could feel the leaf mold dry under her feet. On their second day out of Jatate, they still traveled territory known only to the Lacandons.

A light rain began to fall as they made camp. Kayum told them that by the end of the next day, they would come upon the lake of the ancients where Pancho Balam would be pleased to find ruins in the water. The lake lay in a valley where the trail to the Lacandons of the north began.

"There's a lake in Bishop Landa's history where the Mayans lived on islands. No one in modern times has found it. I think that's where our prince is taking us," Claus said excitedly.

Sitting in her evening bath, Erika watched the air above the stream fill up with night fog. As she emerged from the stream, exhilarated from her contact with the cool, fast moving water, she became aware of a white figure standing on the shore and shrouded in mist. A blue shawl was draped over the head. Erika's first reaction was one of fright and she waded hurriedly to the overhanging branch from which her rubber poncho hung. But on second look she decided that the apparition was unthreatening in its quiet and poise. The mist that curled around the snow white beauty in the blue shawl thinned out and Erika recognized the traditional tunic of the women of Jatate.

"Koh!"

"Doña Erika!"

"What are you doing here? How did you find us?"

"I followed the trails where branches were freshly broken and ran all the way."

"But when?"

"I left home when the sun set on the day of your departure. I knew then that I had to come."

"But why?"

"Why does Kayum come? He comes because he has no home in Jatate any longer. And what am I to do there? Please let me go with you to look for the city of the gods."

"Well, I'd love to have you and so would—but what will become of you?"

"What will become of me in Jatate? When my father dies, no household will take me in. Everyone says I am possessed by devils."

It was hard for Erika to believe that such beauty would be denied anywhere on the face of the earth. Yet she understood the young woman's predicament. But to come away with them, to join her brother now? Certainly Kayum would greet the prospect with horror.

But it was not up to Erika to cast the stowaway into the sea.

"Come, we will have supper and speak with the others," Erika said.

Kayum groaned at the sight of his sister. When Koh made her plea, Claus and the others decided to leave the matter up to her brother.

"Ne Tamacchi! Sister, why do you follow me out into the world? Are you a devil as they say?"

"So you believe it too, Kayum."

"I don't know what to believe. Will our family ever be free of our curse? Go back to Jatate. Here, take some food and go. You can't travel with us."

"My brother, when I gave you pleasure in the milpa, you loved me."

"You needn't remind me of that. Yes, I loved you and look what came of it? Misery and evil for both of us and all our people. Go back, Koh, back to Jatate." He pounded his fist against the trunk of a tree. Koh remained motionless. The others moved away to allow them some privacy.

"It's easy for you to tell me to go back. But can you go back? Believe me Kayum, I don't come to you now for the reasons I came to your hut in the night. Yes, I still hold love for you, you are my brother, but I promise you we shall never lie together again. I will kill myself before that happens."

Kayum threw up his hands. He reminded her that they had both said such things before. How many times had they made suicide pacts only to postpone the time for one last round of love making? He couldn't even pretend to want to kill himself anymore. Now, he had a sacred duty to perform. "Koh, please, leave me alone."

But Koh did not move nor did she flinch at what her brother said.

"I have nowhere to turn. Don't you understand? Even Chankin Stupid of Sak-rum, who wanted to marry me believes I am a witch. And you once told me you would never allow him to marry me. Say what you want about pity. Where am I to go? Our father will die soon."

"Don't speak of it!"

"We must speak of it. The Lacandon men speak of the gods but the women must speak of the things of this world. Now that you are gone, our father will give the knowledge of the counting to Bor and the people of Jatate will not perish in the forest. If I stay in Jatate, what family will take me in? Some married men have already claimed they have seen my spectral soul wander into their huts at night with smiles and hugs to entice them to commit adultery, as the women of Lacanja once did. Even Puxi who is ugly and has albino skin accuses me of seducing him. I would not make tortillas for any one of them."

"You shall not make tortillas for me either."

Koh laughed, even in her desperation. "I'm quite sure you will find a wife to your liking among the Lacandons of the north who will make tortillas for you."

Kayum looked at her fiercely. "Ne Tamacchi! You begrudge me what peace I might find. I would be very lucky to find a woman in Puna."

"Then turn me away. I came because I believed you loved me in a way that went beyond the wish to tread my body. I was mistaken. Very well, my brother, I will leave you to save your soul from such an evil person as myself. I will live alone in the forest with jaguars and parrots and take a vulture as my husband."

Kayum pounded his head with his fists and stamped up and down the ground with his feet.

"Why is the cause of pleasure also the cause of misery?" he shouted to the general company. "I will destroy my seed shooter!"

"Save it for your northern Lacandon bride," Koh said with cold fury. "You needn't worry about me any longer. Yes, brother, you are absolutely right. Whatever trail we take together is a trail to Kisin. I will find him alone." With her head held up high in a manner that would have made a Hapsburg princess proud, Koh strode off into the mist. But before she was lost in the dark fog, Kayum ran after her.

When they returned, Koh was smiling through a tearful face and Kayum had resignation written on his face.

Later, the young man spoke to Erika alone. "Doña Erika, do you have a medicine for the fever of love?"

Erika put an arm around Kayum's shoulder. "The only medicine is time, Kayum, time, and the women of the north."

Chapter Twenty-Nine

Coming off a ridge of tall pitch pines and descending into the deep forest, Erika beheld below them a lake the color of jade, studded with white crystalline islands. The beauty of the sight caused her to gasp.

"This is the sacred lake of the old Lacandons," Kayum said.

They found two dugout canoes beached on the shore and cruised between tiny islands that gleamed like white rock candy. Huge turtles sunned themselves on some of the islets.

Claus told her that the mixing of the sulfur and lime deposits over the ages had produced these islands. They saw evidence of mounds on some of them. Through the water, Erika could see traces of stone and mortar.

Kayum and Koh bounded out of the canoe and gamboled like children on one of the crystal rocks.

"Claus, I see a mound," Erika said prodding a hard relatively flat surface with a stick. Claus looked very pleased.

"Yes, this is Lake Lacandon. I believe it's the very one Bishop Landa wrote about three hundred years ago. This is the last place in Mexico where the Mayans lived together in any sizeable numbers."

"Was it abandoned before the taking of the village the Spaniards named Dolores?"

"It was destroyed fifty years before. The Mayans in that village were probably from here. This was perhaps the last ceremonial site made of stone to be occupied."

"Claus, it must have been a little Venice once!"

Claus told her the story. The Mayans built small temples on the islands. The structures were small and probably crude by the standards of their classic ancestors. But the old Spanish priest was clear on one point. His records reveal that in 1555, some twenty-five years after the conquests of Cortez, the Spaniards, commanded by one dauntless Pedro Ramierez de Quinones, a good Catholic and loyal subject of the Spanish crown, led a battalion of Spanish soldiers and two thousand christianized Aztecs to the lake for an invasion of the last bastion of the Mayans.

The lake was indeed an American Venice then, with glistening white temples trimmed with varied hues of bright color built on many of the islands. There were native huts along the shore. The Mayans may have seen the lake and its isolation as a last refuge. But one day Quinones came. The Mayans sallied forth in their canoes to meet the challenge, and the invaders set out on rafts.

"The good bishop wrote that the Mayans were vastly outnumbered, the invaders came with shotguns of which the Indians knew nothing and against which their bows and arrows were powerless. It was the last great battle between Christians and native people in Mexico."

In her mind, Erika could see the transparent jade turned to an opaque mucky red by the flow of human blood. She imagined the black smoke replacing the morning mists and the sounds of gunfire replacing the night crickets.

Suddenly, Claus gave a little hop on one of the mounds. "Of course! It all fits. Listen, most of the Mayans were killed in the battle. But not all. Now, what would have happened to their survivors? We know some were enslaved by the Spaniards and others settled in a village on the river. But let's imagine that others got away into the forest. Now the ones who escaped into the forest knew they could not survive in large settlements any longer. So, wouldn't it be natural, essential in fact, for them to live in separate caribals deep in the unknown parts of the forest?"

Claus made his case. Being separated, and no longer building large permanent stone structures that would give evidence of their existence, such a people would eventually lose the knowledge of working with stone and mortar. Many ancient temples would be lost. Living in small isolated groups, they would eventually lose the art of writing and pictorial design. All that would remain of their calligraphic writing and monumental sculpture would be some primitive pottery and crude doodles in caves traced over a forgotten history. But the memory of their history would haunt them in dreams and rituals, the original meaning of which they would have lost. Yet, in order to survive, they would have learned to exist in harmony with the jungle. They would live as innocently as children in the dawn of time. "Behold on yonder isle, returning to their ancestral home, the last prince and princess of the underground Mayans!"

Erika looked over the water at Kayum, who was burning incense on a rock, while Koh, laughing freely, held a turtle up to the sun. "Oh, yes!" Erika gasped, quickly drawing her camera out of its case.

Chapter Thirty

In the morning, Koh milled the corn she had soaked the night before. Erika listened to the rolling of the pestle over the stone and the pat of the girl's hands over the meal. The girl seemed content to spend the sun-filled morning so engaged. Her movements were rhythmic as she bent over her task, and her breasts, partially visible in her loose tunic, shook like ripe fruit about to fall from a tree. The men had seen deer tracks on the other side of the lake and had gone out to follow them. Since they expected to spend another day or so on Lake Lacandon, Koh had decided to take the opportunity to prepare some tortillas for the rest of the journey. Claus had estimated that they would be on the trail at least another five weeks. Erika helped the girl place chilis on a rock to dry and, leaving her in camp, took some clothes to the lake to wash. Then she sat on a rock to go over her notes.

It was the first morning of the world. Across the lake, cacao palms and ramon trees rose over the dense foliage. The air was heavy with the scent of blossoms and rotting leaves. The peace of this primordial world was suddenly shattered by a scream. At first Erika thought it was the shriek of a startled parrot. Then it came again, piercing the still air like a spear, racing across the lake like a rocket set off at a Mexican carnival. Then she heard sobs and the laughter of unfamiliar male voices.

Erika recognized the sobbing as Koh's. Erika dropped her notebook and dashed back to camp. She was lacerated by thorns in her rush to get to the source of the scream. As the camp came into view, she stopped, paralyzed by a mixture of terror and rage at what she saw. Quickly, she dropped down behind a cluster of fan leaves.

In the clearing before the *metate*, Koh was struggling with two men who were tossing her from one to the other. They were trying to pull her tunic over her head. When she resisted, they slashed at the tunic with long knives until it ripped off her body in shreds. The girl stood naked except for her short red wraparound cotton skirt. The men slapped at her parts and giggled as Koh tried to escape between them.

"Have you ever seen such a beauty out here in the jungle, Manny?" one of the men said in English. "You can bet this is going to be a treat." He spoke with a rough American accent.

The American took a drink from a bottle as the man called Manny tried to hold Koh. She slipped out of his grasp and ran toward the lake.

"Where you going, sweetie? The party's just starting." Koh had run against a wall of foliage and the two men pounced on her like tackles at a football game.

Erika spotted long nets hanging from a branch. A small alligator was thrashing in one of them, making his prison tighter with each lunge. Alligator hunters! Perhaps they were with Barnes. And if so, where was he?

The American had a grizzly black beard. The other had no facial hair but Erika guessed by his features that he was a *mestizo*. Koh screamed and kicked and the men could not hold her down for long. The man named Manny finally managed to fasten her arms behind her back. Erika guessed that the American was drunk because he was too easily confounded by the thrashing of Koh's legs.

"Fun is fun, but enough of that, honey. Manny, you tell her in Indian that I'm a patient guy, but she's going to have to settle down real soon or I'll get mad."

"You may be the first to mount her when she quiets down, Señor Wills. I know you don't like to feel what another man has left in a woman. I don't mind when the woman has a pretty face."

"The way she's kicking and screaming, I may have to give her a good crack over the head with my revolver. Her friends could be around here some place and hear us. Our friends won't be back for a while. If the boss only knew what he was missing, he'd eat this one up himself. This is your last warning Pocahontas. Now just lie back and enjoy yourself."

Koh's eyes had the look of a stricken deer. She managed to raise herself a little but the effect brought out the beauty of her bosom which excited the men more.

"Christ, she's built like a brick shit house." The man named Wills bent over Koh's breasts. In an instant, Koh freed a hand from her other captor and drew her nails over Wills's face. He slapped her hard. Erika was about to burst upon the scene when Manny stayed his friend's savage blows.

"Señor Wills, enough! Do you want to mount her or do you want to kill her?"

"I'm going to do both. Nobody scratches the face of Charlie Wills. Take that you little gook." Koh ducked and the blow glanced off her head.

"Señor Wills, think a moment. You were right in what you said before. She has friends nearby. Maybe this is Pancho Balam's camp. They may come at any moment. Let us take the girl to the raft and row out to one of those islands where we can take our pleasure without fear of interruption."

"That's what I like about you Manny, always thinking ahead. But won't her screams be heard all over the lake?" Wills was sitting on Koh's stomach now and Manny held her head down.

"Her voice is running out of power," Manny said calmly. "When we get her out on the lake, I will stuff her mouth with banana leaves."

"Ok, but I still say it would be easier to bash her head in."

They picked Koh up by her legs and dragged her behind them, forcing her to walk on her hands to avoid cutting her face with briars.

As soon as they left the clearing, Erika ran into the camp. The mules stood stolidly on the other side of the lean-to, munching on big leaf plants. Erika ran to the boxes that contained ammunition and equipment. She knew that Claus had taken his Winchester rifle and the others had taken shotguns but she remembered an army MI rifle that Kayum had gotten from a trader. The shells were too explosive for game so it was seldom used. It also gave a big kick when fired. She saw the big weapon hanging from one of the cross beams. She pulled it down, filled a clip with cartridges and inserted it into the magazine of the MI. Then she ran out toward the lake.

When she came to the water's edge, Erika could see no sign of Koh or her kidnappers. But she could hear the girl's muffled screams and whimpers coming from the middle of the lake. Erika jumped into one of the beached canoes and poled away from shore. She had learned to row the *cayucos* from the Lacandons and flew toward the cluster of islets ahead of her. She rowed between the white crystalline islands. The cries were close by. They had lost much of their initial strength but the hatred was still in them.

"You bitch. She bit my hand. Lie still you cunt or I'll smash your head in for sure."

"Señor Wills, you must be quiet or you will be heard yourself."

"Ok, but you tell her in Indian that if she doesn't lie still and shut up, I'm going to change her pretty face."

"Wait until I've had my turn before you do that. I like to make whoopee with women who have pretty faces."

"The trouble with you Manny is that you're too sentimental. I say let's kill her now. Her body will still be warm enough for us to have a good time. And we'll have peace and quiet while we're doing it."

"But I don't enjoy fornicating with the dead."

"Then you'd better convince her of the importance of staying alive long enough to enjoy the party because it's going to be nighty-night as soon as it's over."

Erika's canoe skirted a boulder that rose out of the lake. It was large enough to screen her. She knew the scene was taking place on another rock or islet that lay just on the other side.

Koh's cries were muffled now.

"I have her down, Señor Wills."

Erika stood up in her canoe and peered over the rock. On a flat crystalline islet just thirty yards away, the men were bent over what looked like the ruins of an altar. Koh's nude body was draped over it.

The man named Manny was on the altar kneeling on Koh's shoulders and trying to stuff some leaves into her mouth. He was naked from the waist down. Wills was completely naked and trying to wedge his knee between Koh's legs which were crossed. His organ stood up red and gawking like a rooster. He held his revolver in one hand.

In cold rage, Erika raised the MI rifle to her shoulder. She was not an expert shot and had to be careful not to hit Koh. But she was a good shot with her camera and had watched Claus fire his rifle enough times. Yet a miss would give the bearded satyr an opportunity to use his revolver. Erika didn't know if the other man was armed. She was surprised that she felt no qualms about killing either man.

"Her legs are stuck together like glue," Wills complained.

Erika looked through the sight at the end of the barrel. The men were all over Koh now in their struggle with her. Erika waited for a clear shot.

"Turn her around, Manny. I'll mount her from behind. But I promise you this. When we're finished with this tramp, you're going to be looking at her pretty brains."

They managed to roll Koh over on her stomach so that her legs hung over the altar and her buttocks rose in the air. Manny held Koh's head against his thighs while Wills approached his mistress in the manner of a dog. He was an easier target in this position as the upper part of his body was clear.

"I got her, but I keep slipping out. Hold her still."

Erika felt for the trigger. But before she could fire, her concentration was interrupted by a scream coming from Manny who was holding Koh's head between his legs.

"The bitch. She bit my *cojones*. Jesus help my bleeding *cojones*!"

Erika's canoe had drifted clear of the rock and was headed for the islet. She was out in the open and the man who held Koh's head saw her coming toward them as she squeezed the trigger. The head of the fornicator exploded into a shower of blood and torn flesh. The other man released his grip on Koh, picked up his friend's fallen revolver and in the same motion, fired on Erika.

She threw herself down on the bottom of the *cayuco*. She felt a bullet strike the mahogany on the other side of the canoe. The man continued to fire. Erika lay still waiting with her rifle ready. Then she felt the craft changing direction and it drifted away from the islet. Erika could hear the man reload the revolver. She dared not poke her head above the side of her canoe.

Then she heard shots coming from her other side. They were from rifles and some managed to split the port side of her canoe. Water began to fill the bottom of the canoe. Erika remembered the men saying they had friends nearby. They must have arrived because the shots were being fired at her canoe from all sides now. The canoe was filling rapidly with water and listing sharply.

She had to take a chance to see how close her attackers were. As she took a gulping glance over the side, a bullet singed her cheek. In a flash, she saw a military raft occupied by four men who were firing at her. On the rock, the man naked from the waist down, stood alone with his revolver. When she ducked down, she couldn't remember seeing Koh or the dead man.

As Erika crouched low, her body was almost completely submerged in the water that was filling the canoe. Bullets continued to riddle the side that was facing the riflemen. But the other side rose high in the air now and as the vessel tipped, Erika knew she would be exposed to the men on the raft. Then Erika heard shots coming from yet another direction. They were more distant by the sound but in less than a minute they were mixing with the other shots. The air was filled with screams.

Her boat capsized. Erika tumbled out of it, and the canoe turned over. Erika could taste traces of blood in the lake as she clung to her overturned canoe. The sounds of shells whined over her head. Erika could see none of the action but the water around her had turned a muddy red. Black smoke hung in the moist air above her head.

The shooting stopped suddenly, and she saw the faceless head of the fornicator looking like bloodied ground beef, floating toward her. The body floated on its back like a dead fish. The crushed head bumped against Erika's side, and when she pushed it away, the red of the water deepened. Then the canoe turned around slowly. Erika saw two men hanging over the side of a rubber raft, their eyes facing the harsh sun. Then Erika realized someone clung to her canoe on the other side.

Whoever it was swam toward Erika under the boat. She had nothing to defend herself with other than the broken paddle drifting at her side. She reached for it as Koh's bruised face rose out of the bloodied water.

Then she saw a *cayuco* coming toward them filled with the sound of cheering. Kayum swam with the speed of an alligator toward them. The others stripped to their waists and dove in. The swimmers vied for the privilege of taking the rescued girls in.

Back on shore, Erika sobbed convulsively in Claus's arms.

"Claus, what's become of me? I killed a man. Just like that—I killed him. Even in Germany I never killed anybody, not even a storm trooper when I had the chance. But today I killed a man in cold blood."

"But you're all right," Claus said. "You and Koh." Claus shook his head. "And it's all thanks to what you did. Don't feel guilty. You continue to astonish me, Erika. I can't believe you. You're as brave as you are beautiful."

Erika kissed him impulsively and was pleasantly surprised that he returned her kiss, warmly and lingeringly. The muleteers gaped.

Sitting beside the fire, Erika was engulfed in her feelings of horror and guilt, feelings that she had suppressed in the thick of the encounter, but which opened up now like the pain in a frostbitten hand that begins to thaw. Despite some discoloration caused by the bruises, Koh's face had regained its usual composure. She sat placidly, looking like a moon goddess in the reflected light of the fire.

"How many were there?" Erika asked Claus.

"I think there were six in all. There were five bodies floating in the lake when it was over. Was there more than one man on the island with Koh?"

"There were two."

"Then one man may have escaped. He's either drowned or in the woods. We'll have to be watchful and take turns sleeping, at least for tonight."

"Claus, do you think they were members of Barnes's expedition?"

"I hope not. If so, he's traveling with brigands."

"And he's not far."

"But how could he—? He may have made a wide circle to this lake. I'm mystified. What is he up to?"

Erika didn't know, and she didn't say it, but she felt that Barnes wanted to destroy Claus.

Kayum looked disconsolate and sat a little away from the fire, not speaking. By contrast, Koh appeared recovered as if she had done nothing more than take a swim in the lake. Erika went over to Kayum and put her arm around him.

"Kayum, everybody is all right. Koh isn't hurt. Why are you so sad?"

"If the T'sul has left his seed inside my sister, the child of such a mating will be cursed and my people will again suffer sickness and death. Surely the gods will one day destroy all the Lacandons because of the sins of my family."

Koh looked at her brother with an amused smile.

"My brother, you needn't worry. I will not carry the child of the T'sul."

"But did he not mount you?"

"Well, yes and no. You see, the T'sul was weak from drinking the *balché* that comes in the bottle and with fighting me, so when the moment of mounting came, his seed shooter had lost its confidence against my skin and could not rise to the occasion."

Chapter Thirty-One

The Lacandon settlement of Puna was abandoned. They found some empty huts with collapsed roofs over which vegetation climbed. Clouds of flies swarmed over piles of rotted corn.

"It was here that my brother and I came many milpas ago looking for women," Kayum said.

"What could have happened?" Erika asked.

"Let's take a look around," Claus said. "It couldn't have been abandoned too long ago or the secondary growth would have taken over completely."

Erika saw a few scrawny chickens poking about for corn and dry yuccas which were scattered about. She saw a large hut similar to the God House in Jatate and wondered if there was anything in it. As she came to the doorway, a disagreeable odor swept over her. Erika saw a mass of hairy creatures huddled together in the semi-dark. On seeing her, they rose, squealing and grunting. Erika stood back in fright as the herd of wild pigs came storming out of the God House. The animals headed for the bush still squealing and giving off a smell so foul that Erika became nauseated. The men fired upon the pigs and killed several before they vanished in the density of the forest.

In the God House, Erika saw some old censers with heads turned to the wall as in a Lacandon house in which someone has died. There was no incense in the censers and no stones as in the pots of Jatate.

Coming out of the hut, Erika saw Claus and Rogelio standing over the slain peccary, most of whom had swollen bellies.

"We won't be eating these pigs," Claus said. "They're infected with disease."

"What could have happened?"

"Yellow fever. There must have been an epidemic in these parts some time years ago. Let's see if we can find a cemetery."

"Would an epidemic cause the Lacandons to abandon their homes?"

"Not by itself. They know disease is something they can't run away from. But a series of invasions by the people who brought the disease might have caused them to abandon the settlement."

They found a weed-filled milpa and tangles of growth climbing over the blackened stumps of trees. Then they saw rows of grave mounds. The tiny thatched roofs had collapsed or been blown away. Claus estimated that most of the graves were less than a year old.

"Yes, a lot of people died here around the same time. Their survivors took themselves somewhere else, just as Bolon Kin took his people in an earlier time."

"Where could they have gone?" Rogelio asked.

"I have no idea. They might have become extinct altogether."

"What do we do now?" Erika asked.

Claus sat on a log under a tree and removed his hat. The others found similar seats.

He told them they could press on and look for Menche with the scanty information they had. They knew it was north of Lacanja and probably east of where they were. But they needed more information than that. Was Menche in the unexplored region between the town of El Cedro and the Usumacinta River? On the other hand, it might be found in the Guatemalan Peten that stretched out endlessly. "But, damn, I'm convinced it's here in Chiapas, somewhere in this limestone basin that's ringed by the Lacantun waterways."

"Then let's follow your hunch," Lazaro said.

Claus looked up at the surrounding hills. "There's an old *chicle* settlement about a day's hike from here. El Capulin. I suspect it has become a colony for new migrants into the jungle. Have you noticed we've been seeing a lot of burnt hills? We'll need to resupply anyway. Maybe we can find out what happened to the Lacandons who left here."

On the trail to El Capulin, Erika saw many scarred hillsides. In several places, the grey limestone was exposed, making the earth look like it was covered with sores. In some places, they saw hills of red earth burning under the sun.

"Claus, this is horrible, Erika said. "What's the reason for all this?"

"The *campesinos* have come. They are the new pioneers. In their mad scramble for a place in the sun, they are destroying the forest. They don't realize that massive and reckless slash-and-burn farming ruins the soil. Yes, the jungle came back after the Maya collapsed but look up there where the limestone has been exposed on the side of that hill. Nothing will grow there again. Unless this land is reforested soon, the rains will wash away what meager soil there is and fill the rivers with mud."

Kayum looked up at the naked hills. "A world without the jungle is a dead world," he said. "Pancho Balam, who are these people who kill the trees?"

"Tzeltales from the north I'd say. But the Tzoltil-speaking Indians from the San Cristobal mountains are beginning to come to the jungle too. You can't blame them. Their ancestral lands have become worn out or taken over and they don't want to work for bosses who have made virtual slaves of them."

Kayum nodded. "They are the Kah, the people who live mashed together. Now I know why my father didn't want me to trade with them."

"Claus, this destruction is outrageous," Erika said. "How does the Mexican government allow it?"

Claus shrugged. "Mexico has a program of agrarian reform but no agricultural reform. And the jungle is pretty much a no-man's-and everybody's-land."

Erika remembered what Manuel had said about an ulterior purpose to the Lacandon expedition. Were there people in high places who encouraged the destruction that the migrants were carrying out? What was behind it? Certainly, it was right up Barnes's alley.

"At this rate of destruction, how long would it take to destroy the forest?" she asked Claus.

"What does the prophecy say, Kayum?" Claus turned to the Lacandon.

"My father says that unless the gods are worshiped properly, it will happen in my lifetime. When it does, I will see jaguars come out of the sky and devour all mankind."

"The unclothed hills are uglier than an albino Lacandon," Koh said, looking at the limestone lumps.

Erika was busy taking photographs. "These may be the most important pictures I take," she said.

Chapter Thirty-Two

They made camp near the Rio Santa Cruz. Claus set up his lean-to away from Erika's. It had become a pattern. Erika knew he was avoiding physical contact with her. She found herself helping, being careful not to expose herself in going to and from her bath. She was no more physically intimate with him than she was with any of the others. It would be wrong to provoke him. He had made that clear in Jatate. Modesty was the only way she could love him now. But, placing a canvas sheet over one side of her lean-to, she let her mind slide back to the warm, lingering kiss he had given her on the edge of Lake Lacandon. How many alligator hunters would she have to kill to win his love? She laughed to herself. Still, intuition told her he had to love her in some way. They shared too many things. Of course, he shared them equally with the mules. Her mind always rebuked her intuitions. In any case, she would remain demure. Erika slipped into her sleeping bag reimagining the kiss when moonlight had shone on the white bluffs.

In the morning, Erika went to the river to wash. The trees along the banks had been cut and the water was muddy. The brown river threw her reflection back to her. She began to disrobe for her bath when she saw the reflection of a white serape and a face in a flat round hat from which ribbons flowed. She turned quickly to see a handsome young man smiling down at her. Erika had the presence of mind not to appear startled and calmly buttoned up her shirt. She smiled up at him as if it were quite natural to meet handsome young men in one's bath water.

He had the dark looks of Kayum, but his hair was braided. He wore shorts under his serape and huaraches on his feet. The young man announced himself as Juan, the son of the *presidenté* of the village. Erika noticed that his eyes were sad, even when he was smiling. She was able to converse with him as he spoke Yucatec Mayan.

He said he lived close by and would be happy to escort Erika and her friends to his settlement.

Erika invited the young man to have breakfast with them at their camp upriver.

When they sighted the camp through the foliage, Juan stopped and took cover behind a breadnut tree.

"Will you come no farther?" Erika asked.

"I will wait here."

"But we are all your friends."

"But you bring Lacandons."

"They have traveled with us over many mountains and rivers. There are only two of them and they come to be your friends."

The young man nodded when she said this. "My father says Lacandons are beasts of the forest like the jaguars and must be killed."

Erika tugged at the young man's sleeve. "Look at them, Juan. Are they not human, like you and me? They are my good friends."

She saw his eyes fall on Koh. "Yes, the woman. She is not a beast, she is a princess."

Erika smiled. "Very true. Come, Juan."

Erika stepped into the clearing as the party gathered around a shimmering pot of beans on the fire. Juan followed.

"We have a guest for breakfast," she said. The group gazed at the young man in awe.

Kayum got up swiftly, picked up his machete, and advanced toward the stranger. The Tzeltal stood his ground. Before anyone else could act, the two young men dropped to their haunches, brandishing machetes, and began a hopping dance around one another, shouting in a singsong way as they did. In the exchange of looks and shouts, Erika felt the outpouring of centuries of hatred.

"It's all right," Claus said, when she asked him to intervene. "It's an old Mayan way of greeting strangers. They are just trading pleasantries. The custom is in the Tzeltal's background as well as Kayum's."

"Do they understand one another?"

"The way a Texan would understand a visitor from Liverpool," Claus laughed.

Kayum thrust his machete into the ground and Juan drove his next to it. The two men rose and shook hands.

"Buenos dias," Juan addressed Claus and the muleteers in Spanish. But when he gazed at the beauteous Koh, his lips trembled and he stumbled over his words. Erika thought she saw him blush. With a slight, almost patronizing smile, Koh offered the guest a calabash of *posole* and a tortilla.

Juan stepped back unable to take his eyes off the girl and, in his preoccupation, walked backward into a fallen branch. He fell and the *posole* spilled. The young man got up quickly and ran his hands over his reddened face.

"Forgive me, your gods will be angry that I spilled your gift."

Koh fell into a heap of laughter and turned to her brother. "In Jatate, we never saw a Hach Winik who fell over himself. How strange the Kah is. And he spilled all the *posole* I gave him. Do you think he throws away his seed thus?" She spoke loudly enough that the embarrassed young man could hear her remarks, and his pained expression told the group that he understood them.

"Koh, don't be rude. I have traded with the Kah and many are civilized," Kayum reprimanded his sister.

Juan trembled in his embarrassment.

Erika filled another calabash and handed it to Koh to offer again. But Koh set the calabash aside and smiled coyly.

"Doña Erika, we must not waste the food of the gods." Koh resumed her position seated by the fire and gazed abstractedly at the mules.

The young man took his hands from his face and looked at her angrily this time.

"In my village, women do not speak against men. I am told that this is not so among your people."

Kayum blanched at this remark, although it seemed to have no effect on Koh who sat before the fire with the poise of a classic statue.

"Do not speak against my people," Kayum said. "We have come all this journey to worship our god."

"It is good," Juan said, looking at Kayum intently. "I tell my father he is wrong to hate the Lacandons as they are closer to the ways of the jungle. So I believe they are closer to God. I invite you to come with me to my father's house."

Chapter Thirty-Three

Up the valley on the other side of the river, the sky was dark with smoke. Kayum shook his head in disbelief. "Metzabok will be angry. It is the wrong time for planting. He will wash away the earth until the rock is bare and nothing will grow again."

"He's absolutely right," Claus said to Erika. "With the first heavy rains, the top soil will slide down those hills and most of the crop will be ruined. The recent dry spell is only a lull in the rainy season. These migrants have either lost track of the seasons or they always had others to tell them when and where to plant. And I don't know if this fire can be controlled." The smoke so filled the air that the sun looked like a displaced moon. Erika felt as if she inhabited the inside of an oven. She and her friends coughed and rubbed their eyes continually. The surrounding forest shimmered and jiggled through the smoke. They sat down on the banks of the muddy river. It was not much cooler there but they breathed in the moisture that was given off by the water. Before long, they were all grey from falling ash.

"Perhaps Erika and I should go with you first," Claus said to Juan, squinting up at the dull sun. "Your father may be upset to see Lacandons coming from nowhere. We'll explain that they come as friends."

Claus asked Rogelio to take the horse and the mules and establish a camp away from the smoke.

Claus and Erika rowed across the river and entered the flaming hills, their eyes smarting.

They met some Indians in flat straw hats and drill trousers who led them to a village of tightly packed huts, some with corrugated tin roofs and plank floors. An old man who was the *presidenté* and who stumbled as if he had been drinking, appeared. The ashes fell everywhere and they squinted.

Juan introduced his new friends.

The old man looked at the visitors suspiciously. "Who has sent you here?" he asked. "Do you have papers?"

Claus produced some reports of his oil well expedition. There was an official seal at the bottom of the report. As the man squinted at the paper, it was clear that the seal was the only sign on the paper he dimly understood.

"We come with Lacandons who want to make peace," Claus said.

Juan spoke quickly to his father, assuring him of the peaceful intentions of the Lacandons.

The old man shook his head. "Peace with the Lacandons? Can you make peace with jaguars? There were Lacandons in the forest here when we first came a year ago. Our mules wandered in their cornfields and they shot them. So we had to shoot the Lacandons. Many had already died of fever as they are too ignorant to understand medicine. The ones we didn't kill vanished into the jungle. Now we never see the Lacandons just as we never see the jaguars. Do you come with jaguars too?"

Erika could see the pain in Claus's face as he absorbed the news of why Puna had been abandoned.

The *presidenté* went inside a nearby hut. He emerged with a man who had long braided hair and a cotton toga. Erika guessed he the local shaman.

The shaman took Claus's report and studied it. The old man held up a finger to the visitors and the two men went off to the side and whispered together.

Then the *presidenté* returned. "Bring the Lacandons to us," he said.

"They are on the other side of the river. They have never visited a village before. There are many of you. It would be a better sign of your peaceful intentions if you came with us to meet them and then invited them here. You may bring as many men as you wish."

"If you want peace, bring the Lacandons to us," the shaman said.

Going back to the river, Erika expressed her fears.

"Claus, I think we're being led into a trap."

"It's possible. We'll leave it up to Kayum but the Lacandons are going to have to make peace with these people sooner or later. They're all over the jungle now."

Kayum agreed to meet Juan's people. Kayum's father would have opposed the idea but Kayum wanted to show the Kah that the Lacandons were not savages. He was a trader, after all. He would lay down his shotgun in the village of the Kah. He gave Koh a rifle so she would lay one down too.

When they crossed the river again, they observed that the burning fields were empty of Indians. The fire was out of control and Kayum expressed his distress repeatedly.

The village was deserted when they arrived. Erika felt the tingle of dread. The *presidenté* and the shaman appeared in a doorway, but they did not come out onto the grassy square to meet the visitors. Then silently, but quickly, from out of the huts on all sides and from the bushes, over a hundred Tzeltal Indians appeared carrying pitchforks, shotguns and machetes. Erika saw women and small children run out of the huts and enter the church at the other end of the square. Within seconds, the visitors were surrounded. The Lacandons stood poised and waiting.

Kayum stretched out his arms in a gesture of peace. "Put down your guns that are for killing game, and your forks that are for farming. We do not want to make war with you. We invite you to share the jungle with us and our people."

A hubbub went up among the circle of villagers as they watched Kayum empty his rifle and lay it in the middle of the square. Koh, who was not accustomed to using guns, pulled the trigger of her rifle while trying to empty the chamber. The gun went off and the bullet struck the door of the church.

The villagers gave a roar. The circle expanded and then contracted like a giant circular accordion. Machetes and shovels went sailing into the air toward the visitors. As she covered her face to avoid a sailing pot, Erika heard a barrage of gunfire. She was afraid to open her eyes. Unceasing gunfire filled her ears and she wondered how long it would be until she was struck down. As she waited, almost impatiently for her end, she realized that the shots were being fired in ordered sequence. Then all she could hear was the pounding of her heart. She opened her eyes and saw Claus and the Lacandons still standing with her. There were no bodies on the ground and the Tzeltal Indians had fallen back. Some hid in their huts. Others cowered in doorways. Only the *presidenté* and the shaman stood their ground.

"I don't believe it," she heard Claus say.

Erika turned to see a band of two dozen or so men on mule back, holding rifles up in the air. They all had cartridge belts slung across their chests and they wore sombreros. Most of them had heavy growths of hair on their chins and blood-shot eyes. Erika had never seen a more depraved looking group of men in her life. Certainly, they were *bandidos*.

Well, if the Tzeltal Indians respected anyone more than federal agents, surely they respected *bandidos*.

Then Erika felt the shock of recognition. Behind one of the beards hid the craggy face of Barnes. Erika shook with rage at what she saw next. A man on a sore-ridden burro came abreast of Barnes. Erika recognized the grinning face of the alligator hunter who had held Koh's head in his lap and whose genitals had been bitten by the enraged princess. In a flash, Erika saw that the man recognized Koh who returned his telling gaze with a look of cold hatred.

Barnes dismounted his mule and swaggered into the square. The other men stayed on their mules and continued to hold up their guns. One of them fired his into the air threateningly.

Barnes held out a pudgy hand. "I can't very well say 'Professor Boehm, I presume,' because you're not a professor anymore, are you? I suppose one could say you have no more right to be in the jungle than the *campesinos*." He laughed his thin, hissing laugh.

Then Barnes addressed the blind man in Tzeltal. "Yes, Mr. *Presidenté*, I come from your governor in Tuxtla. I want you to hear what my good friend Pancho Balam has to say. We'd all better listen to what he has to say and give his—er—friends a hearing too."

Barnes flashed a stack of papers with seals to the now confused shaman and *presidenté*. "Now, let's all get out of this sun and have a drink somewhere like civilized people. You must have some *aguardientes*, Mr. *Presidenté*."

While the shaman called his people out to the square to meet the Lacandons, the *presidenté* led the explorers to an abandoned schoolhouse. There, he showed them to a row of long plank tables and produced a bottle of rum. Barnes sat at a table with Erika and Claus and the *presidenté*. The alligator hunter and the others took another table and were served by an old woman with a suffering face.

"Where are your teachers? Are there no classes?" Erika asked the *presidenté*.

"We have no teachers," the *presidenté* said. "We had teachers from Tuxtla Guitterez, but when the corn didn't grow, they left. Now there is no one to teach the children or treat those who are sick." He rubbed his eyes continually. "And I am going blind."

"Let me see the sick ones," Claus said. "I will try to treat them."

He told Erika in English that the old man was suffering from an eye disease carried by a species of fly. It was too late to help him, but they might save the children.

"Before you go off to play Doctor Livingston on me, old colleague, have some rum," Barnes said.

"Thanks, Barnes, but I'm not drinking these days."

"Good Lord, this is not the Claus Boehm I knew. Off to save Indian children and not drinking?"

"Barnes, you saved my life just now, and that of my friends. Let's forget past rivalries. I hold no grudge against you. I'm glad you have an expedition. You certainly have a big crew." Claus glanced at the other table.

Barnes rubbed his beard which glistened with beads of spilled rum. "A bunch of renegades for the most part. But they suit my purposes. I have a few good field men, cartographers and mineralogists. They don't like me very much because I won't let them dawdle too long in one place. The others are trail cutters and alligator hunters, picked out of the saloons of Ocosingo. Can't do any serious archaeology with that kind of crew, can I? They're a mean, nasty bunch and just what I need to get through these shit-smelling tropics. I've come to believe the jungle is the hair that covers the world's asshole." He pulled in his lips so that his mouth made a round hole and he whistled disdainfully through it.

Barnes filled his shot glass frequently, and his voice became more strident as he went on. Erika was uncomfortable under his gaze which commanded the attention of whatever it fell on.

He grinned now, his lips wet with rum. "Did you get the note I left you in El Zapate, Claus? You didn't need my warning, did you? Not a bit. You went in and you got through, you old bastard. You came out with two of those pagans to boot. Claus, you're the best damn mule cusser in the jungle, after all. Ah, and you, Madame Boeshure." His eyes swept mischievously over Erika. "You look like you've just stepped out of a beauty parlor instead of having been dragged through the jungle like an ape woman. And, by the way, I understand you're a very good shot with a rifle."

Erika winced. "I feel bad about what I did. But I felt I had to do it."

"Oh, don't feel bad. You did me a favor. Wills created a lot of problems. And he killed Quarles?"

"Quarles? The photographer?" Erika was astonished.

"How awful," Claus said. "How did it happen?"

Barnes lifted his hands in the air and shrugged. "They got into a fight over a card game. The stakes were high, Quarles claimed that Wills cheated. Knowing Wills, I think Quarles was right. Quarles was real angry and, in the scuffle that followed, Wills pulled a knife on him. That was it for Quarles." Barnes shook his head.

"What did you do?" Claus asked.

Barnes opened his hands wide. "What could I do? Call the police? Bring Wills to court? There's no justice in the jungle. That's one reason I want to level it and bring in civilization."

"People like Wills are the worst products of our civilization, Barnes," Claus said. "Greedy, cheating, violent."

"That's enough, about Wills," Barnes said, filling his glass. "Ah, Claus, old friend, it's so good to see you. Rest assured, our rivalry is over. I'll drink to that if you won't."

Barnes drained his glass and filled it again. He fawned over Claus now, and Erika was convinced that an insidious scheme lurked behind the flattery. She would watch Barnes get drunk and give himself away.

He was beginning to slur his words. His manner had more swagger in it. Erika couldn't remember Barnes getting drunk in Ocosingo. She watched his hand tremble as he brought the small glass to his lips, carelessly spilling drops on his shirt.

Erika was struck with a painful recognition. Barnes was the reincarnation of the Claus she had encountered on that fateful morning in the little, cramped room in Ocosingo. Was it possible that their vulnerabilities were reversed, that just as Claus was susceptible to the worst forms of dipsomania when he was taken out of the jungle, so Barnes was turned into a drunkard as he trekked through the wilderness? It was as if the jungle healed one man and afflicted the other. What would happen to Claus when he came out of the jungle this time? Erika wanted to believe that he was healed permanently, but looking at Barnes now, she was extremely disturbed. She never wanted to see Claus like that again. She wished that Barnes would vanish from her sight, but he sat before them, suffusing the air around him with the rank odor of his presence.

Suddenly, Barnes erupted in unexplained laughter. Erika tried to ignore him. At another table, Barnes's men were calling for more bottles from the old woman who brought them. Erika decided that Barnes was a man gone rotten. He sat before them like a decayed tooth. His gaze was fixed on Claus, like that of a rejected lover who finally looks upon the face of his love after a long absence. He asked questions in a manner that was equally captious and reverential. Erika was glad that Claus avoided giving Barnes very much information about their experiences with the Lacandons. Yet Barnes continued to pummel Claus with questions. Indeed, Barnes paid Erika little notice and was barely aware of anyone else's presence.

Finally, Claus cut Barnes short and addressed the *presidenté*. "Why can't they bring teachers and doctors to this settlement?" he asked.

"There are doctors in Comitan. One came here but he left after a week. He said there was very little he could do."

"What are they all doing in Comitan—drinking *comiteco* and showing off their finery?"

The *presidenté* shrugged and rubbed his eyes.

Claus shook his head. He would write to Castellanos and Alvarez. They had to do more than pass ordinances or set up bureaucratic showcases for doctors and teachers to show off their clothes. The problem of immigration into the jungle had to be attacked on all sides. The landless Indians from the highlands who searched for a new life were caught in death traps. They burned and struck down the trees and depleted the thin soil until whole hillsides became nothing more than limestone streaked with useless sand. In the wake of fallen trees, grew scrub that became food for disease-carrying insects. Where were the teachers to teach the immigrants good farming sense?

Erika saw a new intensity in Claus's voice as he spoke. "Doctors and teachers must be given better pay to carry out their mission, but more importantly, those who hire them must make people who work for the public good enthusiastic! If doctors and teachers possessed just one ounce of the passion of the Catholic *frailes*, who converted the Indians, they would save them all from the diseases that came with Christianity."

Barnes produced a full-bellied laugh. "Claus, you are talking of paying higher salaries in the expectation of engaging saints. You are railing against bureaucracy, the dumb beast that carries all of Mexico on its back. The beast may be cajoled and kicked. All it wants is a good meal at the end of the trail. It will run away at the prospect of a breadnut tree to feed off. Old buddy, the doctors and teachers sent to these places are upward-climbing members of the working class poor. For the most part, they are motivated by a desire to better their own lots and shake off the scum in their past. They don't want to have anything to do with the poor, my old colleague. They want to get away from them. Are you sure you don't want some of this rum?"

Barnes filled a shot glass and placed it in front of Claus who ignored it.

"Erika, let's spend a few days doing what we can in this village before we move on. We need to resupply anyway." Claus turned to her.

"I would be happy to," Erika answered.

"Barnes, you have to look at things differently." Claus spoke with a sense of urgency. "Leaders exist among the Lacandons. We must set standards from the top."

Barnes shook his head, laughing almost silently, as if for his own amusement. "Claus, you've been in the jungle so long you don't smell the shit anymore. Ah, I assure you that those who ride the mechanical beast, the bosses, are only concerned with staying on top of the mule. If the load the animal carries is too heavy, the riders are in danger of falling off. Take it from me, you won't get anywhere with a crusade to save the jungle. Listen, my dear old friend, you are that to me you know, Claus—in spite of everything—I assure you that those who ride the mechanical beast, the bosses, are only concerned with staying on top of the mule. Yes, it suits the bosses damn fine. Do you realize the social revolt that would occur if these *campesinos* stayed in the highlands by the thousands, fighting over diminishing acres of worn-out land? Mexico has had enough revolutions. Claus, the Indians are breeding like flies up there and those who don't come here are migrating to dung heaps outside Mexico City. You can smell the shit in the air just walking down the Boulevard Reforma. Yaas.

"At least the jungle is keeping the population down. And you want doctors and teachers in here? There is only so much money the bosses will spend on the welfare of Indians in the boondocks. You might as well start a crusade on behalf of your Lacandons. Those brutes are better off than the million *mestizos* who live in disease-ridden hovels around Mexico City!"

Erika was impressed that Barnes was lucid through his drunkenness. The rum had almost sharpened his mind, honed his razor of evil. But she saw that Claus was waiting to disarm him. "But that's my point. If we help the people in their homes, they won't fill the streets of Mexico City with starving beggars. If the Tzeltales and Tzoltsil speaking people can be taught to work their old lands, if the Chamulas are encouraged to stay in the highlands, if the Lacandons are allowed to live in peace in the jungle, we will keep a lot of weight off the sagging beast."

The *presidenté* brought another bottle of rum and filled Barnes's glass as well as his own. The men at the other table were drunk and arguing noisily. Through the doorway, Erika could see Kayum and Koh sitting with the shaman and a group of Tzeltal elders. They were talking quietly and seriously and there was much nodding of heads. Perhaps what Claus was talking about was possible after all and the realities Barnes spoke of could be turned around. Erika felt proud of Claus.

Claus spoke to Barnes through the haze of rum that scented the air. "Barnes, you know as well as I do that less than one tenth of all the land on the planet is rain forest and that the rain forest produces over fifty percent of all the species of life on earth. If your mule is concerned only with the next feed ahead, the jungle in Mexico will be destroyed before the century is out. This land will be useless for farming then. The jungle stores its nutrients in the trees, not the soil.

"You're a botanist, Barnes. You know as well as I do that with the canopy of the forest gone, the rainwater will wash away hillsides of soil and leach out the soluble minerals that are necessary for anything to grow. And when the rains stop, the solar radiation in these tropics will destroy whatever organic matter is left. Without the big trees to recapture and recycle the nutrients, this soil will contain nothing more than acidic sand and clay. Wild grass will grow in some places but only the scrubbiest vegetation will survive. This is what I've seen and I intend to take my findings to the Department of the Interior in Mexico City as soon as I get back."

Barnes was just drunk enough to be amused. "Don Quixote lances another windmill. Don't be a fool, my friend. You will be laughed out of the House of Deputies. My old Claus, you are a great scientist, but you are politically naive. Why do you think I have come here? Do you think the bosses, the real bosses in this country and north of the Rio Grande, give a damn whether the poor devils who migrate here will be able to farm the land now or forty years from now? These bastards will die in droves here for all the real world cares.

"Claus, this is the twentieth century, you have to learn to live in it. It's the century of Adolph Hitler and Henry Ford. It doesn't matter who wins the war in Europe. It's the century of Hitler and Ford and big industry." He laughed obscenely. "Yes, this jungle will be stripped to prepare the way of the almighty beefsteak. Of course the soil will be no good once the jungle is gone. But wild grass will grow, at least for a time, just as you say. Do you know what that means? I've seen it right here, Claus. Wild grass will grow, and that will suit the big cattle ranchers on both sides of the border just fine. In fact, the sooner the jungle is gone, the better. Claus, you're a prophet whose time is past. Why don't you put on a haircloth and preach your message up and down Wall Street in New York City?"

Barnes laughed shrilly now. Beads of rum flew away from his beard as he did. Erika groaned with the realization that Barnes had won the argument.

But Claus would not let him go. Erika knew that he had a larger truth on his side and he was going to make Barnes see it. "You may be right in the end, Barnes. But what can happen here can happen elsewhere. Suppose jungles vanish all over the planet? Remember, it's the forests that breathe in most of the carbon dioxide in the atmosphere and breathe out most of the oxygen. Jungles are the world's lungs. And consider this before you hail the dawn of the age of the big beef palaces. There are three million species of life that exist only in the rain forest and you know that precious few of them have ever been studied. As a scientist, you know what a vast potential for knowledge will be lost forever when all those forms of life become extinct. Barnes, I can't believe you're just another hungry mule. What's happening here is what's happening in the Amazon. Fifty percent of all the oxygen on the planet is produced between here and the southern edges of the Amazon basin. The industries you speak of are beginning to contaminate the atmosphere as well as the waterways. The Mr. Bigs are cunning, but they don't have time on their side. I think those who are appalled by the increase of insanity in the world have a responsibility to stop civilization from destroying itself."

Barnes stroked his beard and looked at Claus as if seeing him for the first time. An expression of wonder broke through the hostile features of Barnes's drunkenness. "You've changed, Claus, you're not the same man at all. I remember a Claus Boehm years ago who was obsessed with nothing but glory. You reeked of optimism and success. You were Don Quixote taking on paper windmills. What happened to the man who used to say, 'I am the captain of my soul, each man is responsible for himself!' You said it to me after you arranged for my dismissal at Tulane, remember?" Barnes filled his glass from the *presidenté*'s bottle and gulped the contents down.

Claus winced. "You're right. I was ruthless in those days. I'm sorry, Barnes. I was hard on you as I was on others. You knew me when I was winning trophies. It was a long time ago."

The other men had gone outside as had the *presidenté*. The schoolroom filled with shadows as the conversation between Claus and Barnes took on a reflective turn.

"Everything you touched those days turned to gold, Claus," Barnes said quietly with a sudden affection for his old colleague in his voice. "I envied you. Yes, Claus, I even loved you. You were a hero to all of us." Erika decided that the rum had made Barnes sentimental. She reminded herself that sentimentality was a quality often found in the cruelest of men.

"Now I know how much of my success I owed to other people," Claus was saying. "Tozzer, Morely, to name a few. Without them I would have accomplished nothing. I was born at a certain place at a certain time. Had I been born in a Chamula hamlet instead of Copenhagen, Denmark, my life would have been entirely different, wouldn't it? Better perhaps, but different. I was the captain of my fate and then I fell and broke into pieces like Humpty Dumpty all by myself. When you get a bitter taste of failure in your mouth, you realize how much of success is being in the right place at the right time, with help from a lot of people and a heaping spoonful of dumb luck."

Barnes grinned again. "I think we finally see things the same way." He refilled his glass. "I must say this jungle has given me a taste for rum."

They heard shouting outside and they went out into the square. The Tzeltal Indians were sending rockets into the air and the carcass of a deer was roasting over a central fire. Kayum and Koh were smiling amid a cluster of admiring colonists. The feasting and singing lasted into the night.

Chapter Thirty-Four

Claus and Erika entered a hut to find a woman sitting before a *metate* and a little girl in a dirty dress crouching in a corner. The little girl's right eye was red and swollen. There were flies everywhere. Erika could see them buzzing over remnants of food.

"The disease is carried by those flies," Claus said. "I once saw what they can do in Union Fronteriza. They bite human beings and infect their bloodstreams. The disease usually settles near the eyes of the victims and produces blindness. Look at that little girl. There is a tumor near her eye, which is an outward sign that she is infected."

The woman made tortillas gropingly. She stopped from time to time to rub her sightless eyes because they hurt her. On the table, a salad oil can overflowed with flowers.

"Claus, is there anything we can do for these people?"

"It's too late to help the woman, but we might be able to lance the tumor from near the eye of the little girl. We have instruments in our kit but no anesthetic. Of course, the chances are she'll be reinfected."

They asked the woman if they could operate on her child. The woman shrugged in a gesture of indifference, the final stage of total despair.

The little girl screamed in outrage as Erika and her mother held her. Claus cut into her cheek with a long sharp knife. When Erika put antiseptic on the wound and bandaged it, the girl gave in to whimpering. The mother went back to making tortillas. Erika tried to talk to her about sanitation but the woman could only talk about the pain in her eyes. The little girl sobbed incessantly.

Back in the square, many of the revelers were lurching from the ceremonial rum.

Kayum looked grave. "There is peace now," he said. "But I don't know how long it will last. The people drink the whiskey from the bottle that takes away their thoughts."

Claus told Kayum he wanted to stay for a few days to help the people before it was too late. He asked if perhaps Kayum would teach them how to live in the forest. Juan wanted to learn. Kayum agreed.

The fire that raged in the hills illuminated the square. It was so bright that the Tzeltal Indians were shading their eyes. The celebrants lurched and stumbled in the eerie light.

One of the lurchers took on the form of Barnes.

"Would you like us to ride with you tomorrow?" Barnes asked.

"We won't be leaving for a few days. I'll spend a day or so here re-supplying and well, trying to help out."

"I can smell the hint, old buddy. So be it. I'll leave you to your windmills and fairytale temples waiting to be discovered. As for me, I'll settle for a government pension."

"It is as you say, Barnes. God only knows there are no windmills in Chiapas."

They joined Rogelio and Lazaro in the camp upriver away from the burning hills. While preparing supper with Koh, Erika could not help thinking of Barnes and his companions. After taking the evening meal, she confessed her suspicions to Claus while he read through his notes.

"I think he's following us," Erika said.

Claus laughed and waved at his notes. He said there was a time when Barnes might have said they were following him. "Barnes saved our lives just now."

"Why do you think he saved our lives? Not because of any great love for you. He hates you, Claus. But he thinks the Lacandons are leading us to Menche and he'd give his eyetooth to be in on the discovery."

Claus stuffed his notebook into his knapsack.

"Suppose that everything you say is true," Claus shrugged. "Does it really matter if Barnes and his team follow us into the grand plaza of Menche?"

Erika was exasperated. It amazed her that Claus had maintained the innocence of a child right through middle age. She was convinced that Barnes was obsessed with his hatred for him. Couldn't Claus see it? "Just suppose they *are* following us and we *do* find Menche, and I'm sure we will. Claus, they could kill us as we walk across that grand plaza you're talking about. You're the one who told me that no corpse remains long in the forest, that flesh and bones and all are picked clean by jaguars, vultures, marching ants and everything else. We wouldn't be the first expedition reported lost in the jungle, would we?"

Claus wore an indulgent if weary smile on his face as he sipped his foaming chocolate. "Erika, it's a dramatic scenario but absolutely unreal. Yes, Barnes has an old grudge against me. I had him canned at Tulane. He sold artifacts to private collectors before we had a chance to even label them. But the man is not a murderer."

The word sent a shudder straight through to Erika's spleen.

"Claus, *I'm* a murderer."

"Erika, they were going to kill Koh."

"Maybe they wouldn't have."

"There was little doubt. You had to make a quick decision."

"Living in the jungle is an awful responsibility."

"It's the responsibility of being alive."

Chapter Thirty-Five

That night Kayum produced an incense burner from his net bag and said he would burn copal to thank Akinchob for saving Koh's life.

Claus and Erika watched him grind a chunk of copal and place the shavings in the portable god carrier. Kayum poked a stick in the fire to catch a flame. Before he dipped it into the incense burner, he changed the position of the pot so the face peered into the jungle.

"Why did you turn the face away from the fire," Claus asked.

"When you worship a god, his head must always face the same direction."

"Why is that so?"

Kayum shrugged. "My father always told me."

"But why?"

Kayum looked perplexed. "Pancho Balam, I never understand you when you talk about why. Lacandons only try to find the proper places for things in order to fulfill the will of the gods."

Claus gave a sigh of disappointment. "There's a clue in this, but I don't know what it is." He shook his head in frustration.

Erika interjected excitedly. "During the ceremony I attended in Jatate, all the pots were facing the same direction."

Claus turned to her quickly. "Do you remember what direction that was?"

"Let me think, the sun was setting behind us, they faced east. Not quite. I'd say northeast."

"And this fellow is facing southeast." Claus slapped his sides.

"Kayum, if the head must always face the same direction, why is it different here than in Jatate?"

"There you go with the why again. I only know that my father told me that when we are in parts of the jungle north of Puna, the head of the incense burner must be set so."

Claus clapped his hands. "Of course." He turned to Erika. It was possible that the old tradition, now forgotten, dictated that the images of the gods on the censers must face Menche on all ceremonial occasions. They faced northeast in Jatate, southeast here. By using a crude geometry, Claus concluded that the direc-

170

tional planes would meet somewhere east of the town of El Cedro. It was a confirmation of his hunch and fit in with what Bolon Kin told them. "What do you think, Kayum? Is it possible that the incense burners must always face the home of the gods?"

Kayum looked at Claus with amazement. They all looked at the head on the censer.

"Akinchob has revealed something to you that was not revealed to my father," Kayum said. "Maybe he is pleased with you when you ask the question why."

"Is there anything else you remember that your father told you?" Claus looked at Kayum, searching his eyes for one last clue.

Kayum rubbed his head and closed his eyes. "When I was born, Menche was already lost." He looked up suddenly and raised a finger.

"When I was very small, my father told me of his journey to Menche as a boy with his father. I don't remember him saying anything that would tell me where it is. But I had a dream in Jatate during the time my father wasn't speaking to me. It is the same dream I had as a child. In my dream, I see my father making his journey to Menche. He is with his father and they are taking a trail up a hill. Instead of jungle on either side, there are high rocks. My father comes to the top of the hill and one of the rocks becomes a jaguar. My father and his father follow the jaguar. Then I wake up. But I never asked my father the meaning of the dream."

Claus embraced Kayum and shook with joyous laughter.

"Thank you, Kayum! At last, a landmark! Erika, there's a rocky base along an old lumber trail about a two day hike from El Cedro and this side of the Usumacinta River. At the top of the pass is a huge boulder. From one angle it looks like a jaguar head in profile. The trail was used by loggers at the turn of the century. The forest beyond the pass was cut down and abandoned over thirty years ago. The jungle grew back."

Erika wanted to know how Kayum would know about the pass.

"Kayum is remembering something his father had told him as a child. Fact and dream mix in Lacandon reality," Claus said to her.

Erika's mind raced, leaping from one thought to the next. The search for Menche was like a big crossword puzzle and she was beginning to find the words that fit in the spaces. "Claus, isn't it the prophecy of Bolon Kin that the Kah would cut off the head of Hachakyum? He said there was a stone statue of the god in Menche."

Claus looked up quickly. "That's marvelous, Erika. The prophecy of the head may symbolize the rape of the forest or it may tell of an actual event."

"Or both. And it explains the decapitation of Mateo. What does Menche mean?"

Claus looked surprised by the question. "Menche? I don't know. Kayum, what does Menche mean?"

"The full name of Hachakyum's home is Menche Tinamet. It means the City of the Young Forest."

Erika felt she was holding the key word in her hand but she couldn't find the place to put it in the puzzle.

"Why was Menche lost?" she asked, as if the very question would pull everything in place.

Neither Kayum nor Claus said anything. They all looked at the head of Akinchob that gazed at them from the side of the god pot. His expression served notice that he wasn't going to answer Erika's question.

Chapter Thirty-Six

On the morning of the explorers' departure from El Capulin, Juan, his father and one of his sisters came to their camp with fresh mules and supplies. Claus decided to leave the horse with them as they didn't have one and he didn't think the animal could withstand the rigors of the trail ahead. Besides, the children had taken to the horse and the horse had taken to them. The *presidenté* thanked Claus and Erika for the help they had given the people of his village. Then Juan presented Kayum with a new .22 caliber rifle.

Kayum drew back. "My friend, I cannot accept your gift. It is a law of the Lacandons. I have nothing to give you in return."

Juan pressed the rifle into Kayum's hands. "You can offer me the fairest gift of all." Juan turned to face the beautiful Koh who was having her hair braided and *toucan* feathers placed in it by his sister. With a quaver in his voice, Juan went on. "Kayum, I would like to keep your sister here to be my bride. Tell me where I can find the home of your father that I may bring *aguardiente* and do my bride service."

Koh, who was arranging the feathers in her hair and using a pot in which beans soaked as a mirror, looked up when Juan spoke but showed no expression on her face.

"My father lives far away over many rivers and mountains," Kayum said. "He is an old man and will leave us soon to take the trail to the stars."

"To whom can I give the rum and the firewood?" Juan asked.

Kayum was silent awhile and then shrugged. "Lacandons do not drink rum. I will accept the ceremonial firewood and give you my sister as your bride."

Koh came away from the pot of beans and looked angrily at her brother.

"Kayum, what are you saying? You can't just give me away like that. It is against the true customs of the Hach Winik and you know it. A bride of the Kah? Me, living in this filthy place with people who live mashed together and do not worship the true gods? You take to foreign ways too quickly. A girl of the Hach Winik is not to be given away like an ear of corn. You forget your heritage and your obligation to your sister. Do you loathe me so much, my brother, that you treat me this way? Is that how you obey the gods?"

Kayum gave her a look of exasperation. "Koh, our living together as we do is against the will of the gods."

"One sin doesn't justify another. I won't be sold into slavery. And for a few sticks of wood! Why, this stumbler won't even have to do bride service to my father."

Kayum banged his fist against a palm tree and kicked a stone. "Koh, will you listen? I'm not selling you into slavery. Is Juan not handsome? He is the son of the *presidenté*."

"I have a big cornfield and money to buy you a dress so we can be married in the church of Saint Thomas," Juan said smiling.

Kayum shrugged and waved his hands impatiently. "Go with him, Koh. Make tortillas for him and I will pray to our gods for you."

Koh glowered at her brother. "So, am I then to pray to the gods of Jesus Christ and live in crowds for the rest of my days? I, the daughter of Bolon Kin?" Koh pulled the feathers out of her hair and threw them down. Juan's sister drew back in fright.

Juan spoke. "I also hate crowds. We will build our house in the jungle away from the village and I will come to El Capulin only to pray to the saints and buy salt. I will walk with you in the forest and climb the tall trees to pick brightly colored flowers for you. I will bring you cloth from San Cristobal so you can make clothes for the saints and your family. I will make you happy in the night and we will have children who will worship your gods and mine."

"And am I to do all of this and cook with no other wife to help me?" Koh snapped.

Juan looked perplexed but then a flash of understanding crossed his face. "My father will give us a cooking machine that works with the power of Saint Thomas which it takes out of running water. It was given him by a priest who told him it could do the work of two wives."

Kayum looked severely at his sister. "Koh, it is the only hope for us. Juan comes as a sign from the gods."

Koh looked at him as if he had committed blasphemy. "A sign from the gods? How can I make clothes for Saint Thomas and serve our gods? The Kah pray to Saint Thomas to bring the rain. What will Metzabok do to me if I serve Saint Thomas?"

A triumphant smile came over Kayum. "Koh, it was Metzabok who took a foreigner for a bride. The time has come for a princess of the Hach Winik to take a foreigner for a husband. I have taught Juan the true ways of the forest. You can raise his children to respect the forest and the true people. Bolon Kin forbids us to kill the Kah unless they desecrate the shrines of the gods. So we must learn to live with them. This is also taught by Pancho Balam and Doña Erika."

Koh stared at the ground and brooded for such a long time that Erika thought everybody would collapse from the tension. Finally, Koh looked up at Juan and smiled weakly.

Then she turned to Erika. "Doña Erika, advise me, you know I love my brother. What shall I do?"

Erika knew she had to be careful with her answer. "You love your brother and that is good. But look at young Juan. Is he not handsome and noble? In time, you will love him as you loved Kayum. No, you will love him in another way. We never love in the same way twice."

Koh went quietly over to where Juan and his father and sister were standing. Juan broke into a big smile. His father put his arms around his children and Koh. Then Juan's father told Claus he would send two Tzeltales to help break the trail until the expedition reached the El Cedro trail. The half-blind man led his children and Koh to the river where a canoe waited to take them to the village. Suddenly, Koh broke away from them and ran to the arms of Kayum. She buried her head in his chest and shook fitfully with her sobs.

"Koh, please, go from me. I suffer with my love for you," Kayum said, his own eyes filling with tears.

"Will you come back?"

"No. Our dream spirits will meet in the forest at such times as Okna permits. Go now, and be happy with Juan."

Erika watched Juan and his father pole away from the shore. Koh sat in the middle of the canoe with Juan's sister. Snow-white hawks sailed above their heads. Koh looked up at them.

PART V

MENCHE

Chapter Thirty-Seven

After a few days the rains came back. It was November now. They traveled through wet marshy places. A week passed and they still had not come upon the El Cedro trail.

Then the Tzeltales announced that it was time for them to return to their milpas as the harvest season was coming in the next moon when the rains ended. Claus gave them provisions for the trip back. It was just as well that they left when they did. Game had become scarce and they were going to have to ration their food again. Besides, the Tzeltales did not know the trails beyond El Cedro.

After another five days of pushing through *chicle* tangle, the explorers discovered that one of the pack mules was lost in the fog and bush. All their medical supplies, save for a little quinine, had gone on the back of the animal. The remaining mules were in a near state of exhaustion.

Erika drew strength from Claus's dogged determination. Despite the stoicism still shining in their eyes, Erika could see that Lazaro and Rogelio were exhausted too. Even Kayum, who slipped on fallen roots for the first time since Erika had known him, showed signs of weariness.

Then they came upon the El Cedro trail. The spirits of the muleteers picked up immediately. El Cedro was close, only two days away if they stayed on the trail. Savage as it was, it was a piece of civilization with stores, beds, bars, and women.

Claus called the team to a halt.

"This is the crossroads," he said, consulting his maps and peering at some broken branches that made a niche in the forest to his left. "I'm sure this is the old lumber trail I told you about. It looks like we'll have to cut it all over again. We don't have the Tzeltales. I can see you're all tired. Rogelio, how are our provisions?"

"We have enough for two weeks, if we are careful and we find game," Rogelio said.

"We should be back here in less than that if all goes well. But I have to be honest with you. I don't know what to expect in there. And there may be no golden egg after all. El Cedro is just down this trail. We could be there tomorrow. I know you'd all like a vacation. I leave it up to you."

Lazaro spoke at once. "I have agreed to follow you wherever you lead us until the expedition is finished. The expedition is finished when we find the city of the gods."

"Let us pack the mules," Rogelio said.

But on the second day of breaking the lumber trail, Kayum cut himself using his machete, making a deep gash in his thigh. The blood streamed down his leg. Claus was able to apply a bark solution and bandage him with bark strips fastened by vines but the treatment was clearly inadequate. They thought of the mule who had carried off the medical supplies. It would be almost impossible to avoid a fatal infection. It was the reason Lacandons almost never cut themselves. "I have forgotten how to be a Hach Winik," Kayum said miserably.

"He'll need medical attention that's only available in El Cedro," Claus said. "We'll just have to turn back, that's all."

Erika's heart sank. "We're so close to our goal. You're right, Claus, we can't go on with Kayum like this." Somehow she felt that once they were in El Cedro, the momentum needed to come back would be gone.

"Erika, I'm not sure there is a goal anymore. It seems to me I would have seen some traces by now. If we were approaching a big center, we would have found some house mounds near here. Most Mayan populations didn't live in the ceremonial sites. They spread out in the countryside. There's no evidence of anything. And you're tired too. I've been selfish in insisting that we press on, time after time. The Lacandons may be passing on stories of a place that crumbled away from the face of the earth centuries ago." Claus sat down wearily on a fallen log.

"I don't think Bolon Kin imagined it all," Erika insisted. "Claus, why don't we send Lazaro and Rogelio with Kayum to El Cedro? They can get him to a doctor and come back with fresh mules. You and I can continue on foot."

"Erika! I can't permit you to do anything like that!"

"Claus, I want to continue as much as you do. I have no desire to drink in saloons or dance with wild, unknown men. I'm happy right here in the jungle."

Claus gave a sigh of exasperation which thinly veiled his pleasure. "Erika, if the Lacandons can show their gods to you, how can I resist you?"

Claus told Lazaro and Rogelio that he would leave notes in the trees whenever he and Erika took a new trail or broke camp.

So, with huge, bulging packs on their backs, from which dangled pots, pans, canteens, as well as a pick and shovel, Erika and Claus took to the trail on foot.

On their first day alone together, Erika was overwhelmed by the solitude and beauty around them. They passed through banks of coral-colored mushrooms. They saw miniature flower cities of orange frosted lace.

The rains came hard that night. The storm screamed through the night like a nursery of bad-tempered children. "We should be entering a dry season," Claus said, "But when the northeasters come up, as seems to be the case, everything changes."

When Erika tried to joke with Claus about the clamorous rain in the morning, she found him strangely uncommunicative. He made the fire listlessly and replied to her comments with nods and grunts. She got few responses from him during morning coffee and he took little to eat.

Washing the enamel pot in the stream, Erika pondered Claus's silence. He had been talkative for days ever since he had sensed they were approaching their goal. Was he unhappy about being alone with her? It was the first time they'd been unchaperoned in the jungle since the time in Bolon Kin's guest hut. Did he think that she would seize the first opportunity to tempt him now that the others were not continually about? Did he feel more vulnerable?

In a real sense, they were closer to one another now than they had been at any other time on the trip. She had gained his full confidence as a field worker. She understood the needs of the expedition. And she understood him. She'd come to know his thoughts in advance, when he was about to pick up his notebook, scratch his chin, frown, grin, spit. She breathed him in and out like the air. Perhaps that was precisely why he withdrew from her now.

Erika burned with shame and hurt. Couldn't he see that she had been careful not to entice him? She always wrapped her rubber sheet carefully around her body when coming from her bath. She wore her woolen shirt over her blouse whenever it got soaked with sweat and clung to her breasts. And, of course, her blouse always got wet when the heat was unbearable. She had been careful not to come to his lean-to at night for any reason. Indeed, her very efforts to keep a physical distance from him were her only way of showing him that she loved him. And, she did, hopelessly, happily. It wasn't going to be easy to shake hands back in Ocosingo and go their separate ways.

Coming back from the stream with the pot, Erika attempted a few casual questions about the history of the lumbermen in the region. All of Claus's answers were short. He simply didn't want to talk to her.

Claus stared at his notes. Erika went to the *lavia* they had dug together. She squatted over the hole. At least her period wasn't coming on. And she surely didn't have to worry about missing one. Well, he was tired of her at last, that's all there was to it. Now that they were alone together, he was forced to see her as a woman again. And he didn't want her. Her trickle seemed to talk back to her. *The old girl is sticking like chicle sap is what he's thinking.*

Maybe she was imagining it all. But she couldn't go on in silence. She resolved to speak to Claus about it.

When she returned to camp, she was surprised to see that Claus had returned to his hammock and had curled himself up into a ball.

With grim resolve, her heart fluttering, Erika approached the huddled figure.

"Claus, please, tell me," she struggled to control the quavering in her voice. "What is the matter?"

He turned to look up at her as if from the bottom of a deep pit.

"I think I have a fever," he said.

Well, Erika said to herself, *there might be a place in the jungle for the daughter of a Swiss doctor after all.* Erika breathed a deep sigh of relief until her anxiety over his health caught up to her. She wrapped Claus in blankets and gave him some of the quinine they had saved. But after sleeping for an hour, Claus insisted on taking to the trail again.

"This is not a good place to wait for the others," he said. "The ground is uneven and when the rains come again, the shelter will collapse. I remember an abandoned lumber camp about six miles away, it's the only sign of civilization between here and the Peten. There's a good chance it's still there. It will bring us closer to our destination if we have one, and it will be a better place to rest until our friends come back."

"Claus, I don't think you have the strength for such a trip."

"Yes I do. It's the only way."

Erika carried her pack, the frying pan, shovel, her machete, sleeping bag, and hammock. But Claus carried a heavier pack with all the blankets, his heavy rubber poncho, notebooks, clothes, camera, and most of their provisions, plus the pick and his machete.

"Claus, I think we should exchange packs."

"Nonsense, I feel much stronger."

The rains came roaring down, slapping hard against the bark of the big trees and making a racket against the leafy tops above them. Claus stumbled constantly, his pack sliding from side to side on his back, causing him to lose his balance several times. Erika could see that, step by step, his strength was being sapped in his struggle against the suction of the mud. He had to sit on every fallen log.

"How far is this camp from here by a normal walk?" Erika asked.

"About two hours," he said weakly.

"Claus, I hate to break the news to you but the age of chivalry is over. It's obvious you can't continue especially with that heavy load," she put her own load down. "Let me carry your pack until we get to an advanced point, at least a place where you can rest in your hammock. Then I'll return for mine. Even allowing for portage, we should arrive in the camp before dark."

Erika shouldered Claus's heavier pack, and he used the stock of his shotgun for a walking stick. They stumbled over roots and struggled against sucking mud. After an hour or so, they found a level clearing. Erika hung up Claus's hammock. When he climbed into it, she covered him with blankets and the rubber poncho. Then she started back for her pack. Rain continued to pound like cannon on the treetops. It seemed like an agonizingly long time before she came upon her rain-soaked load.

As she started back up the trail again, the forest was darkening around her. The rain, mud and fallen trees made her lose sight of the trail. Night dropped over her in the sudden way it does in the tropics.

Cutting open the cords of her pack, Erika pulled out a flashlight that had managed to stay dry. The light illuminated the shining pellets of rain that fell in front of her. Some rain, dripping off big leaves, fell in streams. Claus had warned her that another trail veered off the lumber trail at some point, but she didn't remember passing it. She had to admit she wasn't sure which trail she was on or whether she was on a trail at all. Then she recognized one of the signs they'd left for Lazaro and Rogelio speared to a branch.

The trail was familiar again. But when she came to the place where she thought she'd left Claus, he wasn't there. She shouted his name. Her voice could not compete with the general clamor of the rain. Where was he? The explanation stood before her like an insurmountable tree fallen on the trail. She had taken a wrong turn. She fumbled in the dark, growing more and more convinced that she had lost Claus. She shouted his name over and over. But the incessant roar of the forest rooftop drowned out her cries.

There was a flash of lightning and in the brief millisecond of light, Erika saw the outline of a jaguar perched on a branch above her head. But the lightning struck a nearby tree and Erika and cat went scampering in opposite directions. She fell on thorns as vicious and merciless as a jaguar's claws. Thorns scratched her in many places, including her face. Only her fear for Claus's survival prevented her from succumbing to her terror and exhaustion. It seemed like she had been wandering for hours. Time itself was as dense and impassable as the forest.

Indeed, Erika lost all sense of time and space as she stumbled on, uselessly calling Claus's name, straining her voice, and finally succumbing to sobs.

Then around a bend, she saw a huddled figure in a hammock. Erika's heart lifted as she rushed to Claus, telling him breathlessly of her adventures. His voice was very weak but he managed to say he was glad she was all right. Erika looked for a nearby stream, but there was none. Then she noticed that water had formed in little pools on the big leaves of trees. She poured the water from the leaves into a cup and made Claus drink it with quinine. Then she got into the hammock with him and pulled the rubber cape over them. Rain fell relentlessly as Erika clung to Claus's body that burned with malaria.

Claus woke up in the morning, still burning with fever.

"I can't go any farther. Go back to the shelter," Claus said.

"Claus, that makes no sense. The lumber camp you spoke of can't be far off."

"I should not have let you take us this far. If you go back, you'll meet the others sooner. Otherwise, they'll never find us. I'll just rest here."

"You can't rest here. The jaguar I told you about should not be far away. We can't keep a fire going all night in this rain. If our fire goes out, he'll be encouraged to attack us. We must find the camp. I'll leave notes on the trees for Rogelio and Lazaro."

"This rain will wash them away."

"It hasn't so far. I saw our notes on my way back. Claus, it's our only hope."

The rains came again as they pressed forward, Claus leaning on his shotgun stock and Erika carrying his heavy pack which contained all they had not abandoned.

Chapter Thirty-Eight

The camp was a refuge against the fury of the wilderness. The plank shelter was built on firm, flat ground and the well-thatched roof was protection from the rain. A small stream gurgled a stone's throw away. Claus was laid up for days while Erika nursed him back to health.

Mercifully, the rains abated. Sitting with Claus, washing in the stream, cooking, Erika found the rhythms of her days merging with the patterns of life in La Selva Lacandona. She felt attuned to the cycle of rain, rotting leaves, fallen trees and the flora that sprang from them. She admired more than ever, the muscular roots that gripped the sides of the forest giants.

She rocked peacefully in the intricately netted hammock of the big jungle. She was a part of it now and she belonged to it as much as it belonged to her.

As the days succeeded one another, she understood why the ancient Mayans conceived of days as good and evil. She was glad the good days prevailed now. Meanwhile, Claus, the stricken jaguar, slipped in and out of his illness. He taught Erika to fish with lianas tied to hooks which they'd found in his pack.

Sometimes Claus raved in the night and threshed about in his hammock like an animal strangling in the undergrowth of the *chicle* trails. At other times, his health seemed to rise as if mahogany roots had attached themselves to his sides and pumped strength into his emaciated frame.

One morning, Erika woke to a ghastly stench that permeated the moist air.

"What is that disagreeable odor, Claus?" It was vaguely familiar.

"Don't mind the smell. It's breakfast."

A herd of wild pigs appeared on the trail ahead.

"The peccaries," Erika said.

"A delicacy for the Lacandons," Claus said. "They have large musk glands on their backs and emit a stinky white substance when they're frightened. Move quickly and quietly to your shotgun."

She heard them crashing through the bush and caught sight of a flurry of pigness streaking across the trail. But her ammunition was wet and the rifle almost exploded in her hand.

Claus was amazingly lucid between bouts of fever. At those times, he was the best company Erika had ever enjoyed. They shared memories of childhoods in Switzerland and Denmark.

Then one morning, thinking him still in the grip of fever, Erika returned from her bath in the nearby stream with her shirt carelessly unbuttoned and her rubber sheet rolled under her arm. She was surprised to see Claus sitting outside the hut, wrapped in blankets and gazing at her. She took to the cover of a breadnut tree. Her underpants and blouse hung on a branch above her. Erika burned with shame. She should have known he'd be outside watching.

"Claus, I'm sorry. I've been careful. Don't you think I've been careful?" She waited while they both listened to a woodpecker hammer on an upper branch.

"I've got a confession to make," she heard Claus say. "I've been watching you come back and forth from your bath the past few mornings from inside the hut. The sight of your gorgeous figure running in and out of the stream is the best medicine I've had during this whole thing. But I'm quite incapable of any molestation. The brute in me is much too infirm."

Erika had thrown on her blouse and utilized the sheet as a wraparound skirt. She stepped away from the breadnut tree in full view of him before she realized her blouse had not dried and the nipples of her breasts could be clearly surmised from its clinging wetness.

"Just pay me no mind," he said, his eyes merry on her now. There was no question that he was gazing at the shapes. She was suddenly shy and wanted to run back behind the tree. But she didn't move.

"Claus, what's come over you. I mean—the rules and everything?"

"I think the statue of limitations has finally run out, don't you?"

Her heart leapt. He wanted her at last, truly wanted her. But a dull foreboding held her in check. Was it just craven desire, an aspect of his sickness? Maybe he was delirious. On the other hand, people slipped in and out of malaria and in the interludes of health, their sensations became vivid.

She wanted to run into his arms but she stayed near the tree. "Claus, I want to come to you but I won't if you think that touching me is doing something nasty. All you know about me is that I showed up on a cow field in Ocosingo looking like a boudoir flower. Do you think I'm a slut? I won't come to you if that's the way you see me. Tell me the truth."

"Erika, I'm insulted. Do you think I have that kind of mind?" His jaw dropped and his face turned red, even in his fever. "A slut wouldn't have stayed with me in this jungle as long as you have. You're a magnificent woman, Erika.

Your being with me through all this is the miracle. You needn't stand half-naked in front of me if I've embarrassed you. I'll look away while you get your clothes."

Erika unfastened the buttons of her blouse and let the sheet drop to the ground. Claus broke into a smile. She was thrilled that he took a delight in her body. She had to admit now that it was what she had wanted from the time she had first seen him climbing out of the plane in Ocosingo.

She knelt next to the sitting man and looked up into his smiling eyes.

"Claus, I can't believe it. What's come over you?"

He took her hand in his. "I just want to tell you how lovely you are," he said.

Erika felt a shockwave cross her heart. "I haven't felt like this for the longest time—. Claus, you make me feel like a schoolgirl with a crush. My goodness, I'm about to become forty."

"I'm almost fifty. From my point of view, you're a nymph. Your body is as delightful to behold as any young girl's. You move like a doe. It's as if you were raised here in the jungle with the Lacandon women."

Erika smiled. She knew it was the supreme compliment. "Have you ever been with one of them?"

"No. My rules, not theirs. The women of Lacanja will give themselves to any man who interests them. In any case, you would be the queen of my harem."

Smiling, Erika leaned her head on his shoulder. But he gently pushed her away.

"Don't come any closer," he said. "I don't want to reward you with sickness." The smile was still in his eyes and Erika thought she would never tire of marveling at their blueness. "You stayed, Erika. You stayed with me and the jungle. That's the wonder. I can't tell you how much that has meant to me. Just sharing so much with you for all these months has given me an extra set of eyes. To tell the truth, I was a one-eyed man before. Now thanks to you, I see in full dimensions."

"It's your fever speaking," she said, feeling the blush on her skin. But joy was spreading across her chest.

"Erika, for your sake, don't come any closer."

She slipped the blanket from his shoulder, kissed it, and ran her hand along his bare back. She rested her head on his shoulder. Her breasts pressed against his arm. "The night we slept on the open trail, I slept with my body on top of yours. But you never knew it."

"I knew it."

They gazed into each other's eyes. Erika knew that Claus wanted to kiss her. She waited for it. They listened to one another's uneven breathing.

"Erika, we mustn't. I don't want to make you sick."

"Claus, malaria isn't contagious. You know that."

He nodded gravely. "I have a cold with it. I don't want to give you pneumonia. It would be fatal out here in the jungle."

Erika shuddered and pressed her cheek hard against his arm. "Claus, I don't want you to have it then. Hold me. I'd rather die of it than you."

They embraced one another and Claus's blanket slid below his waist. Erika felt the gravity of desire drawing them together with its imperial force. It was stronger than anything she'd ever known for it was powered by love. Claus brushed back her hair and kissed the moist crook of her neck.

"You'd better dress before I ravish you," he said.

"Ravish me, Claus."

"Erika, please go away. It's dangerous."

"Claus, we live dangerously everyday." She turned aside suddenly and pulled on a creeper pressed under her leg. "All right. I'm glad you kissed me anyway."

"You know I want you," Claus said. "Besides, something has just happened to me that's the final proof of your charms. Since you're my nurse, I must tell you that the brute in me is alive, and well, standing up!"

Yes, it was compliment enough. Erika decided to seize the moment and the brute.

"As your nurse, I must examine you." She peeled the blankets from him altogether as he lay on his side and replaced them with her warm body.

"Erika don't—that's so marvelous!"

"Your nurse has decided from a purely medical point of view that you can make love to her without kissing her on the mouth."

His skin burned but his organ rose against her thighs like a proud mushroom of the forest. She traced its taut, rigid shape gently with her fingertips, then she lay back smiling up at him as he moved his hand easily over the smooth curve of her belly.

She looked past his head to the gold-speckled morning foliage above them. His fingers explored her pubic mesh.

"I've never known a woman to be so soft," he said, bending over her and lightly kissing her breasts.

"We are softer than young girls. It's part of the body's decay."

"Then *viva la decadencia!*"

Her heart surged with passion as the proud red bulb of his love swayed above her. It was the orchid he had given her in the El Zapote rain ready to be set into the vase of her love. Yes, the orchid was the gift of himself. She knew that if he gave it to her now, he would never take it away. Erika felt a tingle across her abdomen and thighs, like bandages being swept away. She trembled with readiness.

He lowered his body and she opened her legs. The sides of her passage dripped with wanting and stretched to accommodate him. Claus moved inside her in accelerating thrusts. He drove her with such force that she felt there was a god in him. He took possession of her and was possessed by her encompassing flesh. Claus moved quicker as he lunged across her clitoris making her feel him intensely. Her inner muscles pulled him deeper inside her.

Erika wanted Claus in every part of her body. She shot her tongue into his ear and threw her legs over him so that her heels dug into his calves. Meanwhile, the bulging head of the flesh-flower slid deeper into the cave of her passion. Her slick, wet sides pulsated, pinching the head in spasms.

She looked up at the trees while Claus buried his face in her armpit, sucking the sensitive places. The morning light shone as a canopy of royal gold above them. Claus stroked her in tandem with the moaning trees and bubbling arroyo. The jungle was without and within. They rose and fell in its vibrations. It was as if they were being borne home at last to a paradise they had wandered from through lost ages. It was all strange and familiar, dense and ever so light. She was again a woman loving the world—oh, this agonizing thrill of flesh—and suddenly the lovely world tumbled in thunderous quakes and the god in Claus released all of his awesome power into her, hurling bolts of liquid fire until she lay shattered, waiting for the god to collect her scattered pieces and put her back together again.

Erika lay next to Claus under the soft white light that filtered down from the canopy above. With his arms around her, Claus slipped into sleep.

Chapter Thirty-Nine

On the following day, Claus was able to hobble to the stream where Erika washed him with soap and then dried him off. She was now at ease with all parts of his body. After bathing, Claus pointed out exotic flowers and discovered herbs from which they made tea.

"The Lacandons make a tea with herbs they say are inhabited by Kak. In addition to curing sickness, he brings courage."

"You have all you need of that commodity." She reached down and tickled his drooping penis.

Walking along the stream with Claus at her side, Erika's senses were never so keenly attuned to the world around her. It seemed her long stay in the jungle had developed new receptors in her nervous system. She heard sounds she'd never heard before and saw colors that never appeared on the color wheels she studied in school. The world teamed with life. There were no vacuums in the jungle and she lost the sense of herself as a separate entity. She was part of the roots she walked on, the water that dripped on her nose, and the vines that brushed her head. She was the leaf cutting ant and the leaf, the rotting mold and the ferns. And all of it was Claus.

She and Claus sat in silence beside the stream, listening to the sounds of the jungle and to one another's breathing. It seemed that they were sitting on a log in eternity. Maybe the cycles of nature and her daily routines with Claus suggested the theme of returning time to her. She wondered how a Lacandon woman felt, grinding the same corn in the same way in the same place as it had been done by her ancestors for three thousand years. Maybe the woman didn't know about the three thousand years but surely she felt time in her blood. Whenever she asked Claus about Mayan time, Erika found the concept hard to grasp. He spoke of interlocking wheels. It was all very abstract but she was beginning to feel it in her blood.

Erika looked up at some green leaves that sprouted from the side of a zapote tree. Suddenly, her sense of European time came back with a rush. A wheel locked in gear.

"Those leaves are like holly. Claus, I just thought of something. How many days has it been since Lazaro and Rogelio and Kayum left us?"

"Oh, I'm sure they'll be back."

"I agree with you, but that's not why I asked about the date."

"Well, now let's figure it out. They left us the day before I became ill. Hmm. I would say eleven days."

"That's what I count. And they left us on December 13th. In that case, do you realize what day it is?"

"I can't see what you're driving at."

"Claus, have you completely forgotten your upbringing? After all, you were taught to count by the Christian calendar when you were a little boy."

"The Christian calendar?"

"Of course. It's Christmas Eve, silly."

Claus hit his hand against his forehead and laughed. "So it is. Well, now, look around you. We have all the Christmas decorations we need."

"And in just the right colors."

"Look at those lacy fan leaves hanging from the cedar trees. And you see the lianas hanging from the branches like icicles. You can choose any tree you wish for our Christmas tree."

"Claus, look, way up on that mahogany tree. A red orchid."

"I'll climb up and pluck it for you in the morning."

"You can leave it where it is. It's as Christmasy as any poinsettia."

Coral-colored mushrooms and dark green plants added to the holiday scene. Erika plucked some oval fruit from the sapodilla tree. It was a fruit that attracted the peccaries.

"Maybe it will attract some pigs so we can have a Christmas dinner of roast pork," Claus said.

Erika knew he was dreaming. What ammunition they had left was soaked. They settled for a Christmas Eve supper of rice and beans, sugar and watery coffee.

"Merry Christmas," Claus said raising his coffee cup. Erika flew into his arms.

"Merry Christmas, Claus."

"Erika, I still have fever."

"Only Kak brings fever, and he and I are on the best of terms. Give me a Christmas kiss."

Chapter Forty

During the night, Erika woke with a sense of foreboding. The fire outside the hut had gone out and she heard a rustling in the bush just beyond their clearing. There was a swoosh and suddenly, she saw a big cat drop out of the dark trees into the grey moonlit clearing where a feeble wisp of smoke presided over a dying fire. The jaguar was at least five feet long and she knew it could stretch to almost twice its size like any house cat. The beast raised its head high in the air. Erika could see the quivering nostrils and the imperial tail which swatted at an elephant ear plant. The cat made a sound that was between a screech and a growl. Erika could not help but think how graceful and muscular the beast was. She watched in awe.

The jaguar was only thirty feet away when it began a slow, deliberate circle around the hut. Erika could hear its nervous snarls on the other side. She wondered if she would have a chance to run out and relight the fire but realized that any movement on her part could be as fatal as that of the cornered mouse who darts out of his hole into the path of a cat. She tried to waken Claus, but he had slipped into delirium.

The jaguar came round again to the collapsed fire. It stopped, raised its head to sniff the heavily scented air and gave vent to a sound that began with a snarl and ended in a high pitched yowl.

Trembling, Erika reached for a machete. It was the only weapon they had but she knew the speed of her arm was no match for the lethal quickness of a jaguar's strike.

She wanted desperately to waken Claus but she feared that if she yelled, her voice would incite the beast to leap into the hut.

Slowly, imperturbably, the jaguar stalked the hut. Then it approached the doorway and sniffed, raising its head. Erika found herself screaming, To her surprise, the scream caused the cat to walk away from the doorway and resume its circle but the snarls grew heavier.

Claus woke up. Sensing the danger, he shook himself out of his delirium.

"Keep screaming and don't move," he said in a loud voice.

The beast screeched in response on the other side of the tent. Erika was so frightened she could not emit any sounds.

"Bang the pot with the head of the machete. I'll flap this rubber sheet. It's our only chance. They don't like noise and the flapping will confuse him."

The cat continued its slow circumambulation of the hut. Each time it came into view, Erika and Claus screamed at the top of their lungs, banging the pots and flapping the sheet. The beast sniffed and snarled savagely, came to the entrance of the hut and began to lower itself on its belly, thwacking its tail, as if it had finally summoned all its nerve to make its attack. But the continued flapping and beating on the pots kept the animal at bay. Erika remembered a tabby in her Swiss girlhood who had sat all day by a mouse hole without stirring, waiting patiently for the mouse to come out. So this huge spotted cat, larger than a leopard, sat on its haunches and stared at the entrance to the hut, blinking its eyes while Erika and Claus shouted themselves hoarse and beat on the pans.

Eventually, Claus succumbed to his exhaustion. Erika found herself drifting off into sleep for seconds, forcing herself to snap back into wakefulness. Her voice was gone, but her aching arms flapped the rubber sheet at the yellow stare of the cat. If only she could make some coffee—but there was the cat resting comfortably next to the dead fire, and thwacking its tail against a sack of coffee beans. The jaguar yawned in her face. Erika found herself yawning in response and, with the gaze of the spotted beast still on her, she drifted off into sleep.

Erika woke to see the white fog heavy outside the hut. She was surprised to find herself alive. Claus slept next to her. She waited a few minutes, peering through the rising mist, and then realized that the cat was gone.

"Claus, wake up. The cat, the jaguar—it's gone. What do you suppose happened?"

Claus rubbed his eyes. "I don't know. I suppose he got bored. But look, the fire—the fire is going. It must have started again in the night."

"And so he went away. Maybe he was just a great big Christmas pussy."

"Luckily for us."

Erika's spirits rose with the first grey light. The bluish smoke from their fire mixed with the fog as in some ritual reconciling nature and the works of man. Wrapped in blankets and drinking coffee, they watched the fog lift.

Chapter Forty-One

Light trickled down the trees in hues of white and rose. Gem-like spiders glittered across the stream. The leafy floor became suffused with soft color. Night insects stopped their chirping and from afar, curassow birds began to sing.

"A right Merry Christmas, fair lady!"

"*Felicidades, señor.*"

She tickled his ribs playfully and he caught her around the waist.

"For a Swiss doctor's daughter, you've become quite a wanton woman of the woods. Not that I mind, but I think our erotic indulgence needs to be made respectable. If you accept this ring, I'll take it as a sign of our engagement. When we return to civilization, I promise to make you an honest woman."

"Claus, it's the most beautiful ring I've ever seen." The ring was cut out of coral mushroom. "I can't believe it. Are you sure? I thought you were an old mule skinner married to the bush."

Claus laughed, his eyes roving over her in great amusement. "I thought I was. But you taught me what it means to be truly married. I was a part-time lover at best, using the jungle as a port of call. And I've been miserable everywhere else. You made me realize how much I really need the jungle. The jungle is in you now. I love you Erika. If you love us, the jungle and me, marry us. You see, I never had anything to offer you before. So give me your answer so I can begin my bride service."

Erika felt the tears stream down her cheeks, like rain. "Claus, yes, I'll marry you. I'll go anywhere with you, in the jungle or wherever you want to go. But, Claus, if we discover Menche, won't you want to go back to New Orleans and claim all the rewards that will be waiting for you? I'll go even there with you if you wish, but I don't know if I'd make a good university president's wife. Do you want to take me there?"

Claus looked up at the gold dome of the forest. He was silent for awhile and then he turned to her in wonder, as if he had just discovered something startling about himself.

"Erika, it's astonishing, I wasn't thinking of New Orleans when I asked you to marry me."

She felt the slap of disappointment. It was all too good to be true. Of course, what intimacy they had would lose its meaning when they were out of the forest. She wouldn't fit in New Orleans society. She was a sad-eyed doe of the backwoods.

"I'm sorry, Claus. It wouldn't work there, would it? You can take the proposal back."

He gripped her hands and pressed them firmly in his. "That's not what I meant. Erika, when I once told you I was done with all that love business, I didn't know what I was really saying. I meant that I was done with New Orleans. I don't want to go back. I suffered from a kind of mental malaria for almost ten years. This trip has healed me. You and the jungle are the healers of all my fevers."

"Claus, I've never had a lovelier Christmas. By the way, I got up early this morning to shop for your Christmas present." She reached behind the log they rested against. "Here, I bought you this crown of begonias."

Claus laughed heartily as she placed the crown upon his head. "We must have shopped in the same store because I bought you a string of the same flowers for your neck."

They laughed together. "Claus, your present is as beautiful as mine."

"When we get back to Mexico City, I will buy you silver dishes."

"I will buy you a reading chair. And I will wear lacy nightgowns for you."

The mention of Mexico City sent a disturbing vibration through Erika's mind.

"Would you really be happy living in Mexico City? Is it so very different from New Orleans? But if we don't live there, where shall we live? Not that I'm trying to domesticate you with the ring just on my finger, but we will need a home of some kind, won't we? Are we going to start our own caribal and live like the Lacandons? As much as I love the jungle, I came here in European clothes. All that is part of me too. Isn't it part of you? You may not want to go back to New Orleans and I may not want to go back to Switzerland but no matter how well we fit in here, we'll always be people from another world. What shall we do?"

Claus nodded in agreement but his smile told her that his thoughts were well ahead of hers. "You're right. We can't live like the Lacandons. We are all too European, as you say. But there's a place not too far from the jungle, high in the mountains, west of here, a place that combines the best refinements of our civilization with the vestiges of a Mayan way of life.

"San Cristobal Las Casas was established by the Spaniards four hundred years ago. It had been a Mayan trading center but secretly, and surely, over the centuries, the gods of the Mayans in the guise of Catholic saints took over its churches and markets. Today, our civilization is a bright coat of paint over an old Mayan mold." Erika's heart stirred as Claus went on to speak of gentle temperatures, Indians in colorful dress, Ladino shopkeepers, old Spanish aristocrats, the heirs of Fray Bartolme. Claus spoke of a valley of tile roofed abode houses and soft green meadows strung across the rooftop of Chiapas. "There's an old unfinished seminary, built by a Spaniard blue blood and abandoned after he died. It was up for sale for only sixteen hundred American dollars when I went through there eight months ago. Who knows if it's still available, but things don't happen very fast in Las Casas. Erika, we could build our own Lacandon study center there and visit the jungle when we want. Of course, I'm dreaming, but we may as well dream big."

"Claus, it's a lovely dream."

"Your turn to dream," he said.

"I can only dream in the present. Shall we dream of making love?" she gave him a teasing poke.

"That dream will bring my fever back."

"Shall we dream of Menche?" Erika lay back and gazed up at the leafy curtain.

"Yes, it may be only a little way down the trail. It's funny, I want to find it more than ever, but not for the reasons I started out with." Claus lay back beside her.

"Bolon Kin says the gods need men to worship them. I'm a scientist and I'm committed to a certain code of truth. I can't shed that. But I've learned something else. Nature can be understood by the mind. But you have to taste it, feel it, hear it hum in your ears to know it's a sacred place. A lot of people from our world have become numb to it. We have to find Menche before they take the jungle away."

He looked at her with the same intensity that was in his eyes when he first spoke to her of his quest in Ocosingo months ago. But he no longer spoke like a man driven by an obsession, a victim of monomania. He was a man committed to a love and she knew now that she was at the center of it.

She smiled as he spoke of a dream that she knew also belonged to her. "Yes, I've rethought my whole life in these past few months. Thanks to you, I'm not the same person I was." He took her hand.

"You made the difference, Erika. If I've ever come close to having a religion, I experienced it here on the trail with you. I've come to believe that the human intelligence that sends metal birds over the jungle must be charged with the responsibility for ending human suffering. But it's more than human suffering that's at stake. I suppose that now I believe that the gods gave us intelligence to keep the world running for them while they are busy with heaven. Maybe our fate as humans is to be caretakers of the planet after all, weeding a field here, pruning a tree there, preventing one form of life from overrunning another, not just for the survival of our own species, but for all the life that shares this spinning mudball with us."

Erika was stirred more profoundly than at any time in her memory. Claus had opened her deepest feelings. All the inchoate visions that had drifted shapelessly in her dreams, rose up in radiance. She kissed his cheek.

Suddenly, they heard lugubrious shouts above them and they were peppered with avocados.

"Claus, the howlers!"

"Well, at least we won't starve. They certainly have the Christmas spirit. The three wise monkeys. Duck, here comes a breadnut. Thank you. Hey up there, throw down a macaw breast, and one roasted peccary if you please. And while you're at it, you shrieking monsters, boil some maize!"

Claus and Erika sat up laughing while the jungle tumbled down all around them.

Chapter Forty-Two

Lazaro, Rogelio and Kayum arrived that night. Kayum was walking nimbly, even with an ace bandage strapped around his leg.

"*Felices Navidades!*" the lovers greeted them. By now Claus was dressed in a suit of flowers that Erika had wound completely around his body.

"Pancho Balam and Doña Erika, we are sorry," Lazaro began. "We had to wait in El Cedro for a doctor for Kayum. And, uh, we were held up a day or two at the colony of the Tobajalian Indians."

"I'm not surprised," Claus grinned. "There are lovely women in that place who might have insisted that you stop awhile. But your absence gave me the opportunity of a lifetime. You may congratulate me. Meet my fiancée of the sacred stream."

Lazaro and Rogelio brought beans and eggs and chocolate. Kayum brought a curassow he had shot. They produced a hand-operated phonograph they had picked up in El Cedro. Rogelio said it was a big success in the Indian colony. Now Bing Crosby sang "Vaya Con Dios, My Darling" accompanied by a chorus of frogs.

The reunited explorers enjoyed a Christmas dinner of curassow stuffed with beans and beet leaf cake, wild grapefruit and—what had become Erika's favorite beverage—hot, spicy, foaming chocolate. The fire sent long, straight flames into the still jungle night.

"Will we find Menche tomorrow?" Lazaro asked.

"I don't blame you for being impatient," Claus said. "We shall find it in the next few days or we won't find it at all. By tomorrow we should reach the pass Kayum spoke of. I expect to see some house mounds pretty soon. Otherwise, we've lost the needle in the haystack."

"We will find the needle," Lazaro said, contentedly chewing on a wedge of chocolate wrapped in honeycomb.

"Kayum, I'm glad to see you're your old self again," Claus said cheerfully. "How did you like El Cedro?"

Kayum shook his head slowly and rolled his eyes. "Many people and mules live mashed together. Even more than at El Capulin. They put me in a big hut lit with bright torches that give no smoke. In a little hut next to mine there was a white dugout. They filled it up with water that came pouring out of a snake's head. I had never seen anything like it. They put me in it and rubbed me with a bar of grease that looked like the foot of a mule."

"Next to it, there was a big god pot. I offered to burn incense to the gods. But the medicine man asked me to leave my stool in it. I told him I would have to go deep into the woods to leave my stool but he said it was impossible, and besides, he wanted to see the color of my stool in order to cure me. I could not understand how he would know which gods to pray to by looking at my stool. I tried to explain to him that it was a sacrilege to leave one's stool in a god pot. He told me his god would not be angry if I left my stool in the pot. When I did as he asked, the medicine man made strange incantations over my stool and wrote a prayer on paper. He told me he was going to give me some seeds that would change the color of my stool. Then he pulled the handle of the god pot. To my amazement, the god inside the pot swallowed up the stool. Jesus Christ does strange things. I was lucky to get out of there alive. But I knew I was going to be all right when your friend came to visit me."

"My friend?"

"Yes, your friend who saved our lives in El Capulin."

"Barnes!" Claus and Erika said together. Erika felt a surge of dread at the mere mention of the name.

"He asked me where you were and I told him you were in the jungle looking for the home of the true gods. He showed great interest. I was happy to meet someone in that place who respected the gods of the forest. He asked me many questions and seemed pleased by what I told him. Your friend said he would like to worship the gods with us at Menche."

"We'll all have a big party there," Rogelio said facetiously.

Erika was simmering with rage. "I don't like it. Claus, the man wants to hurt you the worst way."

Claus nodded with a shrug. "I know he's following us. So be it. Do you still think we'll be wiped out by his band of desperadoes? I think he was in El Cedro because his gang of bad actors deserted him. Did you see any of them, Rogelio?"

"I saw some of them in the saloons."

"Had they left Barnes?"

"Yes," Rogelio said. "They were angry at him for not having paid them. They said they wouldn't ride with him again. One of the men wanted to kill Barnes, but the others said their only hope of being paid was to let him find the city of gold and then kill him if he didn't give them their share."

"City of gold? He certainly did make wild promises," Claus chuckled.

"Then Lazaro and I saw Barnes in another saloon trying to recruit men to go into the jungle with him. He said he had made friends with a Lacandon who promised to lead him to Menche. There were some strangers in the saloon, about five of them. They were rebel soldiers from Guatemala who had been chased across the border by *federalés* in that country. They asked Barnes if there was much gold in the temples of Menche. Barnes promised them he would make them all rich. The Guatemalans said they needed money to buy guns for themselves and their friends."

"I don't think he can bring it off," Claus said emphatically. "I'm sure those rebels would just as soon kill him as kill the *federalés*."

Or us, Erika thought to herself.

"Well, in any case," Claus yawned, "we'll find out soon enough."

But in the morning, Erika saw that Claus was shivering in his sleeping bag.

"I have chills," he said. He tried to get up but he was too weak and was trembling visibly. He sank down into the hammock again.

Erika knew it was impossible to have the malaria that brought fever and the malaria that brought chills at the same time.

"Claus, you may have pneumonia. We must go back to El Cedro. I know we're almost at the end of the road, but we can come back. I don't want you to die out here."

"There's no coming back. It's now or never, you know that. And there's Barnes, remember?"

"But you can't go anywhere the way you are."

"I just need to rest. I'll be all right by tomorrow. If not, I promise to go back."

Chapter Forty-Three

The chills abated in the morning. However, when he stood up, Claus confessed to Erika that he felt dizzy. It was obvious that he was weak. But he insisted that they press on, and against Erika's better judgment, they helped him onto a mule. The trail was almost nonexistent and the bramble was more profuse than any they had encountered previously.

"It was somewhere out of El Cedro that my father came with the lumber companies," Lazaro said, looking at the thick growth.

"It doesn't take long for a forest to spring up again, depending on how it's cut and whether the soil holds," Claus said. "The truth is, the old lumbermen were less destructive than are the new pioneers."

In places there was no sign of a trail. The expedition went on blindly. Through the leaves, Erika could see they were approaching a steep hill about a hundred meters high. They followed a rapidly moving stream which led them to a waterfall. A little to one side of the cascading water, they found a rocky gorge that formed a pass up the hill.

"The chain of rocks," Claus cried exultantly through his weariness.

Looking at the white, glittering ravine, Erika felt her spirits rise. The collective fatigue and incremental loss of confidence of the group was swept away. Rogelio started to sing. Kayum picked up the tune. So did Lazaro.

It was a narrow pass with sheer walls on either side. They had to climb single file with the animals. Erika kept her eyes open for a rock in the shape of a jaguar.

"There it is, up ahead," Rogelio shouted. It was the highest natural object for miles and was at least eight feet high. Its very position was a curiosity. Was it a stone flung by the Ice Age or hauled to its proud perch by Mayan engineers? As they came close, it took on the form of a huge cat face in profile. The mountain sloped down gently on the other side and was lost in a vast ocean of green that stretched as far as the eye could see.

"Is it a natural formation or a Mayan monument?" Erika examined the feline head.

"The Olmec left giant human-like heads in the jungle but I don't know that the Mayans ever sculpted colossal jaguar heads. It's well worn. I think the sculptor was old Metzabok. But it's the sign we've been looking for. If Menche exists at all, it's down there somewhere under that green canopy that's blowing under us." Claus looked around and Erika could see the vision shining from his eyes.

"Claus, I see a river winding through the jungle, way in the distance."

"The Usumancinta! Beyond it is Guatemala and the Peten."

They were surprised that the trail ahead, which dropped gently through a grove of sapodillas, fig trees, and big green fan leaves, appeared to be freshly cut. It was as if the green sea of tropical flora had parted by divine decree. But the explorers were wary of such a theological explanation.

"Do you think that Barnes is ahead of us?" Erika asked.

They proceeded with almost no resistance through the jungle tunnel. The underbrush had been cleared from the trail on both sides. But after they walked a little over a hundred meters, the forest closed again. They were confronted by a wall of bush.

Suddenly, without warning of any kind, not even the stirring of a leaf, a volley of explosions came out of the bush. Lazaro, who had been leading the bell mule, fell to the ground, writhing and sobbing. Claus slid down from the mule he rode.

Setting his rifle against his shoulder, he fired successive shots at the unseen source of the attack, enabling Lazaro to crawl away behind some fan leaves. Before Erika could think of what to do, Kayum had thrown her to the ground and covered her body with his own. Erika could barely see Claus and the others firing back at the invisible ambuscade. The mules shrieked. The firing from the bush grew heavy and Erika knew it was only a matter of minutes before the spray of shots destroyed them all. Then she heard the cry of a mule in pain.

"There's a lot of them in there," Claus shouted. "Run back to the pass, everybody!"

Kayum ran forward to help Claus and Rogelio pull the mules, using them as shields. Erika and Lazaro, who was bleeding from his shoulder, scampered to the jaguar rock. The firing was fast and heavy as men, woman and mules rushed to the top of the pass and dropped to the other side. The descent over loose, jagged rocks was difficult. They clambered down one at a time. Erika knew that if she fell, she would hold everybody up and conceivably cause the death of the last man to go over the top of the pass.

"Get down to the bottom and take cover under those big rocks," Claus called from the top.

Below him, men and animals charged down the pass wildly. Erika fell in her haste and confusion. She was immediately picked up by Kayum, who tossed her over his shoulder and hopped like a mountain goat down the narrow gorge until they came to the shelter of rocks below.

Looking up the steep, walled pass, Erika saw Rogelio assisting Lazaro to the bottom. Then she saw two pack mules shrieking and tumbling over the rocks. The mules rushed past and disappeared down the forest trail. She saw Claus staggering down the narrow ravine. Blood poured from his left leg. Kayum ran up the pass like a puma, lifted the stricken Claus over his shoulders and carried him down.

Now they all huddled at the bottom of the pass, looking up at the rock stairs, waiting for the first sign of their attackers. There was nothing but silence and stillness above.

"Claus, Rogelio, are you all right?" Erika whispered.

"This is not time for discussion," Claus said. "Reload your rifles and keep them trained at the top of the pass."

Claus gave Erika his revolver and she watched him put a fresh clip of shells into the chamber of his Winchester. Kayum loaded the .22.

Then, at the top of the pass, they saw the outline of a man seated on a horse. He was carrying a semiautomatic weapon similar to those of the type the Germans used at the beginning of the war. His uniform looked like it came from Loyalist Spain. He turned his head and shouted a command at the unseen forces behind him.

"*Vamos Entrada!* The devils went this way."

"Who are they? Is it an army?" Erika whispered to Claus, who crouched in front of her.

"They're not Mexican *federalés*. Whoever they are, they want to kill us."

"Can't we talk with them?"

"I don't think we'd stand a chance." Claus turned to the others. "They'll have to come down the pass single file. Hold your fire and wait til they come closer. Don't shoot until I do and try to make every shot count. We don't have much ammunition. Erika, get behind everybody."

The man at the top of the pass began his descent, his horse picking its way cautiously over the rocks. Another soldier on horseback appeared at the top of the pass behind him and began to climb down. Still Claus did not fire.

"There is a woman among them," the second soldier said to the leader.

"Don't let that soften your heart. She can kill with a gun. We must eradicate all of them. *Todos!*"

More horsemen came down the gorge toward them. The horses tested the rocks as they progressed, some slipping and whinnying. There were at least eight men, all on horseback. They all carried rifles of one kind or another. By the time the last man came around the jaguar head, the leader was so close that Erika could see the piece of gum he was chewing in his mouth. He was young with dark good looks and sad brown eyes. He held the reins of his horse with one hand and, with the other, rested the butt of his rifle in the pocket of his shoulder. The scene seemed tranquil with the men on horses filing quietly down the pass. It was hard for Erika to believe she couldn't just step out and tell the young man that there was some mistake.

"They must be on the forest trail by now," the leader called to the men above him. "We'll catch up to them and shoot them as we see them. The bush is too thick for them to hide in."

The leader spat out his gum just as Claus fired and struck him in his chest. Blood spurted through his shirt. When a second shot fired by Rogelio, hit the leader's neck, he rolled off his horse. Another shot, fired by Lazaro brought down the horse and the next man came in line. He was struck down instantly as his automatic weapon sprayed wild shots and his horse collapsed under him. One by one, the members of the trapped squad toppled like a row of dominoes falling over one another. The last man had gotten off his horse and mounted a machine gun behind a rock half-way up the pass. He was feeding a string of cartridges in it from his protected position when Rogelio ran out onto the pass and fired a shot at the man's head in one swift motion. Machine gunfire ricocheted off the wall of the gorge. The man fell over his gun, and it went clattering down the pass.

Silence fell except for the whinnying of the horses that had escaped to the other side of the hill. Erika ran up to Claus who was bleeding profusely from his leg. On the pass, the bodies of men and animals were strewn like drunks on a staircase. A crimson waterfall splashed over the rocks.

Those who committed the massacre gaped in awe.

"Let's see if any of them are still alive," Claus said limping up the rocky path.

No one was. Claus found some papers in the breast pocket of the slain leader.

"This fellow was a lieutenant in the Guatemalan Army. Here's a picture of his girl."

Erika looked at the picture. The lieutenant's blood was smeared over the girl's face.

"Claus, it's awful. Did we have to kill them all?"

"It just turned out that way. The only other choice was death for us."

"I wonder if Bolon Kin would have chosen death?" Erika said.

"But I didn't," Kayum said. "I was shooting with the rest of you."

"Are we in Guatemala?" Rogelio asked.

"No, but we're not far from the border," Claus said. The men climbed over the dead, taking rifles and collecting papers as if to preserve them was a gesture of respect for the dead.

"I don't want to take the money of the dead," Lazaro said.

Claus nodded. "Then leave it. Others will take it if it doesn't get scattered through the jungle."

"Why did they attack us?" Erika asked.

Claus looked over the bloodied landscape. "They must have thought we were the revolutionaries Barnes had picked up. Maybe they got wind of his expedition and decided we were part of it."

"Will there be others?"

"I don't think so. But we can't be sure."

Lazaro was not hurt badly. The bullet had nicked his shoulder and passed on, leaving only a surface wound. But Claus needed immediate attention. There was a bullet embedded in the calf of his leg.

"You're going to have to operate, Erika." He gave her a confident smile, as she helped him out of his trousers.

Fortunately, the men had brought fresh medical supplies from El Cedro. But there was no anesthesia. Erika washed the leg as best she could. Then, following Claus's instructions, she inserted the surgical knife deep into the swelling calf. Claus shook from the pain and sweat poured out of his body. Erika had to make some artless twists and turns to get at the bullet. Then she bathed the wound in alcohol, made a primitive suture, and with Rogelio's help, bandaged him right away. The bone had not been hit. They helped Claus into a hammock, although he insisted he could hop around. Kayum burned incense to Kak so that fever would not set in.

"We may be amateur medicine men, but I think we pulled it off," Claus said grinning with his leg up in the hammock.

"Claus, we'll have to go back to El Cedro," Erika said. "I'm your doctor now and you have to listen to me."

"Just give me one more day," Claus continued to grin. "We'll be in Menche in the morning or we'll never see it."

"Claus, I don't want to bury you there."

"Are you taking Bolon Kin's prophecy seriously?"

"Promise me we'll go back after one more day."

"If we don't find Menche tomorrow, we'll turn back."

"One more day, Claus."

Claus slept through the afternoon. Erika helped the others bury the dead and retrieve the mules.

Chapter Forty-Four

They were sitting around the early evening fire when night dropped its curtain in the abrupt way it does in the tropics. Erika always felt as if she were watching a play, with the sun as the main actor. The play always ended suddenly, without any hint as to the resolution of the plot. She was again left watching the closed curtain and wondering if the hero would win his battle with the demons of the night. Tonight, as she peered into the dark forest beyond the fire, she wasn't so confident that the hero would win.

Rogelio was playing his Bing Crosby record on the phonograph. "*Vaya con Dios*" the American singer crooned. In her mood, Erika found the song silly and was glad when it stopped.

Then Erika heard a thrashing sound and the breaking of branches in the woods. The camp fell silent as each ear strained to identify the sound. She glanced at Claus, who picked up his Winchester rifle. They all kept their eyes riveted to the screen of nature from whence the thwacking came. Erika heard the braying of mules just at the head of the clearing and the jiggling of big leaf plants. Rogelio and Lazaro held their revolvers in their hands. Kayum had picked up a shotgun and taken position behind a ramon tree. Erika wondered if he had killed any of the soldiers on the pass.

Erika saw the fan leaves part. A solitary burro walked into the clearing of the camp. It was loaded with picks, a shovel, and two *chicle* boxes, one strapped on either side. A second burro followed, this one similarly loaded, but instead of carrying a pick, it carried a camera tripod. A man came behind the second mule, cursing the animal and hitting it with a switch. The man wore a sombrero that shaded his face. A loaded cartridge belt was slung across his chest. The man stumbled over vines and roots, cursing as he did. "Stop I tell you," the man called to the mules, and pulled on the straps. The mules stopped next to the ramon tree. The man was breathing heavily and seemed to have difficulty walking as he approached the fire. His eyes were on the ground and his face was still in shadow under the big hat. Then the man looked up.

"Why all the guns pointed at me? Pancho Balam, is that the way to greet an old colleague?" He removed his sombrero and Erika recognized the glassy eyes and leering grin of Barnes. He made a sweeping gesture with his hat. "My deepest respects, Doña Erika. I see you survive in the jungle as well as the orchids in the trees. It is a victory for beauty to be sure. My former colleague is lucky."

Barnes lurched as he spoke. The smell of rum reached Erika's nose over the fire that separated her from their caller. She wondered when the rest of Barnes's band would arrive.

"You're just in time for cacao," Claus said. He had placed his rifle down at his side. "Sorry for the rude welcome. We thought you were a jaguar."

There was a rustle in the bushes and another mule walked into the firelight.

"Call the rest of your party and we'll all have supper together," Claus said, putting on his best New Orleans accent.

Barnes giggled and ran his hand over his bearded chin.

"My men won't be coming." He laughed again. "You were right, Claus. I never could hold an expedition together. I tried to prevent them from firing on the soldiers. By the way, there are some Guatemalan troops in this forest. They should be passing through here."

"That's interesting news. But how do you know?" Claus asked, appearing surprised.

Barnes shook his craggy head, the incongruous bulbous nose, bright red in the firelight. "I tried to tell those fools not to fire on them. But the rebels are crazy. They were more interested in killing government troops than the promise of good pay I gave them. These half breeds are unreliable. All hotheaded, whether Mexican or Guatemalan."

"Did you lose all your men, Barnes?"

"The ones that didn't get killed by the troops went back to El Cedro. They talked about killing me but they decided to let me go on alone. They said the jungle would give this solitary gringo the death he deserved. Can you imagine? Those half breeds know nothing about us Yankee bastards from the frozen north. I can survive this jungle as well as any of them. Speaking of survival, you don't look well, old colleague."

Claus smiled back. "I had an accident and a slight chill. I'll be up and around after a night's rest."

Erika handed Barnes a calabash of *posole*. He drank deeply and coughed as he erupted into volcanic laughter.

"A night's rest, you say? You'd better look after him, Doña Erika. A night's rest! I think the expedition is over for you, old man. You've been in these woods too long. You're not the kid who once scampered up and down the steps of Uxmal and Palenque. Doña Erika, I'd get him back to El Cedro as soon as possible. I think this shivering old mulepacker has pneumonia. Better put your trea-sure-hunting days behind you, Pancho Balam." Barnes emitted a hissing laugh.

"You may be right there, Barnes. I'm beginning to think I'm on a fool's errand. Pyramids in the fog. You're welcome to spend the night with us if you wish."

"No, I feel strong. I'm going on down the trail."

"But it's night. You haven't taken any food."

"My grandfather built a house out of rocks on the coast of Maine. And you tried to blow it down in the hot air of New Orleans. I'm going to claim my man-sion, Claus. You will be my guest when you come to it."

Barnes slapped the sides of his mules, who shambled obediently into the dark-ness. Then Barnes was swallowed up—mules, laughter and all—into the bush.

"I don't think we should let him go like that," Lazaro said, looking into the darkness where Barnes had gone.

"He's not dangerous," Claus said.

"But Pancho Balam," Lazaro insisted. "By your own reckoning, Menche is only a day's journey from here. He will see signs on this trail."

Rogelio looked up. "I wonder if the soldiers saw anything. They came from Guatemala on this trail."

"They're not archaeologists. They don't know the clues," Claus said.

"Barnes is an archaeologist," Erika said. "He might just stumble on it and claim it as his own discovery."

"That's possible. But I'm far from sure Menche is here at all. We should have seen signs ourselves by now—retention walls, house mounds, something. Maybe it's all pyramids in the fog after all. I'm certain about one thing. If we reach the river without finding any traces, we'll know we've come to the end of the rainbow and found nothing but the wet imprint of rain."

But Claus was out of his hammock hours before the dawn, hobbling about on his leg and stirring everyone out of sleep.

"Claus, have you gone mad?" Erika said, rubbing her eyes.

"We must find Barnes."

"Claus, you must have fever again. No, your body is shaking. Lie down. You need rest. Please."

"Can't rest. Must go on. You know I don't have fever if I have chills."

"Claus, I think Barnes was right. You have pneumonia."

"That's what I mean. We have to catch up with Barnes. Not because he'll beat us to the ruins. At best he can only claim a share of the credit even if we find him sitting in Hachakyum's lap when we get there. No, we must prevent him from killing himself. The rebels are right. He can't possibly survive alone. We must find him."

"Claus, you know he wouldn't do the same for you. He'd leave you to die at the first opportunity."

"Pancho, he would kill you for a bottle of rum," Lazaro said.

Claus grinned. "You're both right, but that's just it. I can't just let him die. Don't you see, Erika, without you, Barnes is the man I once was and the man I may someday become again."

"We will pack the mules," Lazaro said.

Though he loathed the animals, Kayum loaded a mule and pushed it ahead of him with a bamboo stick. The morning birds began to sing.

They didn't have to look far for Barnes. Within hours, they found two mules dead on the trail, blood dripping from their gored sides. Broken boxes of equipment were scattered on the path. A little farther ahead, they found the mauled body of Barnes. His skull was cracked open. His rifle lay three feet from an outstretched hand. The brain case was split open but Erika saw there was nothing inside, only a few lumps that looked like bits of rice in an emptied can of rice and tomato soup.

"His brains! What happened to his brains?" Erika was almost hysterical.

"Jaguars find a supper of brains to be a special treat," Kayum said solemnly.

Chapter Forty-Five

The day passed without any signs of mounds. It was late afternoon. They looked for a flat area by a stream where they could set up camp. There had been little rain in the past week, and they couldn't find any water. It seemed to have all been soaked up by the porous limestone.

Suddenly, Kayum spotted some pheasants in a bush at the foot of a hill.

"Pancho Balam, a good sign of water," he said. "There is a spring nearby." The pheasants flew up and out of sight.

Claus looked about excitedly. "A spring, a hill, a level place. The ideal Mayan site!"

The trail climbed steeply ahead of them. Despite his weariness and the injury that had caused him to limp along all day, Claus scrambled up the incline that led to the hilltop pass. Erika called out to him.

"Claus, don't strain yourself. Remember, you're not well!" But she knew she was wasting her breath. Erika watched him turn right at the top of the pass and disappear into the shrub.

"This is a good place to camp, anyway," Erika said to the others when Claus didn't come back. While the men were taking care of the animals, she found an unusually flat place near the bubbling arroyo. Claus came down the hill with a dejected look.

"A lovely hilltop with a magnificent view, but nothing there. It's just that I was so sure. My intuition has never failed me before. But what could I expect? Any major site along this well-covered trail would be known. Menche isn't here."

"Then where is it?"

"It isn't anywhere. It comes and goes with the fog. Its stones were cut from the collective unconscious of the Lacandons. They needed to invent it when Palenque became a possession of the T'sul. Kayum will tell his father that the gods took it up to heaven. Anyway, I don't think we'll find it in the Lacandon jungle."

In his frustration, Claus paced up and down the clearing, using the stock of his rifle as a cane, jabbing the stock into the earth.

Erika leaned her head against a tree to absorb her disappointment.

"Don't lean against that tree!" He almost leapt at her.

"Why?" She was frightened by his almost vicious tone and jumped away from the tree.

"It's a chechen tree. They ooze a poisonous sap. You always see them around Mayan ruins. Wait a minute!" He hobbled up and down the clearing, pounding the ground with the rifle stock. "This ground is just too level to be natural, isn't it? Yes. It's a perfectly formed terrace we're on, Erika, one that, in these parts, could only have been made by a Mayan. And I think our little hill is a pyramid!"

He dropped his rifle with a clatter when it struck the ground. Then, picking up his machete, Claus bounded up the hill, limp and all, like a schoolboy released by the bell. At the top of the pass, Erika saw him turn left and heard him hacking at the dense foliage with his machete. She followed.

They hacked their way up a steep grade. Erika could see that Claus had little strength in his arm. He was breathing heavily and the jungle was not yielding to the weak chops of his machete. Erika took the machete from him and cleared the vines and spiny palms before them. They struggled with the brush for nearly an hour trying to penetrate the densest profusion of vegetation they'd encountered on the trail. Erika called for help only to realize that her voice would travel but a little distance through the sound-absorbing bush. She saved her effort for the task. Claus swung at the foliage wildly with a branch he had broken off a tree.

Erika began to see blocks of stone under the scramble of growth at their feet. Then they attained a summit covered with trees and twisting roots. They stumbled over a heap of broken stones. Then, the two explorers broke through a clearing between the trees and saw a green panorama of jungle that extended for miles around.

Immediately below them lay the ruins of a Mayan city. Through patches of green, they made out a plaza with many terraced mounds held up by stepped retention walls of stone and mortar. The grey ruins of temples and other edifices rose from the sides. On their rooftops, wild begonias grew. Monkeys chattered and scampered over branches and roots that twisted around stone towers. On the far end of the vast plaza and dimly perceived through a rising mist, a steeply graded pyramid rose majestically. Looking up at its top, Erika could barely distinguish the form of a temple with the remains of a lofty roof comb enveloped in a tangle of roots and vines.

Erika felt her heart rise. Tears formed in her eyes even as she photographed the panorama before her. "Claus, it's so beautiful! And there are no signs of excavation. Why was it never found?"

Claus was panting but could not stop talking in his excitement.

"It's so obvious we should have known. The secret is in the name Menche, or young forest. The people of Bolon Kin worshiped here for the last time almost fifty years ago. Remember that Bolon Kin talked about migrating from Lacanja because of invading lumbermen? Lumbermen worked this area around the turn of the century. They took a lot of timber that made way for a scramble of secondary growth. Zapata's revolution ended the quota system that made Lazaro's father a slave to the companies." Claus's voice shook and cracked in many places but he went on, racing his words. "Luckily, the companies collapsed before the jungle was destroyed altogether. And so, in this wild, dense profusion, a new forest grew. What Bolon Kin saw when he came back in his middle life was Menche, a young forest. Seen from the trail, it completely veiled the city. There were no bent branches, no clues to cause the Lacandons to break through at any place."

"But the lumbermen must have seen this city."

"I'm sure we'll find evidence of their plundering. But it would have held little interest for them. They would have seen only a maze of big piles of stone to make their work more difficult."

"How could they have missed its beauty?" Erika said, her eyes skipping like a child over the wonders around her. She loved the way the vines were wrapped around stately towers, and the pink begonias against the grey stone. "Claus, no wonder Bolon Kin believed Hachakyum made gods out of spring flowers."

"If the jungle hadn't grown back, those roofs would have collapsed for lack of shade," Claus said, almost laughing in his delight.

Erika took a deep breath. "Claus, there are ruins as far as you can see, climbing out of the jungle and the mist."

Claus shook his head, showing he was as dazzled as she was. "We are seeing only part of it. Much more is buried under rotted vegetation and land fill. But let's go down to the plaza and take a look."

"Claus, you're not very strong right now. It's steep and slippery and a long way to fall. The sun is beginning to set. Maybe we should come back tomorrow."

Claus took Erika's arm eagerly. "We have another two hours of sunlight. You're right about it being slippery. I'll lean on you when I need to."

It was difficult going down the stairs that were covered with roots, vines, and loose rocks. They slipped many times, and halfway down, Erika lost her balance. She grabbed a looping root before falling to the plaza fifty feet below. Claus was unsteady but he did not fall.

When they reached the bottom, they made their way across the plaza, stumbling over crumbled stone and surging vegetation. Ahead of them the great pyramid loomed, soaring up to heaven like a man-constructed Matterhorn. Swirls of late afternoon mist obscured the temple on top but Erika swore she saw a flash of light and heard a sound as of someone chanting. The strange murmur fell over the plaza and rebounded on the stones from all quadrilateral points.

"Claus, did you hear?"

Claus seemed to be having difficulty climbing the uneven surfaces of the plaza. Erika rushed to his aid.

She felt that Claus was fading in and out of consciousness. He seemed, from time to time, unresponsive to what she said.

"Did I hear what? No, I didn't hear anything. There are many monkeys up there and bats and who knows what else."

Claus stumbled ahead while they crossed the thorn-filled mound toward the pyramid that rose almost perpendicular before them.

At last they came to the base of the pyramid at the far end of the court. It soared almost vertically and vanished in the curl of mist above them.

The steps were high and the tops allowed room only for the ball of one's foot. In addition, the stairs were covered with vines, powdered stone and dried mud.

"Claus, we can't climb these steps. I thought the Mayans were little people."

"Yes, these steps weren't made for the uninitiated. You'd better wait down here."

"Wait down here? Not on your life. If you insist on climbing them, I'm going with you."

"Take my hand. We'll help one another along."

They began the ascent, lifting their knees high until Erika felt the muscles on top of her legs tighten. It was indeed a climb into the heavens. Through the mist above them Erika saw a continuing flash of light. At first she believed it to be the sun but she realized the sun was a red copper ball on the other side of the plaza. They entered the mist and over thirty feet above them, Erika saw what appeared to be a Lacandon kneeling before a fire. The fire illuminated a sculptured figure of heroic size, ornately dressed and seated with its hands across its chest. Erika gasped at the realization that the figure had no head. Above the headless god, another set of stairs climbed to the temple which was adorned with the remains of a great roof comb. It looked like a crushed spaceship come down after eons of circling in Mayan time.

The chants of the figure worshiping before the headless statue reverberated from all corners of the plaza. Erika caught the scent of copal in her nostrils.

"Claus, it's Kayum. How did he get here before us?"

"He must have come by another route while we were hacking at the bush. Remember, he's young and strong so he's better at using the machete than either of us."

As they approached him, Erika was astonished at what she saw. Resting on its side next to the giant stone body was its head. A serene confident face, adorned with an elaborate headdress in which a jaguar mask was set, presided over the plaza. The mask on the headdress bore a ferocious countenance but the face of the god wore a benevolent expression as it gazed sideways over the jungle and the visitors.

Kayum placed *posole* over the lips of the severed head.

"Claus, the statue was decapitated, just as Bolon Kin prophesized." She could not help but think of the other prophecy that two would die in the search. Many had died, but it could only truly be said of Barnes that he had died in the search. Bolon Kin had seen two jaguars in his dream. Was Barnes one of them? Who would be the other? She tried to tell herself her thoughts were irrational.

"Bolon Kin's premonition was correct," Claus said. "The head was probably severed by the lumbermen who came after the last Lacandon pilgrimage. In their ignorance, the lumbermen probably thought it was an image of the devil."

Erika addressed Kayum. "Have you found a stone to bring back to Jatate, a sacred stone you can place inside the god pot of Hachakyum in your god house?"

Kayum smiled broadly and held out a large, beautifully carved jade pendant. "It was hanging from a necklace around the neck of Hachakyum's head," he smiled. "I have cleaned and polished it."

"It's beautiful." Erika gasped. I'm surprised the lumbermen didn't take it."

Kayum shrugged.

Claus smiled. "They would not have known its value."

"Would it be a sacrilege if I took a picture of you holding the stone?" Erika asked Kayum.

He smiled, holding aloft the jade pendant. "If Bolon Kin allows you to drink the sacred *balché* of the Lacandons, he will surely allow you to make an image of his son holding the sacred stone of Hachakyum." And so it was done.

They all looked up at the sky. Erika knew that night was moving in like a puma who suddenly strikes at the prey he has been stalking all day.

"And the temple?" Claus asked of Kayum.

"I have not visited the temple. My father told me you would care for the temple."

Another flight of a dozen steps or so led to the temple. Erika and Claus looked up at the magnificent corbelled arch. But as they began to climb the stairs, they heard a deep rumble coming from the dark interior.

"Something's in there," Erika exclaimed. It was like thunder but it was coming from inside the temple.

The rumble became a roar.

"Hello up there," Claus called as he mounted another stair.

Claus and Erika were halfway up the stairs when two jaguars appeared from doorways. The huge spotted beasts regarded them haughtily. They were awesome in their size and majesty.

Erika stopped, frozen. She realized Claus had left his rifle in camp.

The beasts delivered plaintive, high pitched moans. Erika could see the pink insides of their mouths and their saber fangs.

"Would it do any good if we made noise the way we did in the lumber camp?" she asked timidly, quite convinced the idea was absurd.

The jaguars roared again, sniffed the air as if seeking final instructions from the gods, and began to climb down the stairs toward the explorers.

"Claus, what shall we do?"

"Just don't move."

Erika thought she was going to faint as the four big yellow eyes regarded her intently in their approach. To her amazement, the jaguars separated and passed on either side of them. The cats moaned mournfully. Then, each jaguar took an opposing side of the stepped pyramid, and, bounding from stone to stone, descended to the plaza below.

Erika's knees were still knocking when the jaguars reached the bottom. She watched the cats disappear into the foliage.

"Why didn't they attack us?"

"They were just angry at us for having disturbed them but not hungry enough to eat us. What do you think, Kayum?" Claus called down to the Lacandon who had resumed his incantations.

"They are the guardians of Hachakyum. It is good. Hachakyum has accepted our offering and will let you enter the temple."

They climbed the remaining stairs and stood before the temple whose walls rose some thirty feet above them. Three doorways opened into dark interiors. The entire structure was crowned by a filigree roof comb. Vines and palm fronds twisted in and out of the limestone comb like unruly hair.

"Duck your head before going inside," Claus cautioned. "The ancient Mayans were little people, as you say, no taller than their Lacandon descendants."

As they took their measure of the height of the doors, the explorers were struck by intricately carved lintels that were mounted over each doorjamb. Although some effects of weathering were evident, the incised details were remarkably clear. Claus ran a damp cloth over the entablature above the first door.

"Amazing! Absolutely amazing!" he exclaimed breathlessly. The lintel showed a male figure with a long headdress, necklaces, and other signs of royal status, holding a torch over a woman who was herself dressed in regal finery. What was extraordinary and caused Erika to shiver was that the woman was pulling what appeared to be a thorn-lined rope through her tongue. Some of the red dye used to represent blood drops remained. Erika winced and experienced a sympathetic tingling in her mouth. Who were they? A king and his queen?

"What do you suppose it means, Claus?" Erika said finally.

The figures were encircled by a text in glyphs. "It's all a story of some kind," Claus said, wiping the second panel. "If only we could read those glyphs." He breathed heavily and Erika saw that his face had become more ashen.

"Claus, please, sit down. Let me clear the next one."

"I'll be all right," he said, gasping in the moist air. "Just a little short-winded from the climb." But he turned over the canteen and cloth. "About those glyphs," he stood with his hands on his hips while his breathing became more normal. "All our efforts to decipher them have failed. There seems to be no rosetta stone, no one key. I'm beginning to think we were all wrong in supposing each glyph is a distinct word and its components are characters in an alphabet. They may represent phonetic elements that we haven't begun to understand. Someone has to try an entirely new tack."

"Claus, look at this middle relief!" Erika was so excited by what her cleaning revealed that she allowed herself to be distracted from Claus's worsening condition. In the panel over the center door, a woman, who was recognizably the same as the one in the first, gazed up at a giant serpent that rose in spiraling coils above her head.

Erika recalled her night of terror with the snake in her sleeping bag. Was she witnessing a reenactment of her own trauma experienced by a queen on a previous revolution of the wheel of time? What was it she had in common with this queen, caught in the coils of eternal return? Yet the woman on the lintel was gazing at the serpent, not in terror, but in a mix of awe and rapture. Then Erika saw that a human-like head peeped out of the serpent's mouth, gazing back at the woman with a fierce intensity.

"Claus, that woman—is she having a vision? What does it mean?"

"I wish I knew. A vision, you say? Yes, yes—of course! It's a bloodletting rit-ual. Each panel tells part of the story, like a comic strip in the newspapers. In the first, she gives her blood in order to have the vision we see in this one. Some North American Indians practice forms of self-mutilation today for the same rea-son. I've seen bloodletting rites on stelae at other sites. But it has always been a king, piercing his penis with stingray spines. The Mayan royalty didn't have an easy time of it. They had to meet their responsibilities to the gods, as well as their people."

"But whose head is peeping out of the serpent's mouth?"

"Who knows? A god? An ancestor? Bolon Kin talked about a vision serpent who comes in dreams, bringing messages from the other world. But this is the first time I've seen a woman as the central figure in a cosmic drama. Is it a renewal myth? Is she sprinkling her blood to usher in a new spring? Or is it a narrative, a representation of actual events? There is so much to know."

Erika was deeply moved by the image of the queen, her tongue dripping with blood as she gazed upward at the god or ancestor who looked down at her from the serpent's mouth. A broken column on the platform was of the right height to serve as a tripod. Erika set her camera on it. She was pleased to be able to photo-graph the lintel.

When Erika was finished, she saw that Claus was shaking from the strain of standing. "Claus, you need to rest. Please! Sit down!"

"Yes, I'll sit down as soon as we go into the temple. But first, let's take a look at the third lintel of this triptych." Erika cleaned it off quickly and effortlessly. The man knelt before the woman who was presenting him with a helmet and shield.

"Like Achilles receiving the shield from Thetis. She blesses him as he sets out for battle," Erika said in wonderment. She wanted to take another picture but she was worried about Claus.

"Were the Mayans warlike, after all?" Claus mused aloud. "It goes against our pet theories. Erika, we are probing into secrets that have been hidden for over a thousand years. I often wonder if we archaeologists have the right to expose them. But I have to believe that after all this time, those secrets belong to the world. All right, we'll go inside."

They stepped inside the middle room and Claus flashed his light on the ceil-ing. A swarm of bats set up a clamor and flocked out of the temple, squealing their grievances until they disappeared under the green cover of the jungle.

Claus played his flashlight on the pitched walls. Erika was disappointed for him that she did not see murals.

"That part of the legend isn't true," she said.

"Wait," Claus said. "If murals exist, they're covered with calcification. Hold the flashlight."

Claus rubbed some medicinal oil over the lumpy surface of the far wall. Colors revealing human figures on a red background began to appear.

"What won't hurt a man's stomach won't hurt a painting several centuries old," Claus said putting the oil back in his pouch. "Do you have any soap in your knapsack?"

"You know I do." But first, I want you to sit down. I'll do the washing." Claus sat on what looked like an altar.

There was a clay pot filled with standing water in one corner of the room. Erika washed large areas of the wall. The colors came out like flowers in the sun. Erika began to perceive a scene of Mayan nobles enjoying a banquet feast. The sure, clean lines of Mayan art were as fresh as if the scene had just been painted. The explorers gaped in admiration.

On the opposite wall, above the door, a procession of nobles appeared, as if summoned by Erika's scrubbing hand.

"Claus, it's beautiful," Erika said.

"Marvelous," Claus agreed. "It may be an accession ceremony. The child could be the heir apparent to the throne. Maybe that's what the bloodletting ritual was about. Asking the gods to sanction the transfer of royal power."

"But the woman," Erika said. "She doesn't look at all like the woman on the lintels."

"You're right," Claus shook his head. "There are so many pieces of the puzzle we don't have. I want to look in the other rooms." He got up with some effort.

It was in those rooms that they saw scenes of war and savagery. Warriors in jaguar headdresses ran spears into their enemy's torsos whose own spears snapped as they fell. In another scene, prisoners, bound and naked, were being beheaded. Executioners gripped prisoners' hair in their hands as they brought obsidian blades against their necks. Trophy heads dangled from the belts of the conquerors.

Claus sighed deeply. "Eric Thompson's picture of the Mayans as being ruled by peace-loving astronomer-priests will have to be revised," he said. "It's clear from all we've seen that the Mayans were very much like the rest of us, human, all too human." Erika took pictures although she had qualms about having to use her flash.

Sadly and without further comment, the explorers went outside and rested atop the temple staircase. The sun was vanishing. Just under them, Kayum continued to pray to the beheaded god. The plaza was forlorn in its emptiness. Suddenly, Kayum stopped chanting.

As they watched, deep shadows covered the rubble that poked up through the mass of vegetation. In the distance the Usumacinta River cut a serpentine track through a forest valley. Then the river became a dull gold. They would have to leave soon if they were planning to go back to camp. Erika stood up, slipping on a loose rock, but Claus reached up and caught her. They listened to the rock tumble down the steps. Then the silence came back.

"Why did they vanish?" Erika spoke suddenly to Claus. "Did they destroy one another in wars?"

"I think it's more likely that the wars were symptom of a general breakdown. What we see up here is from the late classic period. The Mayans built their temples over one another. The new king wanted to affirm the legitimacy of his succession and link himself with his ancestors at the same time. As this temple is the tallest, it may well have been the last one built in Menche. The big mystery of the Mayans is that all the centers were abandoned within a space of twenty-five years of the ninth century. No more dates were inscribed on monuments after that. For the Mayans, time stopped."

Erika took a deep breath, as if time was about to stop again. "How extraordinary. What could have happened?"

"Who knows? An epidemic, a revolution, a general rotting away of things. Surely, increasing warfare would have played a part. But you saw what happened at Capulin."

Erika remembered the bald hills, the burning forest.

The tropical night rushed in. Claus spoke softly, his voice strained and weak. "Think of the thousands of Indians who are coming to the jungle and planting corn. Their method demands the perpetual burning of the forest and rapid exhaustion of the soil. Now, what we've found here suggests to me that the Mayans may have developed more sophisticated farming methods to sustain the huge populations they must have had. They may have built canals and farmed the swamps. But it's my belief that as the growth of their populations created new needs, the Mayans lost their reverence for nature and ravaged the land until they could no longer reclaim it. They turned the forest into a desert and were buried in it."

Erika looked up at the darkening temples that were held in the stranglehold of vines and roots that penetrated the crumbling stone. Roots clutched the remains of one temple like a child's hand grasping the turret of a sand castle. The jungle had won in the end and paid man back for his savage destruction. The Mayan gods lingered to be worshiped by the Lacandons who were too innocent and too ignorant to know of the tragic past. Only some ancestral memory haunting their dreams told them that the old gods must be appeased and that to forget the lessons told in myths and dreams was to bring about the final annihilation of all life in the jungle. The next time, even the jungle would not come back.

Beware, the ruins said. The message bled through the ferns and small flowers that sprang out of the cracks of walls like tears. The wind came up and around them, the centenarian trees creaked. In the distant chatter of parrots and monkeys, Erika heard the warnings of a ruined world.

"Claus, I feel cold and nauseous. Hold me."

She trembled even in the comfort of his arms. Out of the twilight, the moon rose.

Chapter Forty-Six

Erika told Claus that she wanted to spend the night with him inside the temple of the murals. Her reasons were not completely romantic. It was clear that Claus was not well and should not have to climb down the pyramid that night. She would go down to camp and get a sleeping bag for them to share, as well as some food.

"Erika, I don't want to sound like a cold fish, but bring back *two* sleeping bags. No need for you to catch your death up here with me."

"Don't talk about dying. I want to spend tonight in your arms. It doesn't matter if we don't make love. You told me you wanted to marry me. Let's ask Kayum to marry us. Isn't he a priest of sorts? This temple will be our bridal chamber. No queen on earth could ask for more splendor. Will you marry me, Claus? Do it now."

Claus looked down at the intoning Lacandon and smiled.

"Kayum could marry us but I don't have any firewood to offer him. Maybe I can cut some from the top of this temple."

"Save your strength for your wedding night. I'll come back with firewood."

Arriving in camp, Erika found Rogelio and Lazaro roasting pheasants over a fire. The men were delighted by the news of the discovery and said they would be ready to begin excavating in the morning. Erika said they would have to take Claus to El Cedro in the morning. Then she invited them to her wedding. Rogelio and Lazaro sent cheers up into the night and took turns hugging and kissing Erika. The pheasants would be ideal for a wedding feast and there were palm hearts and chocolate. Erika gathered firewood into a bundle.

Then she remembered the incense burner Bolon Kin had given Claus to be used at Menche and asked the men to help her strap the wood and the burner to her back. They made a tumpline out of vines to slip over her head.

The muleteers packed net bags with food and utensils. Lazaro filled all the canteens with water. Rogelio carried Erika's sleeping bag and his phonograph. They all carried flashlights. Erika led the way back to Menche. Climbing the pyramid under the moon, with the firewood on her back, she felt like an Indian woman carrying a cargo of time.

They met Kayum seated crosslegged beside his decapitated god. He said that a girl's father normally accepts the ceremonial firewood at a Lacandon wedding, but since Erika's father was dead and she had no home, he would be her father by proxy and take the wood.

Claus was making a bridal veil out of begonias when his bride and guests arrived. Erika wept when he placed it over her head. Kayum built a fire with the wood, setting aside enough to keep a fire going through the night in front of Hachakyum. Claus burned copal in the censer as he had promised Bolon Kin he would.

Rogelio offered his Bing Crosby record as a wedding present. Erika said she didn't want to take it as it was the only one he had but he said he could get another one in El Cedro. Bing Crosby's voice bounced off the quadrilateral points and Erika decided the song was as good as the wedding march. Lazaro gave Claus a silver ring he had been wearing to give to the bride. It didn't fit, but it was a ring, and Erika thought it was beautiful. Kayum gave the wedding party a mahogany doll he had made along the trail. Then Lazaro and Rogelio carved the pheasants.

In the firelight, Erika saw that Claus had cleared away most of the vast mural on the back wall. An assembly of Mayan nobles banqueted above their heads. The figures were drawn with such clarity of expression, that Erika could almost hear them smack their lips, belch and tell their stories in the shimmering light. Looking at her friends and back at the figures, Erika felt that hers was just another table being set at the eternal banquet on the wall. Indeed, before they began to dine, Kayum passed *posole* over the lips of the painted dignitaries. One of the figures held out a plate of plums in return.

"We are dining with the gods," Kayum said, smiling broadly.

"What of Doña Erika and me. Are we married?" Claus asked.

"Yes. I have accepted the firewood. She has not made tortillas for you but she has served you *posole*. Now she is your wife."

"Is there no other ceremony?"

"None."

"And do the gods approve?"

"You are both loved by the gods and by Lacandons in every part of the jungle."

After smoking a cigar with the wedding party, Kayum went outside to spend a night-long vigil with the beheaded god on the platform beneath them. Lazaro and Rogelio began their trip down the pyramid steps, lighting their way with flashlights. Erika could hear them talking together even at the other end of the plaza. Kayum resumed his incantations.

Erika and Claus sat together quietly, looking out through the arch at the dark outline of trees that covered the opposite pyramid. The fire inside the temple was a soft pink glow.

Kayum stopped chanting. Erika listened to her breathing and the more labored breathing of Claus.

Erika leaned her head against his shoulder. "Claus, just think, we found it. We found Menche."

Claus spoke after a silence. "Yes, we found it. But you know, I think we found it before we came here."

Chapter Forty-Seven

Claus was shaking and his body was cold when Erika climbed naked into the sleeping bag with him. She held him in her arms and wrapped her legs around his so that she could transmit the warmth of her entire body to him. In the morning, she would take him to El Cedro, no matter what he said. Maybe they could hire a plane that would fly them to Ocosingo. Surely Manuel Castellanos had access to the new drug that was saving the lives of soldiers on the battlefields of the war.

Claus drifted off into sleep but Erika continued to hold him, enveloping him with as much warmth as she could. The moon was high and a pale light fell on the feathered headdresses of the ancient celebrants on the back wall. Erika thought about Bolon Kin and the Lacandons of Jatate. In the flickering light of the fire that had burst into flames, the lips of the banqueting Mayans seemed to move. Then a voice whispered in her ear as from a presence outside herself, a phenomenon she sometimes experienced in the twilight between waking and sleeping.

"All things return," the voice said. "But it is given to man to end time."

Then Erika was dreaming. She lay under a canopy of tropical trees. A cold wind came up and blew away the leaves over her head. The sky opened blue and clear. The branches of the trees fell away and Erika looked up into blue empty space. The sky dimmed and Erika saw thousands of stars that seemed to be falling toward her. As they came closer, the stars took on the form of little golden cats. They grew larger and landed on the stumps of trees around her, some landing on fallen branches. Erika saw that they were jaguars, thousands of them settling on the mold leaf floor of the jungle. The specks that fell toward her became snow-flakes. The jaguars on the ground trekked through the snow leaving their prints in the mounting drifts. Erika felt an intense cold in her bones as icicles formed around the dead trunks of trees, and snow fell over the elephant ear plants. Not too far away, she could see the great pyramid of Menche covered with snow. The statue of Hachakyum gazed down at her. The head of the god rested squarely on its shoulders. A jaguar limped through the snow toward Erika. Icicles clung to its coat. The snow fell faintly, steadily throughout the jungle and then Erika was holding the frozen jaguar in her arms. She shuddered. She had never been so cold. Then she was awake, shaking and holding a block of ice. Erika cried hot tears, but as they fell over the cold, inert body in her arms, Erika knew she would never make Claus warm again.

Chapter Forty-Eight

The banquet of the Mayans on the wall continued through the dawn. On a side wall that was dimly illuminated, a triumphant king stood on the neck of a trampled victim. Kayum had made a small bed of bamboo slats and placed Claus's body on it. Erika sat motionless, unable to move or speak as Lazaro and Rogelio came to the assistance of Kayum. The world was strangely silent except for the morning calls of birds. The monkeys on the roof comb had stopped their chatter.

For Erika, time had stopped except for the beating of her heart. She waited for it to stop as the heart of Claus had stopped. What had been uncontrollable grief in the early morning had turned to numbness. She felt as if she were a limestone figure with a mysterious heartbeat. She was a useless thing now, unable, even to mourn. She felt paralysis creep over her as it had taken the body of her dead husband who lay on the bamboo slats.

Lazaro broke the silence. "Well, I suppose we'll have to give him some sort of burial," he said finally. "What do you think, Doña Erika? Kayum says he found a small cemetery in the woods just beyond the north plaza."

"Lazaro, it's an Indian cemetery," Rogelio said.

Erika stirred. She had been listening to the conversation with a peripheral ear, but now it all played back in her mind. She realized why her grief had turned to numbness. She had become emotionally paralyzed because there had been nothing else for her to do for Claus.

Kayum looked at her intently. He had been trying to follow the conversation that was being held in Spanish.

"Doña Erika, do you want to bury Pancho Balam in the cemetery of the Lacandons?"

There was one last thing to be done for Claus after all.

"Kayum, tell me, can one of the T'sul be buried in a Lacandon grave?"

Kayum smiled sadly. "No, but a priest of the Lacandons can. When my father gave Pancho Balam an incense burner so that he could praise Hachakyum, your husband automatically became a priest. So he should be buried as a priest."

Erika felt new tears flow down her face. She embraced Kayum. "Thank you, Kayum. The Lacandons have given my husband an honor greater than any he has received in his life."

Kayum led them to a small Indian cemetery just off the main plaza. Erika guessed it had been used over the centuries to bury pilgrims who had succumbed to exhaustion or disease.

Lazaro and Rogelio brought picks and shovels. Kayum used a pole as they dug a grave two feet deep. They made a roof structure out of saplings and covered it with palm leaves. It was late afternoon when they got back to the temple where Claus's body lay. After a small supper of beans and bananas, Kayum led them in making preparations for the funeral.

"Doña Erika, you must make *posole*," he said, and he told her the things they would have to do in the morning. Then he told her to place a bowl of burning charcoal under the bed where Claus lay. "So Pancho Balam will know that we care for him."

Erika spent the night on the platform outside of the temple. She did not sleep much but she tried to keep her mind on the things Kayum told her they would do in the morning. It was still dark when Kayum summoned her out of her sleeping bag. Rogelio and Lazaro stood by in readiness. Kayum handed Erika a cob of maize which she placed in Claus's dead hand. "This is some maize to throw to the hens of the underworld, my dear husband," she said repeating what Kayum had taught her. Then she cut a lock of her hair and placed it in his other hand, closing his fingers over it. "This is for protection against the lice under the earth."

They removed Claus's Chamula shirt and drill trousers and replaced them with a Lacandon tunic. Then Kayum adorned the body with the bracelets and necklaces of jade, the pendants and ear plugs that they had found in the temple. Rogelio and Lazaro sighed with a mixture of disappointment and resignation as they watched the treasure being returned to the dead. Kayum picked up the obsidian figurines and Erika knew that they too would have to await future looters, even though she was sure that the collection, brought to the Mexican market, would have provided a financial windfall for all of them.

"Here is a bone to give to the dogs of the underworld," Kayum said, placing it in her husband's lap. Then Kayum raised the lifeless body so that it sat up and Erika placed tortillas in the lap. Erika held the body upright and Kayum closed its eyes.

Erika found herself acting as in a dream. Her mind was absorbed in doing all the things Kayum had told her had to be done. Together they doubled the body so that it became a bundle. With Lazaro's help, they tied the bundle with lianas.

Then they placed the bundled body in a hammock suspended between two poles. With Erika and Kayum trailing, Rogelio and Lazaro carried the hammock down the steep grade of the pyramid and across the plaza.

"We can carry you, you are not alive," Kayum said to the figure. Kayum said it was important to constantly reassure the dead of their sorrow and also to pacify the specter that would linger after the soul went to the underworld.

The sun had not yet risen when they crossed the gurgling arroyo and reached the ancient graves which looked like haystacks in the tangle of foliage. Erika continued to murmur assurances as they entered the cemetery.

Rogelio and Lazaro set the poles down across the open grave. The hammock did not touch the bottom. Erika placed a net bag of provisions, including bowls of gruel and fire sticks into the hammock. Under instructions from Kayum she added personal items, Claus's compass; his dog-eared field hat. She decided to keep the copy of *Don Quixote*. Then, on impulse, she added the blouse she wore when they made love in the forest. She spoke the words she had rehearsed during the night.

"I'm going to throw earth on your face, my husband. You are dead. Sukunkyum will give you the judgment of the gods. May the judgment be in your favor, my love." Erika threw a handful of earth over the grave and the others commenced to fill it until a mound of earth was formed under the little palm roof.

"We mean no offense by throwing earth on you," Kayum said.

Erika placed a bowl of *posole* and a tin of dried meat on top of the mound. She added a block of chocolate and some chilis. Kayum explained that the second food was for the journey from the underworld to the trail to the sky, a journey which, all things going well in the judgment of Sukunkyum, could begin in five days. The specter of the dead would wait on earth until then. Kayum handed Erika an obsidian figurine which she placed on top of the mound so that the head faced east. Kayum placed the palm leaves, which represented the dogs, on the four corners of the mound and placed toasted chilis on the trail to ward off demons. Then he lit a fire on the southeast corner of the grave to warm the waiting specter.

Erika could not feel sorrow now. That would come later, she knew. Now she wanted to remember to do everything correctly. As she knelt in her observance of the Lacandon ritual, she felt that she was taking the lifelong burden of Claus on her back, adjusting the tumpline to her forehead as she readied herself to carry it forward in time.

Kayum set out candles he had made from agate fiber and resin the night before. He lit two of them from the fire. Erika knew he did so with the assurance that he was now a Tohil in his father's absence. Erika took the two lighted candles from Kayum and placed them at the head of the mound.

"These candles will light your way through darkness," she said softly. Kayum gave candles to Rogelio and Lazaro who lit them and placed them around the grave until the entire mound was ringed with a string of lights.

Kayum picked up a wooden flute and played a mournful tune. Erika and the others sang forlornly.

"To light your way through darkness. We send you food and all our love for your journey across the River of Tears. May you be judged innocent of sins and find the trail to the sky. May you light a star in heaven for all of us who travel the trails of earth to see by."

They all squatted around the lighted mound, looking at the obsidian doll and the assortment of food until the sun began to lighten the sky.

They left the grave and walked back across the grand plaza of Menche. Kayum pointed to Kak, the morning star, who was pulling the sun up over the jungle.

Erika made *posole* for the living and served it with palm hearts and bowls of steaming coffee. When she finished serving her companions, Erika fell into a convulsive heap of sobbing.

Chapter Forty-Nine

Erika forced herself to assist Rogelio and Lazaro as they packed the mules.

"What will you do now?" she asked them.

"Well, after we take you to El Cedro and see that you're safe aboard a plane to Ocosingo, we're going back to those Tobajalian women we met last week. A life in an Indian colony could be better than being a field hand on a coffee plantation," Lazaro said.

"And it is better than being a *chiclero*. The women are beautiful. We will plant our own fields. Maybe we can teach the Tobajalians what we learned about living in the jungle from the Lacandons," Rogelio said.

Erika found Kayum sitting in the central plaza packing his net bag.

"What will you do Kayum?"

"I will bring the sacred stone to my brother, so that the people of Jatate can worship Hachakyum again."

"Will you stay in Jatate?"

"No, I cannot live there. But I too have found the Tobajalian women to be pleasing. And there is one who finds me so. I will take her into the jungle with me and we will begin a new caribal. She will make tortillas for the gods and for me and we will bring up children who will love the gods. What will you do, Doña Erika?"

Suddenly, she realized what she was going to do. To her own surprise, she found herself answering with conviction. "My first responsibility is to Menche. It is the home of your god and the burial place of my husband. He will not be regarded as my husband by the laws of the T'sul. My first duty will be to see that these crumbling walls are restored and that a caretaker is sent here to look after Menche full-time."

"Do you think the T'sul will send a guardian to care for the home of our gods?"

"I will see to it. Then I will go to a city the T'sul call San Cristobal. It is high in the mountains but not far from the jungle. My people will give me money for the discovery of Menche. I will use it to build a place to teach the world the lessons of the jungle and the Lacandons. I will invite you to visit me, Kayum, and will be happy to visit you in your new home."

Erika and Kayum crossed the plaza in the direction of the trail where Lazaro and Rogelio waited. Before leaving the plaza, Erika turned to take one last look at the great pyramid. The sun was almost directly overhead, illuminating the body of Hachakyum and the severed head.

She listened to the chatter of monkeys and parrots around her. The voices of the forest seemed to be speaking to her. Erika thought she understood. Yes, the voices said, after the world is destroyed, a new jungle will be born. Time will be recreated and the gods, forever optimists, will then make men out of corn.

Epilogue

I gathered my papers and closed my books. It had been three years since my first visit to Casa Balam. I'd come back every summer, using a concrete table in the garden as my study. I read books and old manuscripts from the library, took voluminous notes and sketched early drafts of my book. And yes, Erika finally persuaded me to visit the jungle. A shaggy-haired boy in a white cotton tunic rowed me across a lake in a dugout canoe. I thought I'd gone back to the first morning of the world until I heard intimations of the world's last day in the sound of trees being felled around us.

And just as time finally stopped on Mayan monuments, so I came to the end of my labors in Casa Balam. My reading and note-gathering was done. The rest was up to my imagination and I could exercise that in New York as well as anywhere.

It was late afternoon in Erika's garden. Through the tall pines, I watched the tops of the San Cristobal mountains turn pink. Around me, the hummingbirds continued their indefatigable rounds among the tiger lilies. But my rounds in the garden had come to an end.

I climbed the stairs to the balcony of my room. When I opened the door, I was surprised to see Erika inside. I'd become so much in awe of her, I'd taken great pains to stay out of her way, except for our meetings in the *comedor*. On this occasion, she was spectacularly made up and wore a long, magenta dress with Indian designs.

"What is the matter with you?" she greeted me with severity.

"Are you speaking to me?" I blurted out stupidly.

"How can you write good stories if you have no sense of beauty?"

"I was just admiring the garden—"

"How can you admire the garden when you keep the curtains drawn over the windows in your room? I was passing by and took the liberty to come in and open them."

I muttered something about being forgetful in the morning and ended with *mea culpas*.

"Have you finished the reading?" she asked, her voice softening.

"Yes."

"Good. Come with me to my office."

We walked to her office at the other end of the balcony. Two kittens, guarding the door, ran up my trouser legs. I giggled.

"They are marvelous animals," she said.

With the kittens hanging on, I followed Erika into her office. There were many unobstructed windows but the outside curtain of flora afforded privacy and diminished the effects of the sun. Erika motioned me toward a chair in front of a handsome mahogany desk. Then she draped herself over a chair behind the desk, letting her legs dangle over the sides like a little girl.

"Excuse me, I must rest my legs this way."

The room was lined with bookshelves. Papers were stacked everywhere but the room was not cluttered or untidy. God pots were interspersed among the books. There were ubiquitous photographs. I recognized a print of the one I'd seen in the museum of Claus squatting in a grave, holding a skull in his hand. If anyone was immortal, it was Erika. But she was reading my mind.

"I'm not immortal," she said. "I don't know why I keep going. I wish I'd have a heart attack. It's the only way I'll be able to retire." She did not seem gloomy about the prospect as she glanced through letters on her desk.

"There's a meeting tonight to discuss the future of Casa Balam. I have to think about what will happen to this place when I'm gone. I'm forming a foundation of interested citizens of Mexico, many of them from around here. Some Lacandons are on it. But who knows if the work will be continued."

She gave a shrug of resignation. The light was soft on her face and her voice now was filled with gentleness.

"Do you think the Lacandons will survive?" I asked.

"As well as the rest of us I suppose. I have seen many changes in Lacandon society since I first went into the jungle. It's hard to go along with some things. They are constantly sending requests through visitors for me to bring them batteries for transistor radios." She threw up her hands. "For hundreds of years they were content with their lovely songs and now the dreadful music of Mexico and the United States has become a necessity of life. But I would rather see them alive and colorless than dead and interesting."

"Micheline in the library tells me that born-again Christians have converted over half the Lacandons who live around Lake Naha."

Erika looked at me as if I had brought up the subject of the devil.

"The Lacandons are losing their religion as they see the jungle destroyed around them. It is not that the Lacandons are losing their belief in the old gods. They just feel that Jesus Christ is winning the battle against the jungle and their own gods are powerless. So they are returning the incense burners back to the caves and rocks where their old forest gods have lived for centuries."

"And Menche?"

"Kayum still visits. And Chankin of Lake Naha. But when Chankin and Kayum die, the old religion will die with them. But that's not what bothers me so much."

"What does bother you?"

"I am disturbed by what is happening to the jungle. Hillsides are being turned to useless rock piles. Landholders are fishing with dynamite in polluted lakes. The landless Indians are migrating to the jungle in increasing numbers, going from poverty to despair. What we first saw in Capulin has become widespread all over Chiapas. Behind them come the cattle ranchers and seekers of oil. This has happened even after I used the publicity I got from Menche to convince the government to set aside lands for the Lacandons."

Erika wheeled her legs from the side of her chair and sat up, straightening a crink in her back. I remembered that she suffered from arthritis and had cataracts in her eyes. Old age was taking its toll even of this lady of the jungle.

I watched her thumb idly through the pages of an old book that rested on her desk as if what she wanted to say next was contained in it somewhere. Its pages were yellowed and wracked, some of the corners having broken off.

I was struck by a thought. "That book. Is that the copy of *Don Quixote* Claus brought with him on his expeditions?"

She gave me a surprised smile. "I am pleased that you recognized it. I read from it on nights when I can't sleep. Claus gave me two legacies, this book and a love for the jungle. My old friend Manuel Castellanos was right. Once you've lived in the jungle, it's with you for the rest of your life. I can't imagine the world without it." She closed the book and gave the cover a few little pats. "Oh, I know that saving the Lacandon forest is hopeless, but I try to talk to anyone who will listen," she went on. "I've lectured all over the world. This spring, I got an opportunity to talk to the president of Mexico. I screamed at him for almost an hour. He must have thought I was crazy but he said he would visit the jungle with me this summer so I can show him the conditions there."

She pointed out the window. "Each morning, I plant trees in the hills. I can't keep up with the destruction. Listen, Claus believed that the abuse of the jungle destroyed Mayan civilization. The latest theories are proving him right. There are other theories, of course; overpopulation, wars of conquest, the rise of a middle class demanding power and luxury goods. But in the end the Mayans neglected their environment and were buried in the wasteland they created. Does it sound familiar?" She fell silent and together, we looked at the sleeping cats.

"Do you think western civilization is on the skids?" I asked.

"I saw the first stages of collapse in the war in Europe. Perhaps it is not inevitable. The Lacandons believe that a bad dream can be a warning, a last chance to make amends. So, it all depends on how well we remember our dreams. Do you remember yours?"

"I remember the dream I had on my first night here. It's why I've come back."

Erika smiled warmly for the first time. "I hope you come again soon. I want you to know I consider you to be a member of the house." I was thrilled.

We were silent for a moment. Then Erika looked down at her watch. "It is time to ring the bell for *cena*."

Yes, Erika the Swiss, was a great respecter of time.

"Thank you for the opportunity to learn so much about your life," I said, getting up on her cue. She turned to me with a smile and suddenly I realized how she must have looked sitting in that cafe in Ocosingo, like Marlene Dietrich in the movies, beautiful and wise, yet vulnerable, waiting for the lover who would rescue her and be changed completely by her.

"I have had nine lives like the cat," Erika said. "I have only shown you one of them. Are you going to write my story as a novel?"

"Yes, you will be the heroine."

She beamed. "The last novel I read was *Anna Karenina*. I hope you don't do to me what Tolstoy did to that poor girl."

"Don't worry. There will be no trains."

Erika smiled. "You have my permission to make me beautiful."

We went downstairs and walked to the main courtyard. Erika picked up the baton hanging from the wall and struck the big gong several times.

On the morning of my departure from Casa Balam, I rose at five thirty to meet a taxi that would take me to Tuxtla and my rendezvous with an eight thirty jet to Mexico City.

The kitchen staff bustled about in the *comedor*. Despite the early hour, they let me in and placed a cup of steaming coffee in front of me. A basket of warm tortillas and a plate of fried eggs with frijoles followed. I was told that Erika had already breakfasted.

Waiting for the coffee to cool, I looked up at the tapestry that was mounted on the wall above Erika's chair. I knew it was a gift from a guest who had visited the year before. I also knew it was a woven copy of a lintel Erika and Claus had discovered at Menche. I'd seen the photograph Erika had taken of the lintel in the library.

A woman in royal Mayan robes looked up at a giant serpent that rose in coils above her head. She held a bowl in one hand from which drops of blood spilled as they did from her tongue. Over one arm, a thorn-lined rope was draped. I knew the rope had been pulled through her pierced tongue to make it bleed. But instead of wearing a pained expression on her face, the woman gazed rapturously at a human head that gazed back at her from the serpent's mouth.

I felt a burning in my own tongue as the hot coffee flowed over it. But I had learned something about bloodletting and vision serpents. There had been major advances in Mayan epigraphy and I had read an exegesis of the scene by one of the new Mayan scholars. It was now known that the woman represented Lady Xoc, a queen of Menche who lived in the sixth century. She was a direct descendant of the founder of the first dynasty which was the reason her husband. Jaguar Claws, married her. His lineage was not as pure and he needed this queen to legitimize his claim to the throne. At the same time, he married a noblewoman from Palenque to cement his alliance with that powerful city-state. The newly deciphered text explained that he had designated his son by his foreign wife to be his heir. Lady Xoc, his first and older wife, who was herself childless, performed the excruciatingly painful act of bloodletting to call forth her ancestor from the mouth of the vision serpent. She asked the ancestor to bless the accession to the throne of the child of another woman. She had given her blood unselfishly, not only so that the royal line of Menche would remain unbroken, but so that the conduit between the material and spiritual worlds, represented by the serpent, would be maintained. The rains would fall, the forest would yield its abundant harvest, and the people of Menche would prosper.

Thinking of Lady Xoc, I went out into the patio where my luggage waited. I was surprised to see the aging Indian of my first night in San Cristobal, standing nearby. I had not seen him since my first visit. He clutched a small knapsack that was filled to the brim. He was talking with a young man in the polyester clothing of the ladinos in town. The boy carried a nylon knapsack over one shoulder and a transistor radio under one arm. The old Indian and the boy were holding a heated discussion.

Waiting for the knock on the outside door that would announce my cab, I gazed at the flowers.

Erika appeared. She wore a woolen sweater, riding pants and boots. She held the seedling of a tree in one hand and a trowel in the other. She told me that she and other members of the house were going to plant seedlings of trees on the denuded hills. She wished me well on my journey, allowed me to take photographs, apologizing for wearing no makeup, and then went over to where the man and the boy still argued. She spoke to the boy in an imploring tone but he shook his head at her. Finally Erika sighed deeply, looked up at the sky dramatically, and came back to me.

"He insists on going to Tuxtla," she said, waving the seedling in her hand. "He wants to go there to seek his fortune. There is nothing for him there, nothing. With all the people drifting into the cities, he will become just another beggar in weeks."

"He doesn't look like a beggar. Who is he?"

"He is Kin, the son of Kayum. He was educated here as a boy when his mother died in the jungle. He has visited my house on and off over the years. Now his father wants him to go back to the jungle and help him with his milpa. Kayum lives alone in the jungle with two wives and another son."

I stared at the old Indian in awe. Before me, stood a living hero of the Mayans, Kayum, the redeemer of his people, the retriever of the sacred stone at Menche.

"Kayum will go back to the jungle where his family is waiting. He came here when his incense board failed to cure him of a virus that came with the Tzeltales. It was Kin who brought him here."

"What happened to Koh?" I asked.

"She lived happily ever after, but not in El Capulin. It was destroyed by the eye disease and uncontrollable fires. She and her husband joined the Lacandons I helped group together around Lake Naha. Juan was converted to the old Mayan faith. It happens all too often the other way."

Kayum had given up arguing with his son and was giving him some yucca roots and eggs to put into his plastic mesh bag.

"How will Kin get to Tuxtla?" I asked.

"He says he will walk to the bus station."

"There won't be a bus for Tuxtla until this afternoon. I checked."

"Do you think you can take him in your cab? He can't pay."

"I owe him a trip."

When the taxi came. Kin got into the back seat with me. Kayum continued to shout exhortations to his son through the window as the car pulled off. The driver turned the cab at the corner and I saw Erika standing in front of the house, watching us. She held up the seedling and waved.

I looked at the distant hills behind her that were mantled with trees, the trees Erika had planted over the years. I'd even felt compelled to lend a hand on some mornings. Then I realized that Erika was, indeed, Lady Xoc on another turn of the great wheel of time. Like Lady Xoc, Erika never had children of her own, but gave her blood for children who were not hers. Those she helped were not only the Lacandons. For over forty years, Erika was a lone voice crying in the wilderness, warning us, cajoling us, forcing us to confront the consequences of our carelessness. For we were all Erika's children, deserving of her scoldings.

The boy smiled at me appreciatively as the car rumbled down the narrow lanes of Las Casas. I saw that his profile was that of the classic Maya. He spoke Spanish well and maintained an ongoing conversation with me about the sights around us. As we passed through the *zocalo* in town, I told him that I lived in *Nueva York*, '*un cuidad grande.*' His eyes opened with wonder. He said he had never been to *Nueva York*, but when he was small, his father took him to Menche. Someday, he would go to *Nueva York*.

The mist slipped off the San Cristobal mountains and rolled out of the ravine as we dropped thousands of feet in minutes. I looked out at the scarred hills. The boy pulled up the antenna on his radio and opened a window. In moments, the sound of rock music filled the car. The driver made another turn around the mountain, and in the valley that spread out below us, Tuxtla Guitterez awoke in a golden haze.

978-0-595-47065-5
0-595-47065-3